The Blue Moon

Christopher Webster

A *StoryFix Media* book

Copyright © 2019 Christopher Webster
All rights reserved.

ISBN: 9781794128217

Cover and jacket design by Erick Solis
Interior art by Graham Johnson

Also from Christopher Webster and StoryFix Media

New Horizons: A Novel of Survival

The Pulse: An Interactive Sci-fi Story (Google Play)

For Verity

Part One

The Mouse and the Walrus

1

Paddington Pin tried not to vomit as he steadied himself in his hammock. His stomach was revolting again.

For thirty seven years he'd worked in the bowels of whatever hunk-of-junk transport ship would hire him, preferring the freedom of the Black to being landlocked under Earth's suffocating atmosphere. It was a modest life, hidden away from the eyes of important people; but after all these years he was proud of his humble accomplishments.

He was a master laborer, a mechanic and engineer-in-a-pinch. He'd successfully battled transition sickness more times than he could count, and had clawed his way out of some damn hairy situations that would turn the stomach of even the sturdiest officer.

He was, what his ex-wife used to call, "A stubborn sonofabitch." And yet, here he was, losing his lunch in a hammock that swayed against the shuttering of the Tian's ancient reactor core. As much as he hated to admit it, he was losing his stomach for a life adrift.

Pin balanced himself by grasping a rusty rail that ran down the wall of his cabin. Then he pulled his knees to his chest and clipped his gnarled toenails again, feeling somewhat victorious when a dry husk of one flew into the air and disappeared somewhere on the metal floor below.

"Got you, you yellow bastard," he said through the coarse hairs of his salt and pepper moustache.

He chuckled to himself, brushing the hairs with the back of his finger. Scratchy, the little mouse called it.

She was Emma to her people, but he called the girl Mouse for her habit of travelling inside the walls, coming and going from above and below deck as she pleased. It was a habit that made her father, Captain of the Tian, eternally angry.

Pin would have been fond of the girl for that alone, but he also saw a lot of himself in her. Eight years-old and already she had a mind of her own. She was sensitive, with a ripe curiosity that escaped most people. Even an old mariner like Pin could see the girl was special. The other kid, Adam, on the other hand, was as thick as they came.

As Pin attacked his other toes he remembered the first time Emma had surprised him in his work bay. Someone topside had dropped their guard and the Tian had veered off course and out of range of the satellite beacons that held its trajectory between ports. And when someone topside lost their guard, it usually meant a call down to Pin to come up with the fix.

The Captain needed him to extend the ship's transmission range, which required welding additions to the antennae. Which meant leaving the ship. Which he didn't like.

Not that he was scared. Nothing much scared him anymore. But it was cold in the Black. He felt swallowed by it. It chilled his soul in a way that was indescribable to anyone who'd never faced the sheer magnitude of their own insignificance. But it was his job. It was his place.

Pin remembered where he was when the girl had first appeared. He'd just finished taping the seam along the rivets of his helmet because he didn't trust the seals of the ancient space gear anymore (and certainly not the long-forgotten corporation that had manufactured it). He was about to step into the anti-chamber to begin the countdown to doors-open when he heard a scratching sound behind him.

He turned and scanned the bay, but he saw no one. Then he heard it again: scratching behind the east wall.

Bending down to peer into a long grate, Pin strained to see through the smudges in his visor. Had they picked up a stowaway while docked at Valhalla? That was the *last* thing he had time for. Then the grate popped open and surprised him and he lost his balance, falling onto his back and flailing his limbs like a turtle.

"Who's there?" he asked frantically, unable to flip himself over for the weight of the bulky suit. "Who is it? Show yourself, you yellow bastard—"

He heard a giggle and stopped moving.

"Who's that?"

A pretty little face pressed up against his visor, nose squishing flat as blue eyes peered inside the helmet to get a look at him. The girl laughed again and pointed through the glass dome.

"Why are you wearing that?" she asked matter of

factly.

"I have to wear it to go outside the ship," he answered equally measured.

"Why?"

"Because, you can't breathe in space, that's why."

"Why?"

"Because, there's no oxygen."

"Why?"

This is going nowhere, he thought. "Look, kid, just roll me over."

"I can't. You're too fat."

"No I'm not, and yes you can. If I roll this way, and you push the canisters at the same time, I can get onto my front. Okay?"

"Okay," the girl said, getting to her knees and pressing her palms against his oxygen tanks. "I'm pretty strong, actually."

"Yeah, well, we'll see about that. Ready?"

"Sure."

Pin rolled and the girl pushed and then he was on his stomach. From there, he pushed himself onto his knees awkwardly and pulled himself to his feet by grabbing a chain that hung from the ceiling of his work bay.

He breathed in deeply and steadied himself. Then he looked down at the girl, glad to have his status as the adult back.

She wore a plain white ship's dress that was filthy with dust, and ship's sneakers. It was clear to Pin that she wasn't a stowaway but a topsider— a passenger of some importance by the looks of her.

He sighed and grabbed the girl by the arm, dragging her over to the communicator. "Now I have call up and get you back home. You got parents on board, girl?"

She didn't answer, so he clicked the communicator and waited for someone to pick up on the other end.

"Bloody waste of my time," he muttered, scowling down at her through his visor, now foggy from the hot breath of his earlier exertion.

The girl struggled to pull away, neither of them noticing a small wooden box with a brass clasp tumble from her pocket and slide under Pin's work bench.

"Please, mister. Don't call my father," she said. "He'll lock me in my quarters if he catches me in the walls again. It's boring. It smells, and there's nothing to play with."

"Sounds like the right place for you," said Pin. "Dangerous to be climbing through the walls like a mouse."

"Mouse?" She stopped struggling for a moment.

Pin forgot that children as young as her were rarely born and raised on Earth anymore. Young lungs couldn't take the smog and little eyes couldn't stand the UV. Those with money grew up on ports until they were old enough to work them. Those without means were often deported back to Earth for a short and brutal adult life.

He looked at the girl's eyes, fierce with inquisition. It occurred to him that not only had she never seen a mouse—or *any* animal for that matter—she had likely never seen the green of a grassy field, felt the wind's cool breath on her cheeks, or had her face warmed by the sun's hot rays.

"What's a mouse?" The girl asked, eyes wide.

"Doesn't matter," Pin answered flicking the communicator off and then on again, desperate for someone to pick up and get this girl away from him.

"Why?" The girl asked, pulling at the reflective scales of his space suit.

"Because they don't exist anymore."

"Why?"

"Because when cities ate up all the land they ate up the animals with them. Because humans didn't think mice were worth a worry."

"They lived in walls?"

Pin sighed deeply then broke the seal on his gloves, pulling them off with a hiss of compressed air. Then he peeled the tape away from the seam around his helmet, twisted it clockwise, and pulled it off his head.

He sucked in a breath of stale, recycled air before turning his attention back to the girl.

"They lived anywhere they wanted to. See, they were small critters. So small, they could fit right in the palm of your hand."

"Wow," whispered the girl, eyes wide with wonder as she inspected the size of her own palm. "What did they look like?"

"Some were grey, some brown. All covered in fuzzy fur." Pin put his hands to his head and poked his fingers towards the ceiling. "Their ears stuck up like this and their front teeth stuck out like this."

He puckered and pressed his teeth out, making a sucking sound and moving his nose up and down quickly.

The girl laughed at the impression and he laughed along with her. Then the communicator buzzed and he straightened.

"Ship's porter here," a static-y voice said.

The girl pulled at Pin's leg again and shook her

head, whispering, "Please don't tell the captain."

"The captain?" Pin said. "Why would I tell the captain?"

"He's my father."

"Your father's Captain LaFarge?"

All of a sudden, Pin felt even sorrier for the girl. Captain LaFarge was a real hard ass. He'd never imagined the man had children.

Pin hesitated. He didn't like trouble, and this felt a lot like trouble. After a moment, he pressed the communicator and moved in towards the rusty speaker grate.

"It's nothing, Porter. False alarm," he said and clicked it off. Then he looked down at the girl. "You run along now, back how you came. And I'd appreciate you not saying that we met, or I could lose my job."

"Okay," said the girl crossing her index finger twice across her heart. Moving back towards the grate, she paused and called back, "See you tomorrow!"

"Wait, what's that you say?"

"See you tomorrow," the girl said again. "I want to hear more about mouses and Earth and all the other animals. Bye!"

"I don't think that's—" Pin started but the girl was gone. "I'm a very busy man!" he called into the grate as her little sneakers slipped out of sight around a corner.

Hanging his head, he slid the grate back into place, stopping short of re-fastening it. Then he pulled it away, leaving it off altogether. He didn't imagine he'd see the girl again, not all the way down there, but just in case she decided to pay him another visit, he would keep the chute open. *For her safety, of course.*

The rest of his toenails now trimmed, Pin removed his uniform and lay down on the still swinging hammock. He wrapped himself in his musty old blanket and stared up at a stain on the ceiling.

He found if he focused on the single spot, his stomach settled, so he often watched it until he fell asleep.

He remembered the girl had not visited him the following day as she'd promised. And he remembered that, despite being relieved, he was unable to concentrate on his work that day. Every few moments he'd find himself glancing at the open grate, half expecting her to surprise him again. But she was never there when he looked.

It would be another four days before she appeared again, and when she did she all but ignored him. She pushed through the grate like a rocket and routed about the little work bay like, well, a mouse.

"Where is it? Where is it?" she muttered to herself before finally turning towards him. "Have you seen it? I can't find it. It *must* be here."

"Calm down, girl. Have I seen what? What are you looking for?"

"My box. My treasure. Have you seen it?"

Pin *had* seen it. He'd found it under his oily bench and wondered if it belonged to the girl. He moved towards his jacket, which hung on a hook on the wall, and reached into the pocket, pulling out the wooden box with the bronze clasp.

"I polished it up in case you came looking for it again," he said as he handed it to her.

The girl snatched it away and held it close. "You didn't look inside, did you?"

Pin shook his head.

"It's a secret treasure. It's a treasure just for me. Promise you didn't look?"

Pin ran a finger across his heart like the girl had done days earlier and she smiled and let out a long sigh of relief. Then she sat down and leaned her head on the palm of her hand as though intent on hearing a story.

"Go ahead and tell me about sky," she said. "That's what I want to hear about first. Adam told me his old uncle Danforth said it was blue, but I told him his uncle was playing a joke on him. It's not blue is it?"

"Don't know how blue it is these days, but the last time I saw it it was blue," Pin replied flipping an empty cargo crate onto its side to sit on.

The girl was stunned. "But, that's impossible! How can people see through it?"

"It only looks blue from far away. When you're standing in the middle of it, it's, well, I suppose it's see-through. Like the glass of my space helmet."

"Does it get smudgy?"

"In a way. Gets smudgier by the day, in fact. But not like from fingerprints."

Their conversations went on like this for weeks: Pin doing his best to explain the natural world to a girl who had never seen it, and could never truly understand. After a while he wished he could take her to Earth to let her see it with her own eyes. But the planet had so decayed since he was a boy he doubted it could ever live up to the visions he'd put in her head.

Perhaps it was okay for fantasies to brighten the darkness of real life. It was only a matter of time before she discovered how ugly life really was.

The stain in the ceiling was starting to blur as Pin fell into sleep. His stomach had calmed and it felt as though the Tian had settled into an easy current again.

The reactor had calmed and he could hear its hum now. It was a comfort to him in the night, like hearing a mother's heartbeat in utero. He let it soothe him.

Then a strange smell drifted through the air and he opened his eyes.

2

In the captain's quarters, three passengers sat quietly; two on the floor, one on a stool in front of a long steel table with a glowing top.

Emma LaFarge busied herself with an old rag doll, whispering secrets only the two of them would share. Adam—older than Emma by one year—sulked under the table, bored.

He moved between his nanny's legs, pulling at her pants. She shooed the boy away without taking her eyes off her monitor and he crossed his arms in churlish protest.

The door to the cabin slid open suddenly to reveal Captain LaFarge, face stern as always. He was a sturdy man, severe in demeanor, with broad shoulders and muscular arms. His starched uniform gave him a rigid posture that made him look almost statuesque.

Emma rose to her feet and smiled at him widely. When Emma smiled her eyes shone like paradise, and most who looked upon her were struck by how her face became the absolute purest form of childish beauty. But tonight her iridescence was wasted on a father too preoccupied with adult concerns.

"I think it's bedtime, Nanny," the captain said, barely glancing towards the children.

The nanny's monitor dimmed and she clapped twice to get the kids moving.

"Oh, not yet! Please, we want a story," moaned Adam.

Emma generally thought Adam whined too much, but right now she was in agreement and looked up expectantly as well.

"Not tonight," said the nanny, ushering the children out of the common room and into their bedchambers. "Captain's orders."

As she passed him in the doorway, Captain LaFarge touched her shoulder and asked her to stay behind. She nodded and patted Adam's behind lightly saying, "Hop to it, sailors! I'll be in to tuck you in, and I expect you in your beds when I do."

Both children giggled and broke into a run down the hallway towards their quarters. The nanny turned back and the captain shut the door.

"So, you've decided," she said, not asking, the resolve clear in his eyes.

"I have," he said stoically. "We will not tell Emma about her mother. The girl is too young. She knows so little of life, and nothing at all of death. It would only confuse her, and bring her undue pain in an already complicated situation."

"I see," said the nanny.

"She'll learn the truth in time," the captain said, sensing her disapproval.

"With all due respect, Captain, time only makes pain sting all the harsher, and a lie seem twice as large."

LaFarge ignored this. It irritated him how domestic help presumed to be in a place to question his decisions, as though they were part of his family.

"I'll tell Emma her mother was called away to Earth," LaFarge said and waved his hand dismissively. "Charity work. Children and so forth. We weren't fond of each other in the end, but I'd like Emma to think highly of her nonetheless."

The nanny hesitated and then pressed the control panel to open the door. It slid up to reveal two small children in ship's nightdress.

"Emma and Adam, you get back to your beds this instant!" she said severely.

Adam sighed and crossed his arms. "It's not my fault, Nanny, she *made* me walk her back!"

Emma slid past the nanny and moved to where her rag doll was still lying on the floor. She pushed it aside and then tapped a spot along the bottom of the wall. A panel popped from its rivets and fell to the floor.

Emma reached her arm inside the opening and felt around until she found what she was looking for. Removing her arm, she revealed her little wooden box with the bronze clasp. She tucked it under the sleeve of her nightgown then scooted past Nanny and back towards the door.

The nanny brought her hands to her hips and wagged her finger at the girl. "Oh, that box will send me to the crazy bay. Emma LaFarge, you are too wrapped up in your secrets. What's in that cursed box of yours anyway?"

Emma merely laughed and disappeared down the hallway again, Adam—as always—following loyally behind.

For the first time in a long while, Captain LaFarge smiled. He was glad Emma had a companion. Like a brother and sister, Emma and Adam shared a life on board the Tian. They fought fiercely at times, but also stuck-up for each other when one was unfairly wronged.

They seemed like twins to the crew, their curly blond hair and big blue eyes fooling most everyone into thinking they were siblings. But they were not related.

Adam was a ward of the ship. His parents had joined the Tian to work, but both had succumbed to transition sickness within the first six months of their employment. Only eight percent of humans got sick when they transitioned to a life in the Black, but those that did rarely survived beyond the early stages of the illness.

Many attributed the phenomenon to space's general inhospitality. LaFarge, on the other hand, believed a person's fate was tied to their general constitution. It was a belief he kept to himself out of a sense of propriety, of course, but he felt he'd never seen evolution work itself upon a species so transparently (or as rapidly). Not all humans were destined to inhabit space. It was a hard and empty sort of life, so it seemed sensible that nature would find a way to weed out the feeble.

The captain remembered how happy Adam had been when he'd told him he'd sent his parents back to Earth on a mission of great importance. It seemed a better idea than telling the boy the truth— that he'd bound them in tarp and blown them out the airlock.

There was so little innocence anymore that

LaFarge felt duty-bound to keep his children from the harsh realities of life. At least until the Tian made it to its next destination, Port Miriam, where Emma and Adam would be boarded and properly schooled. At eight and almost nine years-old they were already starting later than other children.

He watched the nanny sigh and pick her way down the hallway after the children. Then he closed the door and unbuttoned the starchy white shirt of his uniform.

"We'll let the teachers teach," he said to himself as he folded the shirt over the chair. Then he sat down and touched his table monitor.

It flickered on to reveal the day's Port news. He liked to keep up with Port politics. When you spent a year sailing between them you could miss the election of a new governor, or the introduction of a tax that could harm your bottom line. It was wise to be prepared for whatever surprise awaited you at the next dock.

It was also reassuring to know that, while Earth was about to die, civilization had persevered and humanity continued to flourish.

The ports were growing every day. Jobs were being created at an alarming rate. LaFarge had even made himself a small fortune since the exodus of Earth began and, for once, the Tian had a full complement of workers. It was a wonderful time to be in the space faring business.

LaFarge had just begun reading an article about a machinist's strike that had turned violent on Port Valhalla when the lights went out. He heard a buzzing overhead and then a sharp *pop* as florescent bulbs cracked somewhere in the ceiling and the room went black.

He cursed and got up, leaving the table monitor on to keep the room lit. Then he smelled a rank odor and decided he'd better call Mr. Pin to bring up his tools and take a look. The last thing they needed was a fire smoldering somewhere between the decks.

LaFarge walked to the communicator and started to thumb Pin's number when his quarters filled with red light and a siren wailed throughout the ship.

"Oh no," is all LaFarge could whisper before his communicator buzzed and the panicked voice of his executive office crackled over the intercom.

"Sir, the ship's reactor—" the XO started.

"What's happened?" Lafarge yelled into the speaker.

"Sir, the ship's on fire!"

3

The nanny was already running back towards his quarters when LaFarge pushed into the hallway wearing only a white undershirt and ship's slacks.

He saw her struggling against a stream of workers scrambling to get to their emergency stations; her hair down, dressed for bed, a look of terror etched on her face. When she saw him, her eyes went wide and she raised her arm and waved it wildly back and forth to get his attention. He waved back and joined the torrent of people, keeping his head up so as not to lose sight of her.

When they finally met, LaFarge pushed her to the wall and grabbed her shoulders. "There's been a meltdown," he said as sternly and calmly as he could muster. In moments like this, it was a Captain's job to remain collected. For the crew's sake. "In the central reactor. The lower maintenance decks of the ship are on fire."

"My god," the nanny said, covering her mouth with a quivering hand.

"We've got protocols to contain it. As long as the

blast doors hold we should have time to put it out."

"What about the children? They're scared. What do I tell then?"

"Stay with them. Keep them calm. I'm needed on the bridge, but I'll keep in contact and come back when the worst is behind us."

"They need their father," she said, grabbing his arm. He looked at her hand and she let him go, realizing her fears were getting the better of her. In moments like this it was her job to be collected. For the children's sake.

She hesitated, then turned and ran back towards the children's quarters.

Emma and Adam sat together on the bed, clinging to each other in fear.

Adam's eyes were shut tight and he muttered, "Shut up, shut up, shut up," over and over, desperate for the sirens to silence.

Emma, on the other hand, didn't shut her senses down. She listened to the commotion through the walls, smelled the hint of smoke, and felt the air tighten around them.

"It's a fire," she said over the noise.

"Shut up, it's not!" Adam squealed back.

"You shut up!" she retaliated and Adam opened his eyes.

"What do we do, Emma?" he asked.

"My dad will put it out," she replied.

"How do you know?"

"Because it's his job, dummy," she replied. "Stop asking dumb questions."

They both jumped when the door slid open and

their nanny burst into the room. She ran and joined them on the bed and the kids parted from each other and clung to her sides instead.

"Is it a fire?" Adam asked her.

"It is," she replied, no hint of distress in her voice.

"Are we going to explode?" Adam asked. He was sobbing now.

"No, of course not, darling. We're perfectly safe in here. You'll see."

The sirens stopped and Nanny smiled. Adam smiled too and she tightened her grip around their little bodies and started humming a tune. Then she brushed Adam's bangs out of his eyes and said, "Let's sing while we wait for the lights to come back on."

So they did. They sang a song that nanny had taught them when Adam was sad about his parents leaving on their special mission. It was an old song that Nanny said her parents used to sing to her when she was little. It went:

"Blue Moon
You saw me standing alone
Without a dream in my heart
Without a love of my own"

Emma liked the song and how Nanny swayed them to the melody. The words made her think of space and the stars and for a moment she forgot all about the red emergency lights and the commotion outside the room. It felt as though they were in a dream.

"And then suddenly you appeared before me
The only one my arms will ever hold
I heard somebody whisper please adore me
And when I looked to the moon it turned to gold"

When they finished the first verse, Emma noticed the hallway was quiet once more. She tapped Nanny on the arm and whispered, "Listen," and nanny stopped singing.

The three of them sat in silence, listening for a sign of what was happening on the ship. But, there was nothing.

Then the strangest sound of sucking began behind the door, like someone had turned on a great vacuum. Emma had never heard anything like it. Nanny moved to get up and Adam squealed and grabbed onto her tighter. She shushed him harshly and pulled herself free and then left the two of them alone on the bed.

The children watched as their nanny slid slowly across the room towards the door to their quarters. The sucking sound grew louder until it reached an unbearable pitch, and Adam and Emma covered their ears with the palms of their hands.

"Come back, Nanny!" they both yelled, but she ignored them and pressed her ear against the door.

Suddenly the sucking stopped and the room was quiet once more.

The nanny turned and smiled and put her hands on her hips as if to say, *Look how silly you've been*, when the door exploded and she disappeared in a ball of blue flame.

The children screamed and covered their faces as a river of fire poured into the room and travelled up the walls.

As the flames drew closer, Adam burrowed himself under the pillows in a pathetic attempt to escape while Emma slid her back up against the wall.

Her mind raced and her eyes scanned the room, but she couldn't move. It was as though her body was paralyzed. *Where is Nanny?*, she thought. Why hadn't she come to help them? It was as though her heart knew they would never see her again, but her mind could not accept it. Then Emma thought of something else and her eyes went wild.

"My box!" she screamed and looked to a long steel table that ran along the west wall of the cabin. Her little wooden box was there, protected by the metal, but fire was slowly creeping up the wall behind it.

She felt a flash of heat on the back of her neck and turned to see flames rising up around the bed. It was creeping up the wall behind them as well. Suddenly Emma could move again, and she knew they only had one chance of escape.

"Come on, Adam!" she yelled and pulled the pillow away from his face. When he saw her, he squeezed his eyes closed and kicked his legs like a grasshopper on its back. Emma grabbed his shoulders and shook him. "We have to get out of here!"

"We'll be burned!" Adam howled, refusing to open his eyes.

"Not in the walls we won't!" she yelled back. "Now come on!"

Adam opened his eyes and sat up. Emma pulled at the sleeve of his bed-shirt and they both slid off the bed and onto the floor.

Heat pounded against the bottom of their bare feet as they moved. Emma grabbed her box, then slid under the steel table and dug her fingernails into the seam along two square wall panels. When the corner popped away, she lifted it off and stuck her head inside the opening.

The air inside the wall was warm and wet, but the tiny crawlspace was free of smoke.

"Where are we going?" Adam asked behind her.

"Just follow me," she replied and crawled into the wall. She turned back and extended her hand. "Come on. I know someone who can help us!"

Fire nipped at Adam's bare feet as he stuffed himself into the wall and crawled after her.

4

Down in the bowels of the ship, Pin struggled to haul forty feet of canvas water hose to the fire team who had taken over his engine room.

It was draped over his shoulders like a sack of potatoes and weighed him down so much he was forced to lean against the wall of the hallway to stay upright.

But it wasn't the pain in his legs that was bothering him, nor was it the way his lungs felt like they would collapse at any moment. There was something else weighing on him besides the bulky hose. He knew the Tian was lost, and it was his fault.

He was responsible for maintaining the ancient engine and for ensuring the safety switch would shut it down if the core became unstable. Not to mention, he was responsible for the alarm that should have sounded if that safety ever failed.

Pin stopped to catch his breath, dropping the hose in a pile at his feet. He wiped beads of sweat from his forehead as he tried to comprehend what could have happened. He inspected that engine daily, cared for it like a father would a child. He gave it everything it needed, so why had it rebelled? He supposed he'd never know the answer and pounded the wall with the side of his fist in frustration.

Manic shouts of desperate fire fighters rang out through the Tian's underworld and Pin stood up a little straighter.

He listened as the ship shuddered and groaned under the heat and pressure of the fire, like a monstrous whale slowly dying, sinking to the depths of some great ocean.

The fire was winning. The Tian was dying.

Pin wondered how long it would take for Captain LaFarge to call for an evacuation of the ship. Not long, he supposed. And when he did, Pin knew the outcome would not be good.

Since the exodus from Earth, the Tian had taken on more workers and passengers than the ship's escape pods could hold. When the ship went down, most of its crew would be forced to go down with it.

An explosion rocked the ship then and Mr. Pin lost his balance. He fell face-first into the pile of hose and became tangled up in it. As he struggled to free himself, anger seeped into his soul.

Why should I be forced to die?, he thought. *I'm no captain, no decorated general. Nobody gave me respected, so why should I live by their code?*

His thoughts were interrupted by the strangest sound of squealing, like rubber not-quite stretched across an open air valve. In a moment he knew what it meant. A bulkhead had failed and the hull was breached.

"Oh my god," he said softly and pushed himself

onto his feet. "We'll rip apart."

Standing next to the length of hose in the middle of that long hallway, Pin knew he had a choice: He could pick it back up and run towards the fire team and aid them in their futile task of saving the ship, or he could steal away on a pod and take his chances in the Black. One was honorable, the other self-serving. Each option would likely end in his death, but Pin hadn't made it this far in life by doing the honorable thing. In his experience, the honorable thing and the right thing were often at odds.

The ship rocked again and Pin made up his mind. Bolting in the opposite direction of the engine room, he looked back down the hallway as he ran and saw a ball of smoke barreling towards him. It quickly masked the length of hose he'd left on the floor of the hallway and he picked up the pace.

There was only two pods for maintenance teams below deck, but he needed to get to his workshop first. It wasn't far. And he needed his space suits.

When he reached his workshop, the air was already thick with smoke. Pin coughed and wheezed as he grabbed his canvas duffel bag and filled it with rations enough for his escape into space.

He didn't have much: twelve liters of water, forty-two leathery protein bars and a bottle of vitamin supplements he'd been given by the ship's doctor. He also threw in a thick roll of tape and a bundle of cloth-bound tools.

He looked at the supplies and sighed. It wasn't much, but he'd been lucky before. His pod could float into a shipping lane. It was unlikely, sure, but not outside the bounds of probability.

Pin clasped the bag closed and slid it across the floor until it hit the wall next to his clunky maintenance space suit which hung alongside a row of others by the door. Some were newer, but Pin only trusted his own.

He coughed again and grabbed at his chest. The smoke was getting thicker. He didn't have long. The smoke would move to choke the upper decks by moving up through the vents soon, so Pin knew the call to evacuate would come shortly. Once it did, his chance of getting to the pod would be all but gone.

He grabbed his suit off the wall and flung it over his shoulder. Then he picked his duffel bag up by the handle and opened the door to leave.

For some reason, he stopped then and turned, scanning his smoke filled workshop one last time. It had been his home for so many years, and just like that, he was leaving. He let his mind burn an image of the scene and then turned back towards the exit.

He was about to leave when he heard a familiar noise behind him. Someone inside the wall was working at the panels at the far end of his workshop.

Without turning, Pin dropped his bag and hung his head in despair. *Oh God, please no*, he thought then heard a panel hit the floor with a reverberating clang.

He heard the patter of tiny feet, the wheezing of tiny lungs, and then finally felt the thin fingers of little hands pull at the back of his uniform.

He looked down at Emma and Adam, their faces streaked with tears. They said nothing. They didn't have to.

Pin pulled two more space suits off their hooks and flung them across his shoulder. All of a sudden he felt weighed down again. He picked up his bag and kicked the door fully open with his right foot.

"Follow me, children!" he called as the three of them left the work bay and made for an escape pod.

Emma found it hard to keep up with Mr. Pin and Adam as they ran down one smoky corridor after another. For one thing, the hallway kept rocking and throwing her off her feet. And by the time she rose again, Pin and Adam seemed almost too far gone to catch up to.

But each time she fell behind, Adam would turn back and cry out for Pin to wait and then Emma would run to them again.

"Keep on your feet, girl!" Pin yelled at her once as she rejoined them.

"I can't!" she replied, "grabbing his arm for support. The floor keeps moving!"

"The stabilizers are out! The ship's heeling. Move your body the opposite way of the floor and you'll stay on your feet."

As he said this, Emma sensed the ground moving again and suddenly it felt like they were climbing upwards. She waved her arms and felt like she was about to fall back when Pin grabbed her around the waist and forced her upper body forwards.

"Lean into it, like this!" he yelled over the alarms.

Adam tried too, bending at the waist and holding his arms out in front of him.

"Now keep walking. We're almost there," Pin said, and the three of them trudged up the hallway towards a steel door labelled EMERGENCY ACCESS.

When they reached the door, Pin began typing

something on a keypad on the wall. Emma watched as he tried to remember what number came next, muttering between each press of his crooked finger.

Before he could finish, a voice boomed from speakers hidden somewhere in the ceiling. The words came quickly and deliberately.

"Attention all passengers and crew of the Tian. This is your Captain speaking."

"Here comes havoc," Pin muttered, turning back to the keypad.

"Daddy!" Emma cried out, recognizing her father's voice.

Pin ignored her and punched two more numbers into the keypad as Captain LaFarge continued.

"With this broadcast, I am giving the order to abandon ship. All passengers, go to your designated evacuation bays in an orderly fashion. Crew will meet and assist you there."

The keypad emitted a harsh buzz and Mr. Pin punched it. "Don't tell me you forgot the code, you old fool!" he scolded himself. Then he took a calming breath and started punching the keypad's buttons again.

Adam looked up and pulled at Pin's shirt, but the man waved the boy away.

"Someone else might know," Adam said, ignoring Pin's disinterest. "Maybe we should wait—"

Two more explosions popped like fireworks in the distance and the ship rocked again. They all repositioned themselves as the floor levelled off and Pin looked around wildly.

"She's tearing apart!" he said, returning his gaze to the keypad and pressing buttons quickly. "We can't wait for anyone else."

"Why?" asked Emma.

"Don't you start that now!" Pin yelled as he punched in the code's last number.

The keypad beeped twice and Pin stepped back. The door came alive with a whir of gears followed by a loud *ka-chunk* as the lock mechanism gave way.

He grabbed the thick metal handle and heaved it from right to left and the door cracked open, releasing a gust of smelly ozone into the hallway. Without a word, he ushered the two children into the cramped evacuation bay.

It was darker inside than the hallway and Emma began to feel nervous that they would be worse off than if they waited for others to arrive.

When they were all inside, Pin pulled the doors closed and locked them from the inside. Then he turned and elbowed an emergency box that hung on the wall. Glass scattered across the floor as he reached in and punched a big red button inside.

Yellow emergency lights flared and the round door to the old maintenance pod rolled open.

Pin threw his duffel bag into the pod first and then stacked the three space suits on one of two small benches. He turned to Adam and lifted him up and over the lip of the door.

Emma watched the boy sit on one of the benches dutifully and was suddenly struck by a strong desire to run away.

"My dad!" she said as Pin lifted her towards the pod. She struggled against him. "We have to get my dad!"

Pin's brow furrowed with determination as he pushed her into the pod and blocked the door with his wide body.

"Do as I say, girl!" he yelled over the alarms. Then he bent over and ducked into the escape pod.

Emma tried to sneak past him, but Pin held her back with his arm and forced her onto the bench next to Adam. She tried not to cry, but tears poured from her eyes freely and she began to sob.

Adam slid his hand across the bench and their fingers intertwined. He didn't like seeing her cry, but it was all he could think to do.

Pin hardly noticed their tenderness as he groped along the wall of the dark pod. Finally he found a long latch and pulled it down hard.

The pod doors rolled closed and sealed shut with a hiss. Then lines of tiny lights flickered on along the floor and ceiling. Able to see now, Pin moved to a panel of levers, studying each until he found the button to launch.

He looked back at the children and for the first time noticed Emma was crying. Moving away from the panel, he knelt down and pulled her chin up with the knobby knuckle of his index finger. She looked up reluctantly, anger and confusion in her eyes.

"I know you want your father, Emma, but it's his job to stay on board the ship," Pin said.

"Why?" she asked.

"It's just what captains do," he answered.

"I don't understand," she said in a deep sob. "Why?"

"I don't know," Pin replied. "But I know he would want you and Adam kept safe."

Another explosion—this one much closer—rang out and the pod began to shake violently.

"So, we have to go," Pin said to the girl. "Do you understand? For your father's sake."

She nodded her head and cried harder.

Pin told Adam to hold onto her tightly and Adam hugged Emma around the waist. They were both crying now, eyes shut tight with fear.

Pin looked at them and wondered if he was doing the right thing. Once they left the ship, they would be at the mercy of space. Rescue was improbable. Starvation was likely. Perhaps fire was a better end. Then he saw the ceiling of the evacuation bay tear apart through the pod's little window and the room filled with fire.

Pin punched the launch button.

Moments later Emma opened her eyes. The escape pod was far enough away from the Tian that she could see the massive ship spinning wildly and breaking apart through its little round window.

A thousand fires across the ship spewed liquid flame into space and she thought it looked like blood flowing from a million tiny paper cuts.

She stood up and pressed her nose to the glass, in awe of the Tian's beautiful and silent destruction. From far away, it hardly seemed scary at all.

Adam moved beside her and the two of them watched as fiery pieces of the ship tore away like flaming scraps of paper that extinguished as though hitting a pool of water. Then a flash so bright they had to shield their eyes flared across the stars and Pin grabbed them and turned them away from the window.

"That's the reactor core gone," he said quietly. "It'll all be over soon."

When Pin let them up again, Emma and Adam returned to the window to see the Tian tearing down the middle. Passengers and crew poured into space and flailed like one of Emma's rag dolls, smashing into debris, their tiny bodies popping open in puffs of red, like a splash of food coloring hitting water. It was a sight that both terrified and exhilarated the two children who had seen so little in life.

They watched until the Tian became so lost to space that it seemed like another flickering star among millions.

Adam turned away from the window and sat back down on the bench next to the space suits. He ran his finger along the helmet of one, leaving a greasy little smear on the glass faceplate. Then he looked over at Pin with the oddest expression that Pin could only read as boredom.

"I'm hungry," Adam said. "How long do we need to stay in here?"

Pin ran his fingers through his greying hair and let out a long and thoughtful breath. "Well, the truth is, I don't rightly know. Until we're picked up by another ship, I suppose."

Emma turned away from the window and sat on the bench next to Adam. She reached into her pocket and pulled out her little wooden box, inspecting it for damage.

"How far away is it?" Adam asked. "The other ship, I don't see it."

"We can't see it," answered Pin.

Emma leaned forward. "How do you know it's out there at all then?" she asked, feeling as though she was getting hungry as well. "How do you know we'll be saved?"

Adam and Emma looked on expectantly as Pin sat against the back wall of the pod and placed his duffel bag on his lap.

"I don't, children." he replied. "I'm sorry."

5

Adam sulked. He thought Mr. Pin was being far too stingy with the protein bars.

He'd seen more than enough in the man's bag for each of them to have their own, but Mr. Pin had made them share only half of one. Even worse, he'd made them wait hours to eat at all and his stomach was already grumbling!

"I'm still hungry," Adam said, folding his arms across his chest and frowning.

"We all are," replied Pin without taking his eyes off the control panel's gauges and blinking readouts. "But we have to keep as much food as we can for as long as we can. We don't want to run out."

He turned to the boy and pointed to the floor where Emma was sleeping peacefully under one of the bulky space suits. "Why don't you try and get some sleep," he said.

Adam huffed and slid off the bench to curl up next to Emma. "I'll try," he said.

Pin shook his head and turned back to the control

panel. He was too distracted to worry about Adam's discomfort just then. After going through the escape pod's life support systems, he calculated the craft could supply them with oxygen for no more than fifty six days. If they were still adrift after that, each of them would use a space suit, but that would only give them, at most, another eight to twelve hours of breathable air.

He sighed quietly. Of course, if they were still adrift in fifty days it also meant their little pod had gone completely unnoticed by any craft that might have been in the shipping lanes, and the option of rescue had long since passed. As far as he knew, no ship had ever travelled that far from the regular transit zones between space ports. Why would they? There was nothing worth visiting in the middle of space.

Pin confirmed the pod's distress beacon was transmitting at full frequency and then leaned against the wall.

He looked at Emma and Adam, both asleep, curled up together like a pair of kittens, and let his mind wander back to his own childhood; to a more innocent time when space wasn't just cold and black, but offered hope and the promise of a better future.

Back when he was a child he'd been obsessed with the government's search for a second Earth. The project was called Eden Star, and the scientist in charge of it was Dr. Charles Le Guin.

No expense was spared to ensure the Eden Star's success and—despite outcry from Earth's struggling and starving populations—Le Guin captivated the world with bold claims that she and her team would launch the human race into the stars and toward salvation.

Hundreds of long range probes were launched, their sensors beaming back amazing images and sounds from the farthest reaches of space. Pin remembered his family huddled around their monitor for each broadcast, itching to see what new planets and systems were discovered.

"See, Pin" his mother would say, planting a kiss on his cheek and pointing to each Technicolor orb that popped up on the screen. "That's where we're going to live one day. A whole new planet. A fresh start."

For a while, these images were enough to give humanity hope again, to make them forget that Earth's fate was beyond their control. But, after years of searching—and out of hundreds of new planets discovered—Eden Star remained elusive.

Earth, it seemed, was indeed a miracle.

Out of necessity, Le Guin's focus shifted away from discovering a new planet and towards moving humanity off-world and onto space ports. After that, space lost its wonder for Pin. It just seemed mundane and, well, empty.

The probes had sent enough information back to Earth to send ports into a vast array of systems to capitalize on the few planets that could be mined for gas and minerals; a dangerous business, it turned out.

Pin shuddered, remembering his own experience as a young man in the Deep Space Mining Corp. His first three years off-world he'd manned a drill ship for a company called Mariner Ore. To this day, he still didn't know which was more dangerous, the job or the other miners— criminals most of them, driven to rum and violence by the brutality of the work. Of course, he'd done more than his own share of drinking then. Back when alcohol still existed.

Pin licked his lips, remembering the sweet bite of alcohol. *Just another pleasure lost forever,* he thought and looked around the small pod. It suddenly felt a lot more like a coffin than a space craft. *I could sure use a bottle right now.*

Pin returned his thoughts to the situation at hand and took stock of their other supplies.

He'd only packed enough protein bars for sixty days and enough water to last thirty days. But that was only for himself. He hadn't anticipated caring for two tiny companions. With heavy rationing, he thought he could double the food rations, but their calorie intake would be dangerously low. Vitamins would help off-set the malnourishment, but alone they were useless.

Adam snorted and turned over and Emma shifted onto her back. It seemed as though the children would rise then, but they settled back into sleep a moment later.

After all they've been through, they need it, Pin thought. *After everything they've witnessed.*

He'd seen in their eyes that—while they were dazzled by the strange spectacle of the Tian's destruction—they were unable to understand the violence of it all, or the magnificent loss of life. He wondered if Emma understood the fate of her father and secretly hoped the topic never came up again. He wasn't what you would call adept at cheering people up. *Luckily children rarely dwelled on the past,* he reminded himself. Instead they seemed predisposed to focus on the moment, on where they were and what the future had in store for them. Living in the past was a pastime exclusively held for the old.

Pin's eyelids felt heavy and he decided he'd better get some sleep before the children woke up. Careful not to disturb them, he lay down next to them on his back and folded his arms across his chest.

He listened to Emma breathing through her nose, each inhale followed by a soft whimper as the air left her nostrils. At first, the sound was a comfort to him, but then it reminded him of how little air they had left. Then he fell into a restless and dreamless sleep.

6

"Am I asleep?" said Pin, waking with a start.

He couldn't remember falling asleep, but reasoned he must have. Did he hit his head?

He looked around, but it was dark and his eyes had yet to adjust. His fingers felt rough fabric on his body and he looked down to see his old space suit draped across his shoulders. He blew out a sigh of relief, deciding he must be in his work bay and still aboard the Tian.

"What a horrible dream I had," he said aloud. "The Tian destroyed, gone up in flame and torn apart."

"Mr. Pin!" came a tiny voice from somewhere in the darkness.

Pin straightened for a moment, surprised, and the truth came flooding back to him: the fire, Emma and Adam and their escape into space.

He rubbed the sleep from his eyes and turned on the pod's interior lights. It was as it was before, the children there with him, Emma awake and perched on the slender bench along the wall.

"Mr. Pin," Emma said again.

"What is it, honey?" he answered, still groggy.

"Where are we?"

"Space, of course. Where else would we be?" he answered the child.

"Where's daddy?" she asked.

"He'll be along shortly," said Pin, not knowing what else to say.

"I want a drink," the girl said.

Mr. Pin pulled a liter canister of water from his bag and poured the girl a cap full. She drank it down quickly and demanded more by pushing the cap into his face. He denied her request, shaking his head and taking it from her. To her credit, she didn't resist him, but watched closely as he twisted it back onto the bottle.

"Is it night or day?" she asked, settling back down next to Adam who had not stirred as far as Pin could tell.

"Reason it must be night still," Pin replied, relying solely on a gut feeling. "By human standards, that is. No such thing as night or day in space."

"Oh," was all she said, already close to sleep again.

"Why don't we get some more sleep and see what the morning brings?" Pin said and turned the lights off in the pod.

Emma mumbled an inaudible reply and faded back into sleep, her tiny whimpering breath filling the blackness once more.

Unfortunately for Pin, sleep would not come as easily. His bladder was full and his back was aching from the metal floor. He envied the children's young, nimble bones.

Moving to the waste system, he opened a small

drawer and pulled out a long plastic bag. Peeling open the top, he turned away and relieved his bladder into it until it was full and warm in his hands. He inspected it to see its coloring was dark and there was a murkiness to the liquid that made him nervous. He knew it meant his water intake was already far too low.

Careful not to spill any urine, he sealed the bag and slid open a panel along the wall to reveal the round opening of the waste disposal tube. He slid the bag into it and sealed it shut again before pressing a little green button on the wall and releasing the bag into space.

Pin watched the bag undulate for a second before freezing and floating away into the distance. Then, casting his eyes around the horizon through the pod's little window, he tried to find a sign of life. But no movement or a ship could be seen, or sign of a planet, only an eternity of stars. Of course from the limited view of the window, Pin had a very small horizon to study. In the vague and limitless world of space, it was possible that there were ships just out of sight that could sneak up on them at any moment.

He chuckled as the thought entered his mind. Such positivity was uncharacteristic of him. He looked back at the two sleeping children and wondered if they had inspired it somehow— Emma and Adam entwined beneath a dirty old space suit. At that moment he wanted nothing more than for them to be safe and enjoy as long a life as he had.

He sat on the bench with a groan and cast his thoughts back to the days of his youth; to blazing bar fights on Port Valhalla, the oily decks of monstrous drilling vessels and, of course, the choking smoke from the mines of Rhea, Saturn's moon. Such men and women he had known. Derelicts of the Earth they were, charged with taming a new frontier.

After almost forty years of trips on so many different ships it was near impossible for him to remember which was which and who was who anymore. Why was it, for example, that he remembered the bloody face of his old friend Jack Rafferty, but not who'd thrown the punch? Or why for that matter?

Pin sighed. "Thoughts of youth may be long, long thoughts," he muttered. "But none are longer than this old mariner's, lost in space. Right now they seem as long as the world is round and as infinite as space itself." Then he nodded off to sleep, where youth waited to greet him in his dreams.

"Daddy!" Adam cried suddenly, sitting up and rubbing at his eyes. "Where are we?"

"Alright, Adam, my boy!" said Pin, who had been awake for some hours, watching the horizon in another vein endeavor to spot ships. "Your daddy's safe, I'm sure, and he'll be here soon enough and bringing a ship with him." He put his arms around the boy's shoulders to comfort him and noticed Emma was awake and sitting up against the wall. "So, you're awake too, little mouse."

Emma nodded and pulled her feet under the warmth of the space suit. Another child might have supplemented Adam's inquiry with questions of her own, but she did not. Was it because she sensed the subterfuge in his answers? Pin couldn't quite tell, but guessed by her nature that she was less likely to be fooled by false comforts.

"Ahoy!" called Adam as he stared out into space through the pod's little window. "I'll be a captain one day, like Emma's old dad, won't I, Mr. Pin?"

"Could be that's true," Pin replied.

For the first time, he noticed how dirty the children were, their faces covered in a thin layer of grey ash. He could only imagine what *he* looked like after fighting the fire in the engine room. Even though he knew they couldn't spare the water, he felt compelled to wash them all so, moving to his bag, he poured some water into his hand and tried to wipe Adam's face.

"I don't want to wash!" the boy said, pushing Pin's hand away and almost spilling the water.

"Stick your face in this water right now!" Pin said, pulling the boy towards him and rubbing his cheeks roughly. "We may be the only three fools for light years, but we're not sitting around with faces like bags of soot and coal."

When Adam had washed, Pin beckoned Emma forward. "You too," he said and the girl slid off the bench and walked over to them without protest.

Pin knelt down to her level and Emma titled her head, casting her eyes upwards. As he washed her forehead and cheeks, watching the dirty water drip over her chin and bead down her porcelain neck, Pin was struck by the ceremony of the act. He'd never been much for religion but just then he felt like a priest performing a baptism, the girl, like the Virgin Mary, washed of sin and speaking silently to The Lord.

When she was good and clean, Pin let Emma skip back to her seat and watched her slide back under the space suit. She peeked her head under it for a moment to check on her secret box, which was there safe and sound, and then sighed contently to herself.

"Mr. Pin?" came Adam's inquiring voice from beside the window.

The man turned to the boy as he sat down to ease his aging knees. "I suppose you can both just call me Pin from now on," he said. "Since we're all becoming fast friends."

"That's a funny name," said Adam, wrinkling his nose.

"Well I prefer it to Paddington, my first name. Pin will do for us all if it's all the same to you, Adam."

"Emma is a short name for Emmeline," the girl said enthusiastically, happy to be sharing in the conversation. "It was my mother's name."

"A fine name to be sure," Pin said, noting the sweet smile that crossed the girl's face. And what about you, Adam, my boy?" asked Pin.

Adam shrugged his shoulders. "I'm just Adam," he said, flatly.

"Nothing wrong with being just Adam," Pin replied. "Just Adam is just fine. Now what were you wanting to ask old Pin?"

Adam turned back towards the stars as he continued. "Well, I was just wondering about animals."

"What about them were you wanting to know?"

Adam shrugged again. "I don't know. *All* about them, I suppose."

"*All* about them is a lot, so I'll start by telling you this: There were three kinds of critters that used to roam the Earth before people wiped them all out."

Adam ran across the pod and sat on the bench

next to Emma, excited to hear all about the three kinds of animals.

"First, there were the ones that walked on land. Some had fur, others had smooth and shiny scales, and some were as bald as you and I.

"Then there were ones that flew in the sky. Birds we called them; some of which were made up of so many colors you'd think you were looking at a rainbow. They were called Parrots, or Robins, or Woodpeckers, and people would keep them in cages on account of their beauty."

"I wish I had a parrot in a cage," said Emma dreamily.

"And what in the world would you do with a parrot in a cage, Emma LaFarge?" asked Pin.

"I'd let it out, of course," replied Emma.

Pin nodded and chuckled. "I believe you would, little mouse," he said. "I believe you would."

Pin continued, telling the children all about the third type of animal, those that swam in the waters of Earth's vast oceans. He described how schools of fish moved together in the currents and how whales— some larger than even the pod they were in— could swallow the whole lot of them at once.

He loved the way their eyes lit up with wonder at his memories and couldn't recall a happier morning.

When the children grew tired of hearing about animals and Earth, Emma asked Pin to tell them a story, and seeing no reason to deny the girl her wish, Pin began to weave a tale as old as time about a land before everything, where people lived in glorious gardens and slept among green trees and colorful flowers in an endless valley surrounded by tall mountains.

"In this land," Pin said, speaking in a low and serious tone, "two royal children—a twin brother and sister—ruled justly with a shared heart. They were so close they could read each other's thoughts, and feel each other's joy and sadness.

"When they were awake, the world was light. And when they slept, darkness fell across the valley. As long as they were together, the valley was in perfect harmony and their subjects were happy. They were both equally beautiful, and kind, and forever young and their subjects loved them fully."

"I like this story," said Emma as Pin described the world to them.

"Me too," said Adam with a big smile.

"Not so fast," warned Pin, a stern look crossing his face. "For you see, on the other side of the mountains, there were people who lived a very different kind of life. They had nobody to watch over them, so they lived with terrible hardship. They were always hungry and thirsty and lived in great fear of fierce beasts and terrible monsters that hunted them throughout the land and gobbled up their children."

"That's terrible!" blurted Adam, unable to control himself.

"Indeed it was, Adam, very terrible indeed!"

"What happened next?" both children asked almost simultaneously.

"Well, if you'll both hush up and let me go on then you'll know, won't you?"

The children nodded and lay down into one another as Pin continued his tale of the royal twins who ruled their world as one.

"One day, two travelers appeared in the valley. They appeared sickly and indeed were on death's very door on account that they were at the end of a long and treacherous journey over the mountains. They were met with great kindness by the people of the valley, who fed and clothed them and eased their pain with heavenly potions and ointments.

"When they were finally in good health again, the two travelers asked how it was that the valley people lived in such glorious splendor. The people told them of their rulers, the beautiful twins who lived atop a silvery tower in the very center of the valley. The travelers were intrigued by this and asked to see the twins for themselves, and so were taken to the great tower to meet these sacred children."

"Did they see them?" asked Adam.

"What did they say to them?" Emma piped in.

"They did see them, Adam, but they did not speak a single word, Emma. They couldn't, in fact, because the twins' beauty was so wondrous to their eyes that mere words would not come to them. Instead, having been raised in the violent world beyond the mountains and knowing nothing but treachery, they grabbed the girl and stole her away from her brother, away from the silver tower, away from the valley and back across the mountains, where they hoped she would bring light to their dark world."

Both children sat up straight, their mouths agape in disbelief.

"But—" Adam started.

"Why? I mean, why didn't anyone stop them?" Emma finished for him.

"Well, I suppose it's because no one had ever seen such a thing. Couldn't even imagine something like that could happen."

Adam leaned forward, dissatisfied. "Will her

brother get her back again?"

Pin rubbed his chin as though unsure of the answer. "Well, suppose she *could* bring light and happiness to the people beyond the mountains. And chase away the monsters and demons. Would that be a good thing?"

The children fidgeted as they thought about this. Finally Adam said, "But you said the twins were sad when they were apart."

"Indeed they were. And while they could feel each other across the mountains, they only shared a deep sadness between them. But, they could also share the sun and moon equally with everyone and while the valley people were a little bit less happy than they once were, the mountain people were a little less sad and scared. So, you see, to steal his sister back, the prince would have to be willing to also steal away the happiness from the mountain people."

"I think he should get her," said Adam. "Those rotten mountain people were bad!"

"I don't like this story at all," said Emma with a huff.

Pin chuckled and rose to his feet with a grunt. "Well, chew on that for now. There's more of this story to tell, but you'll have to wait to hear it," he said. "Right now there's work to be done and there's no point putting it off any longer."

With that, Pin turned to the control panel to study the pod's readouts. He was determined to find a way to save some air time, somehow.

When he heard whispering behind him, he turned slightly to listen. Adam and Emma were continuing the tale of the estranged twins, wrestling with the dilemma he'd set for them, and trying to figure out how everyone could live happily ever after. He marveled once again at their innocence, and smiled to himself as he continued his work.

Over the many days that past, it often occurred to Pin that most people in their situation would find the total absence of privacy intolerable. But surprisingly, the things that most people might call indecent, or would shock them under normal circumstances, seemed like nothing at all when herded together in a little shuttle and forced to live face-to-face with eternity.

Since he had no more convention than a walrus, Paddington Pin cared for his two little wards like a nursemaid would a baby; that is to say with no mind for modesty or decorum.

He helped them with their bathing and toiletry needs and fed them on a strict routine. He helped them fall asleep when their little minds wouldn't settle and soothed them when they were cold, or scared of the dark, all the while entertaining them with more tales of the royal siblings who ruled their kingdom with love in their hearts and learned the hard lessons of life.

While none of them said it, it seemed to all three castaways that they had become something of a funny little family drifting all alone in an endless sea of stars.

Part Two
The Red Giant

7

Some days later, while he was taking stock of their dwindling supplies, Pin decided the children would need to die before he did.

The notion was something he'd been struggling with for weeks, but no matter how he conceived of their inevitable demise, it just didn't seem right to leave them to their end alone and confused. When the time came, they would need a shepherd into darkness. It was simply a matter of kindness.

Watching them now, as they occupied themselves with some childish game he was unable to understand, he could already see the hunger taking its toll. *Growing little bodies need more than they're getting*, he thought glumly as he stacked the rest of the week's protein rations into a jiggling tower of beige gelatin.

Adam's cheeks, once plump and healthy, had become so sunken that Pin could trace the shape of the boy's skull under the tight pink flesh of his face, while the sockets of Emma's sapphire blue eyes had darkened so that she seemed to have aged five years since their escape from the Tian. Her blonde hair, once shiny and thick, now sat flat and dull atop her head.

They were wasting away before his very eyes, and Paddington Pin felt a stirring of self-loathing in his heart, as though he were solely to blame.

"Guess what, children?" he said suddenly.

Adam and Emma looked up, curious and expectant.

"What are we guessing?" asked Emma.

"Is it a game?" Adam chimed in.

"No, it's not a game. Today is a special day, is what," said Pin. "It's our anniversary. One month we've spent together in this cramped little pod and I wouldn't trade a single day of it."

"Is that like a birthday?" asked Adam.

"I suppose it is, considering it's celebrating the start of something special."

"On birthdays you get a surprise and something sweet," said Emma.

"Well, we'll have both those things in one then. The surprise being each of us will eat an entire protein bar to ourselves tonight."

"You mean it?" said Adam, greedily. "No sharing?"

Pin nodded, then looked into Emma's hungry eyes. "I suppose it isn't sweet like pudding or a tart, Emma, but tonight we'll sleep with full bellies for once and that's a sweetness to me."

With that, Pin handed each of them a slender block of protein, which they ate slowly, savoring every bite like it could be their last.

When she'd eaten half her bar, Emma's stomach gurgled loudly and she let out a little burp. Her face turned bright red at once and she covered her mouth with her hand, but not before Adam chuckled and pointed at her, tauntingly.

Not liking to see her embarrassed, Pin sucked in a deep breath and belched the air back out again. It sent such a low sound through the pod that Adam thought it sounded like the rumbling of an old ship engine and said as much with a laugh.

"Let's see if you can beat that, Adam, my boy!" bellowed Pin, his heart swelling with joy to see a bright smile return to Emma's face.

"I can!" shouted Adam and jumped to his feet.

Just like Pin, he inhaled a mouthful of air and swallowed it down into his belly. Only, instead of letting it out, he let it sit there for a moment, holding out his finger as if to say to his two spectators, *Just wait until you see this! I know I ain't much more than a scrawny boy nobody ever wanted, but I can belch as well as any king!* And indeed, when the boy opened his mouth, the air came forth like a hurricane, and was just as loud as the old mariner's had been.

Pin clapped his hands and Adam bowed. Then the old man turned to Emma and gave her a little wink. She smiled and winked back and they all returned to their special anniversary dinner.

For the rest of the night, neither one of them spoke of what the future might bring. Instead, they spoke of the past; Emma of her mother, wondering aloud if she thought of her from time to time in her charity work on Earth.

When the girl spoke of her, a flash of longing crossed her face. Pin could tell the girl thought highly of her old mom and wished upon wishes that he felt similarly about his own. But his had been a hard woman, made harder by a drunk of a husband. She used to say she had a cinderblock in her gut and seemed to make it her mission to ensure that Pin was weighed down by one as well.

While his was a mother worth running from, it seemed from the way she spoke of her, Emma's was a mother that would wrap you in her arms and keep you safe from ~~the~~ all the world's troubles.

"Your mom sounds like a fine lady, little mouse," Pin said when Emma had finished speaking. "I'll bet she thinks of you all day long and dreams of you when she's sleeping. And if she were here now I bet she'd be mighty proud of how brave and smart you are."

Pin turned to Adam, who'd remained silent during Emma's talking. "You too, Adam. I'll bet your parents would be some surprised at the little man you've become, strong and helpful to others. I see the way you care for Emma, putting her before yourself when things get tight. It's a good way to be, my boy."

Adam looked away bashfully and Pin was struck by a sudden sadness. With no children of his own and an ex-wife who'd fallen out of love with him so long ago he doubted she'd remember his face if they met the next day, Pin realized no one would think of him fondly when he was gone. Or think of him at all, for that matter. He began to wonder if, without that, life was a waste, when Emma's voice chased his thoughts away.

"What's wrong, Pin?" she said, her mouth curling down at the corners in concern.

Pin grunted and ran his fingers through his grey hair, greasy from so many weeks without washing. "Oh, nothing to concern a young mind like yours, child. Just the old thoughts of an old man. Now, why don't you go ahead and sing us a song to stop my mind from wandering and fill my heart with love."

Emma pressed the tip of her index finger to her chin and thought about what song she could sing to make Pin feel happy again. When she decided on one, she told Adam he could help if he remembered the words, but he said he didn't feel like singing.

So Emma sang alone. Her voice was high and breathy, like a light breeze blowing across the top of crisp blue water. She sang:

"Blue Moon
You saw me standing alone
Without a dream in my heart
Without a love of my own"

And Pin closed his eyes and was transported away across the vastness of space. Like a rocket travelling at the speed of light, he shot through constellations of stars, past ships and planets and the hot fires of suns until he was alone in a sea of black, lost to oblivion.

And his heart was full.

Six weeks later their food and water were gone, and their oxygen was almost depleted.

Emma was curled up on a bench, sweaty and sick, her arms folded across her stomach in response to hunger pains. She'd been all but delirious for days, muttering half-words and random thoughts to no one in particular.

Adam had given Pin permission to use the last of their water to wash her forehead and ease her fever, but she still felt hot to the touch.

Adam sat under her on the floor, his eyes closed

tightly, though he was not asleep. Recently, night terrors had robbed him of a decent night's rest and now he seemed to exist in a kind of waking sleep; his mind neither in this world, or the next. But he found if he stayed close to Emma he felt a little better, so the two of them had become inseparable.

At least they'll leave this world together, Pin thought as he watched them helplessly. *At least they'll have that.*

The old man shook his head and heaved a deep and burdened sigh. He knew he wasn't helping them by prolonging their suffering. He knew it was time to end it once and for all.

"Children, I know you're weak," Pin said quietly. "But the air is almost out and it's time to put on your suits."

Adam opened his eyes and stirred, but when he tried to rise, his legs gave out from under him and he sat back down. "I can't walk," he said, tears forming in his eyes. "And Emma's asleep still."

"No bother, boy. You just sit right there and old Pin will get you sealed into your suit."

Pin brought both suits over to the children, laying Emma's over her body as he helped Adam up. He laid the boy's upper body over his shoulder like a bag of coal and lifted his right leg into the suit, followed by his left. Then he held him up and stuck both his arms into the heavy sleeves and sealed the suit up the front.

Pin looked into the boy's eyes and gave him a little kiss on his flush cheek before popping on the glass helmet and sealing it along the neckline.

Reaching around the boy's back, Pin turned the valve clockwise on the oxygen canister and air flowed into Adam's space suit with a sharp hiss. Pin watched him take a breath through the glass visor then helped him sit back down against the wall under the window.

When Pin sat Emma up, she half awoke; her eyes fluttering open momentarily and then closing every few seconds. And as the old man helped her into her space suit, she spoke to him as though the two had met in a dream.

"Do you smell that, Daddy?" Emma whispered.

"It's not daddy, child. It's only old Pin helping you into your suit."

"Do you smell it?" the girl asked again.

"Tell me what you smell, little mouse," he answered, lifting her onto his lap and hoisting the heavy suit up her torso.

"A sweetness, Daddy," she said, her eyes fluttering open for the briefest of moments. "Like perfume on a wind. Do you suppose it's flowers and trees?"

"Could be it is, Emma. It could be that," said Pin through tears.

All at once, Emma's eyes opened wide and she twisted and grabbed Pin around his collar.

"I see it!" she yelled, eyes wild. "Do you see it? Do you see the colors? Red, Daddy! Deep red in a blue sky! I see it!"

Pin held the girl to his chest and cried. "I see it, Emma! I see it, too. It's beautiful! It's enough to steal your breath away."

"We're saved," Emma whispered finally before slipping back into a restless sleep.

Pin rocked her a moment longer, until his tears dried and he could allow himself to let her lay down again. When he did, Pin sealed up the front of Emma's suit and slid the helmet over her head. Then he turned on her oxygen and watched through the dirty visor to ensure she was breathing properly.

With the children in their suits, it was time for Pin to get into his. As he pulled his legs into it for the last time, he thought about all the times he'd needed to wear it over the years. He'd always hated it as a reminder of humanity's fragile existence among the stars. So now it seemed fitting that, in the end, he would die wearing it.

His life had always had a way of working out for the worst, and yet, as he watched the children asleep in their suits, he felt a strange joy to be going out this way; together with them. He had saved them from a violent death aboard the Tian, and they were sparing him from dying a lonely old man. Perhaps it was just too much to ask for them all to be saved from death, but at least they would all die peacefully and together.

Pin sealed his helmet along the neckline and turned the valve on his oxygen canister. He took a breath of stale air then moved over to where Emma was sleeping, still restless and muttering about flowers and blue skies.

He scooped her up in his arms. She felt as light as a newborn baby. Bending down, he laid her on the floor next to Adam. He thought they looked like angels lying there together. Or like ancient alien children floating through the heavens, asleep for eternity. And in that moment, he realized he loved them more than anything else in his miserable life.

Pin bowed his head and let himself cry. He cried for a long, long time. He cried for Emma and Adam. He cried for himself. And he cried for everyone who'd perished on the Tian. He cried for every child alive and yet to be born. He cried for the very end of humanity, for at that moment he saw its demise in the faces of the children laid before him.

Finally, sobbing, his face wet with tears, Pin reached down and turned the valve of Adam's oxygen canister counterclockwise. The flow of oxygen to the boy's suit stopped at once. He knew it would only take a few more minutes for the boy to lose consciousness and slip away forever.

Unable to look upon their faces any longer, Pin shut his eyes as he reached for Emma's oxygen canister. He paused before turning it, wondering for an instant if there was another way. Something he hadn't considered. Anything other than *this*.

"Just do, it you old coward," he whispered to himself. The words bounced around in his helmet, sounding like various voices cursing him at him all at once. "For once in your miserable life, don't you run away."

Pin turned the valve of Emma's oxygen tank slowly, the air flow becoming a slow hiss as the suit's intake reduced by half. His hand shook so violently he found he had to grab his wrist to steady it and finish the job.

But it wasn't just his hand that shook. The pod was rocking. It shuddered so slowly at first that he barely noticed, until it became so violent he could hardly stay kneeled before the girl.

Pin fell flat on his back and then rolled across the floor of the pod, crashing against the far, steel wall with a loud clang. Whatever force had captured the pod seemed to be hurling it through the stars at an enormous velocity so Pin was pinned to the floor and couldn't move for some fifteen or twenty seconds.

Then a bright flash of light erupted all around them and, as quickly as the madness had started, the pod was still again.

Pin blinked as though waking from a nightmare. His cheeks were still wet with tears and his vision was blurry. He struggled to move from the floor, but his muscles felt taut, as though he'd just run a marathon.

"Look," Adam's quiet voice said somewhere in the dark.

Pin rose up and looked over at Adam, still lying across the pod. He was awake and looking up at something on the ceiling. He lifted his arm and pointed upwards.

"Look, Emma. You were right," he said again with a breathless squeak.

Pin followed Adam's gaze upwards until he saw what the boy was looking at— a muted red glow that spread across the pod's ceiling like flowing blood. Pin watched it grow quickly, until the ceiling was covered and the pod was filled with brilliant red light.

Jumping to his feet, he shielded his eyes and stared out the pod's window. There, off in the distance, was a red giant. Not believing his eyes, Pin rubbed them roughly before taking another a look. But when he opened them again the planet was still there, ten times as large as Earth and waiting to swallow them.

"Children!" the old man shouted. "Children, the gods have saved us!"

In an instant, Pin remembered everything. He dove towards the children and turned Adam's oxygen valve back on. The suit began to fill once more, but Adam had since passed out. Picking him up, Pin shook him roughly until his eyes fluttered opened.

"Breathe, boy!" he yelled at Adam. "Breathe!"

Adam breathed in and coughed and Pin sat him back down.

"Now you, my little mouse!" yelled Pin as he

reached behind Emma and turned her oxygen back to full flow. When she didn't move, he pressed the glass of his helmet up to hers and watched her face carefully. In a moment, he saw her eyes move under their lids and knew she was still asleep.

Deeply relieved he fell back onto his backside. He pressed the rough fabric of his gloved hands against the glass of his helmet and let out a loud and agonizing cry.

"Oh, children! Children!" He shouted over and over, rocking back and forth as tears of joy flowed from his eyes freely. For even though Pin didn't know anything about this planet—whether it would help or hinder them—he knew it was something special. He knew it had brought them there and saved the children.

He was sure it was a sign.

8

As they approached the red planet, Pin used the pod's scanners to examine its atmosphere. While they were still more than 4000 Kilometers away, he knew it wouldn't be long before the giant began pulling them into its orbit. If he needed to maneuver them away, he would need to act quickly.

    The children sat against the wall, still in their suits, the pod's oxygen now fully depleted. Emma was groggy but awake, stimulated by the excitement of the planet's appearance. Adam shifted uncomfortably in his suit. He was getting frustrated by how long it was taking to get to the planet, but had learned not to complain while Pin was working.

    Finally, the pod's control panel spoke its electronic language, spitting lines of numbers and elemental signs across its dusty old monitor. Pin muttered to himself as each line appeared, reading every character carefully.

    "Nitrogen. Argon. Helium." he said quietly as text continued to appear. "Okay, okay. We can work with that in the right amounts." He pushed his face closer to the monitor and squinted as new information appeared. "What's this now? Hydrogen at eighty percent... surface mass is... molten."

Pin gripped the panel's thin metallic edge and hung his head. For a long while he didn't move and Emma was beginning to wonder if he was feeling sick.

"What is it, Pin?" she asked him, her voice muffled through the glass helmet.

Pin didn't answer her directly, but came alive at once. He shook the electronic panel violently, cursing and kicking at the controls. Then he pounded the monitor with his fist, yelling out in pain as his knuckles cracked against the hard glass.

"Stop!" Emma yelled, frightened by his outburst. She gripped Adam's arm and shook it as if requesting him to help her understand.

"Pin, stop!" Adam said and rose to his feet. He shuffled across the pod until he reached the old man and pulled at the back of his suit. "I'm scared! Stop!"

Pin either didn't hear him or couldn't comprehend the words, because he reached back and shoved Adam away and continued to rage against the pod, pulling down cables and punching open compartments until the once pristine and ordered interior was a jungle of wires and broken panels.

Finally, he stopped and threw his face towards the pod's ceiling. "Why did you bring us here? What do you want from me?" he cried out before crumpling to his knees.

After a moment, Adam stood back up slowly and walked to where Pin was huddled and breathing heavily. He put a gloved hand on the man's shoulder and bent down to look upon his face.

"Pin?" Adam asked, but the old man did not look up. "Pin, will we land on the planet soon?"

Emma was surprised to hear Pin begin to laugh then. It was a quiet sort of laugh and first, high-pitched and whimpering. But when Pin looked up at Adam's expectant face it turned hearty and rich and seemed to roll along the pod's ceiling as he grabbed at his belly and cried tears of rich irony.

"What's funny, Pin?" Adam asked confused. "Is it a joke?"

Pin grabbed the boy's hand. "Help me up, boy," he said calmly, and Adam helped him back onto his feet.

Looking around the messy pod, Pin felt ashamed that he'd let the children see him act so destructively. He looked at Emma, still weak and sitting up against the wall, and then down at Adam whose hand was still in his.

"I'll tell it to you straight, children. We can't land on the planet," he said.

"Why not?" Adam asked, disappointed.

"Because it's full of poisonous gas and lava so hot we'd burn to a crisp before we even touched it," Pin answered moving towards the pod's window. "In fact, we'll need to thrust ourselves away quickly, or be swallowed up whole in no time flat."

As Pin moved back towards the beat-up control panel, Adam stepped up to the window and peeked out. The planet was closer now and he could make out violent swirls of gas and dust storming across its atmosphere.

So impressed he was by the beautiful severity of it all, he wished Emma could see it too. But, when he looked back at her, he could see she was too weak to join him.

"I'll tell you what it looks like, Emma," he said and turned back. "Swirls like draining water are dancing across the red surface. But it's not water, it's gas. Pin says it's poisonous. And there's flashes of light sparking all over. It's like a laser show. Boy, I wish you could see it."

When Adam looked back at Emma again, her eyes were closed and he could see she was crying. He was about to ask her why, but lost his footing and fell over as Pin engaged the thrusters and the pod blasted away at a 90 degree angle.

Keeping low, he crawled back over to Emma and sat with her against the wall. "We're moving away, aren't we?" Adam asked as Pin looked out the window again to make sure they were on course to miss the dangerous planet.

"We are indeed," answered Pin. "Like old Jonah fleeing the beast's belly."

"Where will we go, next?" Adam's questions continued. Only this time, Pin wasn't the one to respond. Eyes wet with tears, Emma turned to Adam.

"Nowhere!" she shouted, surprising her companions. "Don't you get it? We're all going to die!"

"No we're not!" Adam yelled back, pushing her away. "You don't know that!"

"Yes I do," Emma said.

"Pin, are we going to die?" Adam called across the pod.

Pin sighed and looked towards the boy and his expectant eyes. "Everything and everyone comes to an end and that's the honest truth," he said slowly.

"What does that mean?" Adam answered.

"It means I'm right and we're going to die,

dummy," Emma said mockingly.

Pin cut in quickly saying, "The hardest part of it is not knowing when, or how the end will come." Then he moved over to the children and kneeled down to meet their eyes as he continued slowly. "It could come today or maybe not, but I'll tell you this much: I never believed life had a plan for any of us. Always seemed to me we were all just particles zipping through space without any rhyme or reason. But now, well, let's just say I'm not so sure there isn't some kind of plan working itself out all around us."

"What do you mean?" Emma asked quietly.

"Well, life brought us together didn't it? And we've managed so far, haven't we?"

Pin put Emma's hand in his. Then he grabbed Adam's and squeezed it tightly, the three of them locked in a tight circle.

"I almost lost you once, I don't intend to lose you again," he said to them softly.

Emma cried harder then, overcome with emotion. She lowered her face, unable to look into Pin's eyes. "But, I saw it," she said. "Blue skies and flowers. I could smell it. I know I could. But, we can't land on the planet."

"Emma LaFarge, you look at me this instant," Pin said sternly and Emma looked up at him again. "In all my life you two children are the most important thing that's ever happened to me. And if there's one thing I've learned since meeting you it's that you never know what's waiting just around the corner. So don't you give up hope on me, because without you I reckon there's no hope in this whole damned universe."

They were quiet then, the hum of the pod's

exposed mechanical systems the only sound filling the silence as they drifted away from the poisonous planet.

Pin watched its reflection in the glass of Emma's helmet. Her face was on fire with the red glow of it. All except her big blue eyes, which were a striking contrast to the violence of the receding red gas giant. They were powerful and pure, and pulled him in with their youthful intensity and fear, purity and wildness.

Then, as though her eyes had the sublime power to conjure miracles, the red began to drain from Emma's face. It was slow at first—like a curtain being drawn to let sunlight into a dark room—but soon the red glow was completely usurped by a new light that bathed the girl's face in rich blue.

Moving away, Pin looked down in shock to see that he too was being washed in a natural blue light. And indeed, so was the pod's small interior.

He looked back at Emma to see her focus was now on something behind him. Something outside the window was reflecting in the glass of her visor. A blue orb, tiny in comparison but no less impressive in scale, was emerging behind the red planet.

"Pin, look," Emma said, breathlessly. "Is it sky?"

Pin jumped to his feet and rushed to the window. What he saw made his heart pound in his chest and blood pulsed through his body like a dam bursting and releasing a flood across dry land.

"It's a moon!" he yelled and bolted towards the control panel. "Hold onto something, children!"

Pin programmed a change in their trajectory quickly and slammed the ignition. The pod jerked violently as the thrusters threw a puff of ozone into space and pushed them in a new direction. Then, working to get a readout of the blue moon's atmosphere, Pin trained the scanners towards it and waited.

A moment later, the panel beeped aggressively and he cursed and slammed a fist against it. Then he knelt down and picked at a bundle of wires strewn about the floor under his feet.

"Blast you and your temper, Paddington Pin! You fried the bloody scanners!" he shouted at himself as he tried to determine where the problem might lay. Unable to find it, he rose and turned to Emma and Adam who were now standing at the window and watching the moon grow larger.

"We've got no choice but to go in blind and hope that life's got bigger plans ~~than~~ for us than to choke to death on a poisonous moon in the middle of uncharted space," Pin said as he pushed the children towards the far bench where they sat down.

"You two strap yourselves into a landing harness and hold onto each other. And when we land, you keep your suits on until I say so. In fact, don't do anything without my saying so. We don't know anything about this moon and after all this I'll not have you killing yourselves doing something stupid."

Adam helped Emma strap herself to the wall, clipping four straps into a single round harness point at the center of her chest.

When she was good and secure, Pin harnessed Adam in and pulled the straps tightly around his emaciated frame before sitting down on the bench across from them.

The pod began to shake as Pin strapped himself in. He yelled that the moon was pulling them into its orbit and it wasn't worth worrying about, but Emma felt sick and woozy like she might pass out.

As they continued their descent, the pod shook worse and worse until the three companions could barely make each other's shapes for the vibrations.

A moment later, Emma felt hot inside her suit and saw wild flame outside the pod's window. She screamed and shut her eyes as they entered the moon's atmosphere and plummeted towards its mysterious surface. It wasn't long after that she passed out completely.

9

Screams and rushing water.

Pin was standing over her when Emma came to, wild eyed and panicked. He was out of his harness and trying to keep steady as the pod rolled head-over-tail as if someone had stuffed them in a drum and sent it rolling down a mountainside.

Adam was still next to her, safely strapped to the wall but screaming bloody murder. In a moment, Emma saw why. The pod was filling with water.

Amid the chaos, she scanned the interior until she found the source of the leak— a wide tear in the pod's fuselage was letting in gallons of frigid water, the level of which was already past their legs and over the top of the narrow bench.

"We touched down on water!" Pin yelled. "We're rolling to the bottom! Stay in your suits! And pray we're not in the middle of a goddamn ocean!"

As if looking for proof, Emma's eyes shot to the window where, sure enough, a storm of bubbles raged outside, drummed up by the pod's turbulent descent.

Pin was right: they had made it to the planet's surface, but the pod was submerged and moving further into the depths of a great body of water.

Eventually the pod stopped rolling and settled into a deep sandbar, the currents dragging it steadily downwards along the seabed.

Water still poured in through the fuselage, the level now sitting just below the children's shoulders and rising.

The moment the pod stabilized, Pin slapped the center of Emma's harness and the buckles released with a *snap*, the straps zipping back into their wall sockets. He pulled her to her feet and helped her steady herself before moving to Adam and doing the same.

Emma shivered in her suit as she watched Pin help Adam off the bench to stand beside her.

"We have to evacuate!" he yelled over the noise of rushing water and sloshed towards his small duffle bag. Reaching inside, he pulled out his package of clothbound tools and secured them inside his suit. When he was done doing that, he moved towards a small panel beside the pod's door and, turning back, he said, "Don't fight against the water when it floods the pod or you'll end up topsy-turvy and breaking your visors against something. Give in to it until it settles around you and then kick your legs and move your arms like this until you're outside the pod."

"Then what?" Emma yelled back. She had never done anything like swimming before.

"Then you look straight up and kick your legs as hard and as fast as you can until you reach the surface! And don't look back for any reason! Do you understand?"

Pin didn't wait for their reply before slamming his palm against the red release button and bracing himself for the impact of incoming water.

The door hissed loudly and gears whirred and kicked up bubbles as its three deadbolts began to release one after the other.

When the first two were unlocked, the door rolled slightly and water gushed from the open seam. Pin yelled, "Here we go!" but then the last bolt squealed painfully and stalled, the door failing to open all the way.

Pin pressed the red button twice quickly then cursed and dove under the water.

Emma watched his shape jerk back and forth as he tried to release the final bolt by hand. Then, without knowing why exactly, she clasped her arms across her chest and hugged herself to stave off a punishing anxiety that was beginning to gnaw at her.

What she didn't know was that, since the water level had risen to the bottom of her helmet, the first pangs of claustrophobia were creeping in, and all at once she felt as though the walls would close in to crush them.

To ease the sensation, she breathed in slowly and cast her eyes towards the window to get a sense of the larger world outside. But, instead of being calmed, a cold terror struck her and she screamed at the sight of an inky black tentacle that slid across the glass outside.

The tentacle pulsed and sucked at the window with a hundred bulbous appendages before removing itself with a sickening *pop* and slipping back into the darkness.

Pin burst from the water then and swam towards

the children. Ignoring Emma's panicked cries, he lifted them onto the bench before the water covered their helmets and huddled them all together.

"The door won't open!" he yelled. "Hydraulics are shot and I ain't strong enough to fight against them."

"Are we going to die?" Adam cried out.

"Not if one of you squeezes through the tear in the pod and opens the door from the outside," Pin replied. "It's a failsafe designed to override the pod's systems so those inside can be rescued during a bungled touchdown just like this. Problem is, there's nobody outside to rescue us."

"There's a monster outside!" Emma blurted pointing to the window.

"How's that?" Pin asked, quickly turning to look, but seeing nothing but dark water outside.

"I saw it," Emma continued. "A big arm hugging us. It wants to get us!"

The desperate look in Emma's eyes told Pin she'd certainly seen *something* outside the pod. But right then, faced with knowing they would definitely drown versus the not knowing what was outside, he didn't see they had much choice but to follow his plan.

"Did you see it too, Adam?" Pin asked the boy.

Adam shook his head and gulped. "I don't want to—" he began, but stopped short of finishing.

He looked at Emma and saw the fear and exhaustion in her eyes. Even amid the chaos, he didn't want her to be scared. He thought back to how she'd pulled him into the wall and saved them both from the fire on the Tian. She'd saved him then, despite his protests, and now it was his turn to do the same. All of a sudden Emma's fear made him feel brave in comparison and he wanted to be strong and protect her.

"I'm not scared, Pin!" Adam said finally, though he knew it was a lie.

Pin grabbed his shoulders and pressed his visor against the boy's. He could see hesitation in Adam's eyes and feared it would turn to panic once he left the pod and found himself alone in endless, dark water.

"I know it's a lot to ask," he said, "but you'll hear my voice over the communicator and I'll talk to you the whole time. You won't be alone out there."

Adam nodded quickly and Pin helped him down.

Emma watched, terrified and helpless, as they swam to where the pod had torn apart. Since the gash was now underwater, it wasn't long before both were under the waves and she was alone and scared in the claustrophobic water coffin.

Before letting him go, Pin explained to Adam what he needed to do. The pod had slowed its descent but they were still being dragged by the currents, so there was a risk of being left behind if he didn't keep a good hold onto it from the outside.

"Pull yourself along the outside of the pod until you reach the round door," he said firmly. "Then look for a square panel. It'll be somewhere close and latched shut, so you'll need to open it up before you can trigger the door. Once you open it there will a button of some kind. Press it to release the hydraulics and the door should open. If you get in trouble out there, just holler and I'll talk you through it."

The more he spoke, the more Pin could see Adam was beginning to hyperventilate, which meant he was taking in too much carbon dioxide and could end up passing out.

"Breathe slowly, boy," Pin said sternly. "Focus on

what you're doing and you won't be scared. It'll all be over soon and we'll be out of this blasted thing once and for all."

He waited for Adam to calm himself before patting the back of his helmet, saying, "Okay, let's do it," and swimming with him to the gash.

Floating next to the opening, Pin gripped a jagged portion of damaged fuselage and pulled it forcibly away to enlarge it enough that Adam's body could squeeze through. The strain on his already tired muscles was immense and his forearms shook almost immediately, and he began to lose his grip.

Adam swam to the hole and pushed his face to the opening to look out into the dark abyss. He scanned the depths for a sign of danger but could see no shapes or movement in the water outside the pod save the sandy seabed that flowed beneath them.

Meanwhile, Pin was about to release the piece of damaged pod. "Out you go, before you get caught up! I can't hold it much longer!"

With that, Adam flashed Pin one last worried look then ventured outside the pod and into the blue darkness.

Twisting his body as he left the pod behind, Adam kicked his legs and quickly reached for a thin pipe he saw running along its side. Grasping it with the tips of his gloved fingers, his grip slipped immediately and he was left floating just out of reach as the pod continued along the bottom.

"Pin!" Adam yelled.

A moment later, the communicator in his helmet clicked on and Pin's electronic voice filled his helmet.

"Where are you?" Pin said.

"Floating!" Adam replied, panicked.

"Can you see the pod?"
"Yes!"
"Then swim to it. Kick your legs and move your arms. You can do it, my boy!"

Adam did what Pin said and kicked his legs ferociously until his body was an arrow pointing towards the moving pod. Then, using his arms to guide him, he swam madly through the water until he was close enough to make out the mechanical details along the outside of the pod.

He saw the tear along the fuselage where he had ventured out, bubbles trailing from it as the pod made its way along the sandy bottom. He saw the pipe that was too narrow for him to hold onto then, looking up from it, saw a spindly metal hook that jutted from the pod and hung out over the side, like fruit hanging from a tree branch.

Narrowing his eyes and keeping them trained on the hook, Adam kicked harder until he was close enough to grab for it. He smiled when his fingers touched metal and made a bold move to snag it when the pod was swept up in a current and began to roll over, taking the hook along with it.

Adam kicked harder and followed the hook as it moved upward, no longer on the side of the pod now, but on top of it.

Planting his foot against the side of the craft, he launched himself up and on top of the rolling pod, scrambling along until the hook was finally within reach. Grabbing it tightly with his right hand, he pulled himself into a sitting position and straddled the top of the pod, using his left arm for balance.

"I did it, I'm on top!" he yelled once he was finally stable.

"Good boy!" Pin yelled hurriedly. "You'll have to slide over the front to get to the door. Hurry up now, there's no room for water in here anymore!"

And indeed, Pin was right. As Adam worked to catch the pod outside, inside had completely filled with water.

Emma, scared and crying, clung to Pin's body like a baby marsupial would its mother. They had swum to the door in anticipation of Adam opening it, but the wait was proving agonizing. Each time the walls of the metal machine groaned under pressure from the depths, Emma was sure the monster had come for them again and kept her eyes shut for fear of seeing the fearsome creature.

"It's okay, little mouse," Pin said to her soothingly. "Adam will get us out in no time. He won't let you down. You'll see."

Outside, Adam had shimmied onto his belly and was working to slide his legs over the front of the pod. His right hand still holding the metal hook, he felt along the front with his feet, searching for a sturdy foothold. When his right foot finally felt secure, he let the hook go and fell in front of the moving pod.

Unfortunately, the weight of his suit and boots forced him down more quickly than expected and he was unable to grab anything before his feet slipped from the bar and he landed in a heap on the sand, the pod dangerously close to rolling over him.

He looked up wildly to see the round door bearing down on him, threatening to smash against his helmet if he didn't act fast. So, pulling hard against the water with both his arms, he swam straight up until he was on his feet. Then, turning his body, he shouldered the heavy metal pod as it was thrust forward, carried by another strong current.

His elbow crunched against a square bolt in the metal door and he screamed out in pain, but didn't hesitate to clasp his fingers around a maintenance ladder alongside it. Another strong tug upwards and his feet were safely on board as well, and he was within reach of the door's main control box.

"I'm here!" Adam said into the communicator. "I'm opening the box now."

Adam reached for the control box and saw the latch Pin had mentioned. It was a thin strand of metal, twisted into a figure-eight and threaded through the round ends of the box's strike. He grabbed it with the tips of his fingers and pressed to twist it apart when a great shadow overcame him and the water around him darkened.

Adam stopped moving, paralyzed with fear. He felt a rush of turbulence as a mass above him threw a great gust of water downwards with what felt like the flick of a massive appendage.

"Adam?" his communicator crackled as Pin's voice filled his helmet? "Adam, are you there?"

Without opening his eyes, Adam whispered, "It's the monster."

"Okay, don't move," Pin said. "I'll wager it ain't got good eyesight, so you just stay still and we'll see if it swims away. Emma said it already had a good suck on the pod, so it knows we're not tasty. It's just making sure. Be patient now."

Adam did his best to stay perfectly still. He could sense the shape above him, lurking and feeling around with its bulbous tentacles, sending wave after wave toward the pod as it swam around in a sickening circle, like a vulture waiting on death from above.

Just when Adam thought it was safe to look up again, the beast threw a thick tentacle against the pod, missing him by inches and striking the metal door.

The pod jerked and rolled as the beast pulled at it, tasting through touch. Adam weaved to the right as the tentacle moved across his path, ducking before it could connect with his side. Finally, it curled itself into a circle before releasing with a *suck* and *pop* of fleshy suction and flying back upwards. Then the darkness vanished and the monster swam away with one last flick of its three long tentacles.

Adam twisted the latch as hard as he could and the top of the box floated open to reveal a green button that read EMERGENCY USE ONLY. He pressed it down with all his might and bubbles exploded all around him as the final bolt sprang loose and the round door rolled open.

Pin and Emma burst through the door in an explosion of bubbled and Pin pulled Adam by the suit as they passed him by.

"Everyone look up and swim as fast as you can!" he said, dragging Adam by his suit until the boy began to kick his legs and swim on his own. "And nobody look down, no matter what!"

Bubbles raged around the three survivors as they swam furiously towards the lightless unknown surface.

The stronger of the three, Pin lead the way, moving through the dark waters quickly. Scared of being left behind, Emma did her best to keep sight of his heavy boots as they kicked ahead of her. She could see Adam just below her out of the corner of her eye.

Worried he would lose sight of them, she looked down momentarily and saw the monster wrapping itself around the empty pod. It was even bigger than she'd thought, a grey mass of inky flesh surrounded by three great arms that swirled around it, manically searching for food.

Before she turned away, she saw its body flip inside out to reveal a repulsive mouth full of hundreds of bone-white teeth. They bit at the pod twice, sending a reverberating *clang* through the depths, before recoiling again. Then the beast let loose a deep, agonizing bellow before vanishing down a long trench, dragging the pod behind it.

Eyes wild, Emma looked back towards the surface and prayed they would soon leave the dangerous depths for good.

She kicked her legs and moved her arms as quickly as she could muster until finally she saw a twinkle of light dancing somewhere above them. At first it was dim, pale white amid the darkness, but soon it shone like a star on fire in the night.

She trained her eyes on the light as she swam upwards behind Pin, towards what she hoped would finally be safety for them all.

10

Hard rain washed over Pin when he broke the surface. It poured sheets down his visor, obscuring his vision in the already obscured dark of night, leaving him panic struck as he treaded water and searched furiously for land.

He wiped at his glass helmet uselessly with waterlogged gloves and turned circles to scan the horizon. But his heart sank when his eyes met nothing but endless waves that evaporated into the pitch black distance.

Two tiny splashes erupted close by and he turned to see Emma and Adam break the surface. He swam towards them as they struggled to keep their heads above water, holding onto Adam just as the boy sank under the waves.

"Lay on your backs," he told them, using his legs to steady himself as he lay Adam down across his arms. "You can float that way. You won't get tired."

Emma lay back too, her helmet anchoring her to the rise and fall of the waves with its buoyancy.

She closed her eyes and let the rhythm calm her until her heart slowed and her breathing normalized and she could sense the flurry of rain showering around her, kicking the water into a deafening veil of organic vibration. Such a sound was wholly new to her and she opened her eyes and stared into the stormy night sky with raw curiosity.

Even through the heavy drops of water bouncing off her visor, she could make out the stunning red silhouette of the gas giant watching over them from above. It was the light that had guided her up from the depths, she realized, both a monster and a savior.

Meanwhile, Pin continued his search for land. He strained to see in the dark, but the storm was proving impenetrable beyond a few meagre leagues.

"Which way will we go?" Adam asked breathlessly over the communicator.

"We may need to stay put until the storm passes," Pin replied, his breathing heavy, his voice weary. "Maybe even until morning. If there *is* a morning on this moon, that is. Could also be it's always night for all we know of it."

Adam didn't like the notion of an endless night. Living life in darkness, ignorant of what was right in front of you seemed like a horrifying existence.

As though in response to his thought, a great burst of lightening flashed across the night sky and, for the briefest of moments, the world burst into view.

"Children!" Pin cried suddenly, his voice muffled by the crash of resounding thunder that followed. "Land! Right behind us! Look there!"

Pin pointed and Emma and Adam searched the darkness for what Pin had seen. But if there was land in the distance it had been swallowed by the darkness once again.

Pin stroked his way back towards the children, passing between them and pulling at the backs of their suits to help them move through the waves towards the land he'd seen.

"I'll pull you until I can't. Kick your feet to help me now!"

Both children did as they were told, struggling to kick their heavy boots amid the waves as thunder crashed and rain poured down around them.

No more than an hour later, Pin's vision was proven right when his boots touched a long sandbar and he was able to walk along the sandy ocean floor.

Since it was still too deep for the children, he flipped them onto their fronts and showed them how to paddle their arms as he pointed out the dark outline of land that had finally shown itself from behind the curtain of night.

Even at a distance it looked vast and wild and they could make out many strange and wondrous shapes; the most startling of which were towering, multi-armed goliaths that flailed violently in the prevailing winds and tempestuous rain.

"Monsters!" Emma cried at the sight the terrifying figures. "They've come back!"

"Not monsters, my girl," replied Pin. "Trees! Great and wild beasts to be sure, but trees nonetheless! By god, I've never seen any so big in all my life! Adam, do you see them?"

"Hurrah!" Adam cried joyously. He was not sure what trees might be like, but Pin's voice was jubilant and the strange moon was proving to be full of fresh visions.

"Land ho!" Pin yelled out again. "I see the beach right before us. Can you touch the bottom, children?"

Adam stopped paddling and let his lower half sink until his boots felt the lose sand beneath them. The water level was still well above his nose, but with his helmet on he was still able to breathe freely and make out the beach before him.

Being shorter than Adam, Emma had more trouble steadying herself against the push and pull of the waves, so Pin had her ride upon his back as he and Adam trudged onwards through the water.

As they drew nearer, the sea grew more active and savage, and the thunder of the surf became clearer. The breakers were fierce and threatening, pushing and pulling at them until finally the opening widened and invited them upon the dark beach where they climbed and fell to the wet sand.

Fighting the urge to collapse and let precious sleep claim him, Pin ushered the children up the open beach and inland a ways.

The storm showed no sign of letting up and, in fact, the wind seemed to wage a personal war against them as though venturing to push them back out into the great sea. But, hunched together and moving as a single mass, they managed to defeat its best efforts, and were soon picking their way through thick and tangled foliage that lined the border of the sand.

Eventually they came upon the mammoth trunk of an almost endlessly tall tree and Pin ordered the children to stop, but keep their helmets on.

"There's too much interference in the storm to read the air, so keep your suits on until it passes," he said as he sat them up against the tree.

Protected by high overhanging branches covered in human-sized fronds that reached out in all directions, the rain had all but reduced to a sprinkling of drops against their helmets. The sounds of the storm had also dimmed to a constant drumming patter that raged on somewhere above them, like a war being fought in heaven.

Emma and Adam were too overcome to take in the details of the savage world around them, or imagine what dangers may be lurking just out of sight. Instead they watched Pin work—as they had become so accustomed to doing—tearing at the bushes and smaller trees close by and stripping the larger branches of their leaves.

Digging shallow divots by striking with the hard heel of his boot, Pin set the ends of each wooden stake in front of the children and leaned the tops against the tree until they were fully protected from the harsh wind and rain. Then he covered the leaning structure with leaves and smaller sticks.

When his crude shelter was complete, Pin crouched low and squeezed himself inside to join the children.

"It's not much better than a pod, but it'll keep us safe from the storm until morning—" he said, stopping suddenly when he saw Emma and Adam huddled together and already passed out and sleeping deeply.

He sighed heavily and closed his eyes. Against all odds they were free from space, the pod, and had escaped an endless ocean. He didn't know where they were, or what new complications the morning might bring, but, watching the children safe and sleeping, it struck him that they had come from worse places.

"Sleep now," he said quietly, feeling his eye lids grow heavy. "Yes. Sleep."

"Pin!"

The scream infected Pin's sleep, turning a perfectly fine dream into a perfect nightmare.

"Pin!"

That voice. A boy's. I know it. It almost sounds like Adam's, only far, far away. And, no matter where I look, I can't see a soul.

"Pin! Please, come quick!"

At that, Pin's dream ended and the old man opened his eyes.

He was dripping sweat in his suit and felt the slap of sweltering humidity immediately. He coughed and shifted and felt a body next to him. It was Emma, still asleep, her head resting against his shoulder. She was also sweating, her hair soaked and sticking to her brow in clumps. Then he noticed the two of them were alone under the shelter.

Pin sat up and looked to where Adam should have been, but the boy was gone. In his place, a glass helmet and space suit lay derelict on the forest floor.

He strained to listen. It was achingly quiet. The storm had passed, the wind no longer howled, and thin beams of bright light penetrated the cracks of their little shelter.

"Pin!" came another scream from far off in the distance.

"Adam," whispered Pin quickly. "I'm coming for you! You hear me, I'm coming!"

Pin shook Emma awake and told her to stay hidden until he returned.

"What's happening?" she asked, groggy with sleep.

"Adam's in trouble somewhere," Pin answered swiftly. Then he crawled out from under the shelter and into the bright, sunlit open.

All at once, Pin's senses were overcome with the sights and sounds of the wild jungle before him. An electric buzz of insects swam inside his helmet, while the heat of the sun beat against his suit, turning it into a hot oven, his body into cooking meat.

He looked towards the sky as he moved forward, marveling at the scale and height of the trees around him. Their massive leaves reminded him of Earth's palm trees, but their trunks were much wider at the base and blood red. And by god they were tall! Six hundred feet at the low end, the tops of them so high they became lost to the human eye.

Alarms rang out from his suit then. His oxygen was almost gone.

"Adam! Where are you?" he called as he moved towards the beach.

He stopped when he heard a skittering of motion somewhere ahead and positioned himself into a ready stance. *Whatever has Adam might be coming for me now*, he thought nervously.

Then a tangle of waxy bush parted twenty yards ahead and Adam burst forth and ran towards him. The boy beamed, his eyes wild and arms waving.

"Pin!" he cried as he moved towards the old man.

Pin ran forward, ready to sweep the boy up and whisk him back to their shelter and away from whatever might be chasing him. But when they finally met, Adam grabbed his hand and pulled him back the way he'd come, back towards the beach.

"Pin, come see! You won't believe your eyes!" he

yelled.

Pin pulled the boy towards him and bent down to his level.

"Why aren't you in your suit?" he asked harshly.

Adam gave a puzzled look as though he'd forgotten Pin's warning the night before. "Oh, it was too hot in that old suit," was all he could think to say.

"You can't run off like that! Not here. You get that? We don't know anything about where we are," Pin continued.

"Okay, okay, but Pin— look!"

Adam pulled and Pin followed until finally they broke the tree line and were looking upon the most glorious of wonderlands.

In the light of day, Pin saw that the ocean they'd travelled the night before swirled around coral piers and flooded into a heavenly, sheltered lagoon.

On either side lay a great sweep of waving blue water, but the lagoon was a calm oasis; a lake of sapphire and aquamarine with water so clear that even at a distance you could see branching coral and great schools of passing fish casting long shadows across the white sandy bottom.

But the soul of it all, the heart-stopping thing about this blue lagoon, towering trees and sky, was the light.

In space, light is cruel. It comes in two varieties: man-made fluoresce so unnatural it inspires sickness in the pit of your stomach, or blazing constellations bright enough to burn your sight away forever. In space, light has nothing to focus itself upon, nothing of beauty to exhibit or illuminate to a beholder, only infinite emptiness and desolation.

But here, the light was glorious. It turned the air

into a crystal through which Pin saw the loveliness of the land and reef, the green and red of mammoth trees, the bleached white coral and, of course, the lagoon, all heart-achingly beautiful.

Pin looked down at Adam who was smiling and shielding his eyes from the harsh light as he stared out across the lagoon. Without his suit, the boy looked as natural a figure as could be imagined.

Slowly, Pin closed his eyes and twisted his helmet. It let out a great hiss before he lifted it off and held it at his side. He breathed in slowly, letting the fresh air fill his lungs fully before breathing out again and opening his eyes.

The lagoon, the great ocean beyond, and the jungle behind them were all still there, as real as he was.

As he and Adam stared, awestruck at the sight before them, Pin knew they had found the soul of eternal happiness and youth. Pin knew they were saved.

"Where are we?" asked Adam in hushed reverie.

Pin put his arm across the boy's shoulder and looked down at his young face.

"It's everything," he said quietly. "Come on. Let's get Emma. We have a lot to do."

11

Too tired to walk herself, Pin carried Emma back through the jungle towards the beach.

Before scooping her up, he'd stripped her of her suit and left it under the tree where they had spent the night. Then, marveling at how light she felt without it, he'd carried her out of the shelter and made his way back towards the beach where he'd left Adam, mad with delight, running along the beach like a dog let off its leash.

As they approached the tree line, Pin warned Emma to shield her eyes from the bright sunlight. She covered them with her hands and waited for Pin to tell her when it was safe to look again.

All at once she felt a peaceful heat swell across her body and rays of light peeked in through the cracks between her fingers, forcing her to squint. Then she sensed the two of them sink slightly as Pin took his first step onto the loose, white sand.

"Okay, Emma," said Pin sweetly. "Look now and

see where we've ended up."

Emma separated her fingers slowly and peeked out from between them. What she saw filled her with such curiosity that she pulled her hand away quickly so she could see everything all at once.

"Oh, Pin!" she exclaimed as she scanned all there was to see. "Look at the sky. It's blue, just like Adam's uncle Danforth said. And the water is so clear and still, it looks like the glass on Nanny's mirror."

Loud chattering erupted behind them and Emma looked back to see a flock of winged creatures burst from the tall trees. They pecked at each other and squawked wildly as they flew in formation, seemingly right towards them. Emma cried out and covered her head as the whole flock swooped down upon them, and Pin laughed heartily and dropped her to the sand where they both ducked as the beasts flew low and rose again to soar over the great blue lagoon.

"Watch how they fly!" Pin cried, pointing to where the flock was now moving together in a great circle over the water. "They want to catch some fish for breakfast."

Adam, red faced and puffing heavy breaths, ran up to them and pointed out to where the birds circled.

"Are they parrots? He asked.

Pin squinted and looked out to study the makeup of the large bird-like creatures.

"Not parrots. They're certainly colorful like Parrots, Adam, but they don't have feathers that I can see. And can you see how their colors sparkle in the light? I'll bet they got scales on their bodies more like a snake. No, I'd say these are something altogether new. Something no one has ever seen before."

"Except us," Adam replied with a wide grin.

"Except for us, indeed," replied Pin. "I'd say that makes us very special, wouldn't you, Emma?"

Emma was dazzled by the not-parrots and how they flew together without knocking into one another. And the way reds, greens, and blues shimmered across their bodies in the light. To her they seemed like something altogether magical.

Suddenly, as though knocked from the sky by an unseen bullet, one of them tucked its wings tightly by its side and fell like a stone towards the water. Then, hitting the surface like an arrow it barely made a splash as it disappeared from view.

"See, they're hunting!" cried Pin, dancing a little on the spot.

He seemed so overcome with joy to see such a thing that Adam couldn't help but ask, "What's hunting?"

"Everything eats something else, and hunting is when you look for the thing you eat," replied Pin.

"Even us?" asked Adam with a glimmer of boyish devilishness in his eye.

"Yes, even us!"

At the thought of food, Pin glanced at the surrounding vegetation and knew there was likely enough edible plant life and fruits to feed an army. A fresh water source would likely be close, somewhere uphill no doubt. He would search it out in due time. For now, he would enjoy paradise.

He flung himself under the shade of an overhanging tree and watched the children chase each other along the dry, white sand and splash along the shallow shore of the lagoon.

"In all my life," he chuckled to himself, "through all my troubles, I never imagined I'd end up in such a place." He closed his eyes and let the sun warm his face. "The only thing missing is a pipe stuffed tight with tobacco and a tall drink of rum. But I'll not complain about that now."

The next thing Pin knew he was awoken by Emma, who had crawled up and sat herself next to him in the sand. He could already see her skin browning from the sun and thought she looked much stronger than earlier that morning.

Adam ran up to her, waving a large purple crustacean with three clawed arms that he'd dug out of the sea. The creature's eyes bulged and its claws snapped as the boy pushed it towards Emma, pretending it was about to bite her.

"Take it away!" cried Emma, holding her hands out, fingers widespread, to wave it away. "Pin! Pin! Make him take it away!"

"Leave her alone, you little devil!" Pin said, waving Adam and the sea creature away from her.

Adam laughed and, despite Emma's fears, Pin couldn't help but laugh along at the playfulness of it all. Then he waved Adam off and hollered, "Go and put that back where you found it, before I give you a whipping!"

"What's a devil?" asked Adam, still panting from exertion.

"I'll answer no more questions until you get that wretched thing away from here and back into the water from where it came. Can't you both see I'm trying to rest for a change?"

Adam moaned but turned away, leaving Emma to contemplate Pin as he rested with his eyes closed, taking long breaths of fresh air. Then a great thought occurred to her and she ran away from the beach and into the trees as quickly as she could.

Adam watched her disappear from the water where he'd let the clawed creature back onto the rock he'd found it on. He thought about following her, but became distracted by a thin worm, longer than he was tall, that swam circles around his bare feet. He reached down to grab it but, when it sensed him, the worm burrowed itself under the sand and vanished.

By the time Adam looked up, Emma had returned and was sitting next to Pin again. A small package was in her little hands. Curious to see what she'd found, he ran back up the beach to see what it was.

Pin pulled one eye open and peeked at what the girl was holding. It was small and wooden and Emma was busy brushing it free of sand.

"I see you still have your little box," he said to her. "I should have known through everything we've been through you'd keep it safe."

Just then, Adam came into view and dropped down in front of Emma. He looked at the box and made to grab it, but the girl pulled it away from him.

"Will you open it?" he asked Emma.

"It's only for me," she replied. "It's a secret treasure."

"Oh, open it!" cried Adam, mad with curiosity.

"Maybe I will," she said quietly.

Pin sat up and gestured towards the natural world around them. "Perhaps, since we're the only people on this whole moon, you'll share your secret with us. What do you say to that, Emma?"

Emma thought about this for a moment and then said simply, "I will open it."

Turning the front of the box towards herself, she undid the clasp slowly and let it hit the metal bottom with a tiny *clink*.

"Open it!" cried Adam, and Pin shushed him quickly.

"What's in it?" asked the old man, becoming curious himself.

Emma opened the lid and an electric hum sounded. Adam moved in to get a closer look when a crisp blue light shot from the box and morphed into a tiny hologram of a beautiful woman.

Emma turned the box for everyone to see and Pin noticed that the woman's beauty—much like Emma's—came mostly from a wide smile that sang with happiness. In her arms was a newborn baby, asleep and perfectly peaceful.

"Huh," huffed Adam in slight disgust. "I don't care about that. I thought it might be something fun to play with." With that the boy rose and ran back to the water where he continued to search for aquatic critters.

Pin, however, marveled at the pretty woman, so tiny she could fit in the palm of his hand.

"Well, I'll be," he said.

"That's my mother," said Emma, staring at the hologram. "And that's me in her arms."

"You sure were a pretty baby, Emma," said Pin.

Emma stared at the image before her. Then, as though becoming sad, she closed the lid and the woman vanished.

"What's wrong?" asked Pin.

"I'll never have a baby now," Emma said, suddenly sad.

The notion took Pin by surprise coming from a girl so young and he found he was stuck to know how to respond.

"Nanny told me doctors grow babies in science laboratories. So I suppose I'll never have one now that we're here on this moon."

"Well, that's true," Pin responded thoughtfully. "Growing them like that is most popular these days. Only what your nanny didn't tell you is that babies can also come from more than just doctors and labs."

Emma perked up at this. "Is that true? Where else do they come from?"

"Well, uh, the truth is... How do I say this now? They come from a natural place. You see—" he stammered.

"Natural? Like trees and flowers?"

"Well, I suppose that's right to a point. They grow from a seed and eventually, well, just—*pop*—there they are."

Emma stared up at Pin, confused as ever, and the old man jumped to his feet in a shot.

"I'll need to rig a better shelter for us in case we get a storm during the night," he said quickly and called for Adam to join them. Then he looked down at Emma and winked. "But first, let's go on an adventure to find water and food. I certainly am hungry. What do you say?"

Emma smiled and slid her box into the pocket of her already tattering ship's pajamas. Then Adam joined them and the three entered the thick jungle to search for food and water.

Entering the jungle was like stepping into a tall and endless temple made of trees that arched themselves into holy passageways. The pale green roof above sparkled and flashed with points of light as the breeze blew the green fronds back and forth. Under it, they were protected from the heat of the sun.

They had been walking awhile when Emma asked, "We won't get lost will we, Pin?"

"Lost? Heaven's no. And besides, how can we get lost when there's no one place we're coming from?"

Emma thought about this as they continued through the jungle. While they hadn't set up camp yet, she'd come to love their secret beach and inlet and didn't want to lose it.

"Right now we're moving uphill," Pin continued. "When we want to find our way back, we'll just walk back down again. So don't worry about getting lost, Emma."

Something fell from above then, hitting the dirt with a loud *splat* and splashing them with sweet smelling juice.

Adam cried out and rubbed thick pink liquid from his face before looking at what had nearly missed them.

"What is it?" he asked Pin and the old man knelt down to get a better look.

Examining it with his fingers, Pin could see the object had a thick hide, dark blue and covered with microscopic fibers. Inside, the flesh was bright pink with a core of small seeds.

He swiped at it with the tip of his finger and touched some of the liquid to his tongue. It was sweet like honey.

"It's a fruit of some sort. Come and have a taste, children."

After sampling the fruit's sweetness, both children tore into its pink insides like predatory animals, stuffing handfuls of delicious pink flesh into their mouths and chirping sounds of enjoyment.

Pin chuckled and warned them to eat slowly or risk a stomach ache, but they ignored him, eating until all that remained was the thick, hairy husk.

Staring up into the trees, Adam saw that more plump fruit hung hundreds of feet above. He wondered how they could get more.

"Think you're able to climb up and drop more down?" Pin asked as he watched the boy.

Adam nodded. Right about then, he'd do anything to eat more of the strange and wonderful fruit.

"We'll make a chore of it later then," Pin said as he continued through the jungle. "After we find us some water. Come along now, the both of you."

Not long after leaving the grove of hanging fruit, the three explorers found themselves in a dense area where a deeper sort of twilight hid them in shadow. The trees where closer together here, their blood red trunks nearly touching to form long walls of wood and twisting vines.

Pink and yellow flowers travelled the ropes of wild vine strung tree-to-tree and Emma marveled at their long stamen, waving in the air to tempt bulbous buzzing insects that flew from each in search of tasty pollen.

Suddenly, Pin stopped and gestured towards the children to do the same. Adam made a sound, but Pin hushed him as he listened to the sounds of the jungle. Cutting through the murmur of insects and the reef's faint song, a quiet rippling sound made itself known to them.

"Water," said Pin quietly, listening again to make sure he had a good sense of its bearing. Then, without looking back at the children, he made for it quickly.

After pushing through another area of thick trees, the three castaways finally emerged along the edge of a grassy clearing where—fifty yards ahead and over a high rock of polished black stone—a cascade of water poured into a glittering pool below.

Purple leafed ferns grew all around and great ropes of colorful flowers hung down from the trees to kiss the waterfall's refreshing spray.

A great tree covered in long, yellow-jacketed fruit sat at the top of the waterfall and Pin leapt forward in an instant, running up the rocks until he reached the top of the waterfall.

Adam laughed at his sure-footedness, then cried with joy as Pin plucked the fruit and tossed a few down towards them.

"Hurray! Look at Pin, Emma!"

But Emma wasn't watching Pin and showed no delight in where they'd ended up. For she had just discovered something wedged between two black rocks and was studying it with immense fascination and curiosity.

12

"Emma, what are you doing?" Adam asked for a second time when she didn't answer him.

He'd tore a strip of bright yellow skin from the long fruit to reveal a red pulp underneath. It was not juicy like the blue fruit had been, but it was still sweet to the taste.

Emma knelt low to examine the strange object nestled between the two black rocks. It was round and smooth, and the top was covered with slimy green lichen. It could easily have been mistaken for a stone but for the keen precision of Emma's inquisitive young eyes. She didn't know why, but there was something about it that seemed out of place in their surroundings.

Sticking two fingers into the thing's two round holes, she pulled until she'd forced it from its resting place.

"Look at this funny thing I've found!" she called to

Pin who sat eating, his legs hanging over the little waterfall.

"What is it?" he called back to her. "Can't you see I'm washing my tired feet?"

"I don't know," Emma said and held it over her head for him to see. "It's got holes in it."

Pin squinted to make out the shape of Emma's discovery.

"Give it here," said Adam suddenly, grabbing it from her and turning it over in his hands. "Why, it looks like a face with no parts!" he said aloud.

Pin saw what it was then and jumped to his feet as though poked in the back by a large stick.

"Drop it!" he yelled gruffly as he picked his way back down the rocks to where the children stood. When he reached them, he plucked the thing from Adam and hollered, "Where did you find this?"

The boy looked at Emma who pointed at the rocks just below the surface of the little stream.

"Just there," she said. "What is it, Pin?"

Pin tucked the object under his arm then pulled them away from the waterfall and back through the trees towards the lagoon.

"What happened?" cried Emma. She felt as though she'd done something wrong.

"Hush up, girl!" whispered Pin as he weaved them quickly between the thick trunks of jungle trees.

Despite more protests, he didn't slow until they'd reached the spot where their crude shelter still stood against the trunk of the great tree. Then he pulled them inside and made them promise to be quiet, or he'd give them each a whipping.

After listening to the sounds of the forest for a few moments longer, Pin pulled the strange object from under his arm and held it up gingerly for examination.

Despite the green lichen, he could see it was a skull. Two empty eye sockets looked back at him as he examined the front, and when he turned it around he was shocked to see a deep dent in the bone where it must have been struck by something hard and heavy long ago. Or, he supposed, the damage could have occurred from a high fall. The rocks around the waterfall could certainly have done the trick. But, if that were the case, where was the rest of the body?

Without warning, Pin threw the skull as far as he could into the trees and wiped his hands on his pants as though they were covered with a sickness. It shattered somewhere in the distance, its pieces cascading against the rocks and trees of the tropical underbrush.

He sat back against the trunk and scratched at his chin as he thought hard. A skull by itself wasn't something to be concerned about. There must be an abundance of animals on the blue moon and, though thankfully they hadn't met any, some would be predatory. No, there was something else that disturbed him about the skull. Something about it struck such a fear and confusion in his soul that he could barely breath. The skull—preserved by the cool water for who knows how many years—looked almost human.

"Impossible," he whispered to himself, shaking the thought from his mind. "It's just... it couldn't be."

Emma and Adam looked at each other, confused by Pin's strange bout of introspection. But before they could speak a word, the old man crawled from the shelter and started pulling at the ropey vines that covered the tree.

"What is he doing now?" Emma asked Adam. But the boy only had time to shrug before Pin poked his head back under the shelter, pulling two long vines behind him.

Moving beside Emma, he looped one of the vines around her waist and tied it into a tight double knot. It rubbed against her skin uncomfortably and she squirmed and tried to free herself.

"What are you doing? I don't like this," she said as Pin forced her to stop struggling.

Pin didn't answer right way. Instead he tied the other end to a thick branch outside and moved to do the same to Adam. Emma pulled against the vine, but there was little slack.

"Why are you tying us up?" Emma cried. "I'm sorry if I did something wrong. I don't want to be tied up!"

"You'll stay tied up until I get back," said Pin sternly. "If I could trust you to stay hidden and not follow me I wouldn't have to tie you like this, but I can't. The both of you would be on my heels in a moment, and you know I speak the truth."

"Where are you going?" Adam whined as Pin finished tying him to the tree outside. "What if you don't come back?"

Pin pressed a callused palm to each of their cheeks and sighed deeply. "Stay here. Stay hidden. And, for goodness sake, stay quiet."

Pin left the children and ran back uphill, muttering anxiously as he went. He passed the grove of close-growing trees, this time ignoring the beauty of the flowers that grew in rows on their sides.

When he came to the little waterfall he didn't stop to wash his feet, or eat from the yellow fruit tree. Instead, he scaled the rocks quickly until he reached its top and kept moving higher through the jungle.

The higher Pin climbed the thinner the jungle became. The trees grew farther apart, allowing easier movement and a better line of sight. He passed through a patch of cane, twenty feet tall, that sprouted from the earth in alien rows and dripped with sticky sap. But he didn't stop to investigate.

Then, finally, the trees parted and Pin stepped into a desolate area where a sun-bleached plateau of white stone welcomed him to the jungle's highest point for miles around. Beyond it lay a deep valley surrounded by rolling hills patched with the green and red of towering trees.

As though his presence had caught Nature by surprise, a great flock of leathery not-parrots burst from the trees below like multi-colored fireworks and then disappear again.

Pin stepped to the plateau's edge and surveyed the terrain in the distance, looking for signs of intelligent life among the thick vegetation. He wasn't exactly sure what to look for, but unnatural movements were obvious in a natural world.

He looked for smoke rising, listened for human chatter, but nothing met his gaze. No handmade dwellings littered the horizon, nor ships flew across the skyline. It seemed that he and the children were indeed alone on the moon.

He turned around and looked back down towards their lagoon. He could make out its half-moon outline far in the distance and could imagine the sound of the water lapping peacefully against the sand and rocks.

It felt strange being surrounded on all sides by nature and to feel the hot breeze blow through his hair. They were in a place completely unknown to anyone but the alien birds and beasts who owned it unknowingly, completely indifferent to the petty affairs of Earthly men.

Pin sat down on the warm stone and hung his legs over the edge. He wished he had a pipe to smoke. Tobacco crops had held out well through Earth's years of endless drought, but had eventually died along with the rest. It struck him as interesting that, though he hadn't smoked in more than forty years, he could still remember how tobacco's earthy sweetness turned to pepper and spice in your mouth upon taking a first full drag.

He returned his thoughts to the skull Emma had found. Looking into its empty eye sockets had sent a shock of electricity through to his soul. It smelled of death and reminded him of the decaying world they'd left behind.

Perhaps he was mistaken and it was not a human skull after all. Simian perhaps? Some celestial descendent akin to Earth's monkeys? Maybe. But something felt too familiar about the structure of its face and the size of its cranium for Pin to completely resign himself to that.

Two options seemed to present themselves: Either the skull belonged to a creature that was indigenous to the moon, or it was a visitor from the stars like they were. As far as Pin knew, this moon had never been recorded by Le Guin's probe program.

Perhaps it was hidden by the electromagnetic energy of the much larger gas planet it orbited. Pin remembered the strange event that had rocked the pod, and the flash of light that had occurred just before the planet had revealed itself to them. Perhaps the same phenomenon that had saved them then, stood between them and salvation now.

Pin sighed and rose to his feet. It was a mystery beyond his ability to solve in the moment, so he decided he shouldn't let it consume his thoughts. Until they learned more about their new home he would remain vigilant, of course, watchful and alert. But, for now, he and the children had a lot to accomplish. A sturdy shelter and a good meal would be a good start.

After that, he would need to create some rules.

13

At Adam's request, they all spent that night on the sand listening to the water's natural rhythms and pointing out shapes in the constellations around the electric red of the gas planet.

No sooner had the sun set than they realized a great many amazing things happened in and around the lagoon at night. First, the water along the shore came alive with the brilliant twinkling of blue and green algae that lit up the surf like a tree at Christmas.

Drawn to the vision, the children ran down the sand to examine the strange phenomenon. Adam, ever one to explore through touch, stuck his finger into a squishy bulb of light and was shocked to see it extinguish at once. Then, when he pulled his finger away, it lit up again and he sent a high-pitched laugh cascading across the crisp water.

More prone to immerse herself into the wonders of their natural surroundings, Emma tiptoed along the shore-lights, splashing and pirouetting happily as she hummed a merry tune.

The woods came alive with nighttime lights also, the flowery orchids hanging from ropey vines glowing in the dark as though releasing all the heat they'd absorbed throughout the day. Night insects with swollen abdomens hummed loudly and flickered iridescence like lightbulbs on the fritz as they flew between them.

Watching the blue moon's dark world come alive in such a pleasing and magical way made Pin all but forget the day's concerns. He thought there was nothing quite like surrendering to nature's embrace to forget all the useless bric-a-brac that consumed his old mind. The simple act of digging his bare toes into the cooling white sand had power enough to make his mind purge modern troubles: his meagre wages, Port politics and the general rank-and-file imposed upon him for so long by human civilization. Here, all men, women and children were equal, and the very passage of time was rendered irrelevant by the surf's sweet lullaby, the warm night air, and the sound of Emma's lovely singing.

For the first time in their lives Emma and Adam would sleep in the open air, curled up on the sand like dogs, and covered by the veil of a beautiful night. For the first time, they would all be free.

The next morning, before the children had risen, Pin set out in the twilight to make them a better shelter; one that could withstand the sea winds, provide some security by blending them into their surroundings, and would be large enough to hold the three of them comfortably.

Marching into the jungle, he studied the trees'

hanging limbs until he spied the perfect place to get started.

From across an open area between the trunks of two tall trees, the branches of both had long ago intertwined to form a great knot across the divide. Pin thought their gnarled form would provide a sturdy crossbeam for a tall A-framed roof he could build from there to the ground below.

For siding he would lash sticks of hardy cane together with vines and cover them all over with eight-foot palm fronds that littered the forest floor. There was certainly nothing better than the natural wax of the fronds to resist rainwater. He could also use cane to manufacture a raised sub-floor to keep them off the dirt and allow water to run underneath them in the event of a flood, or the run-off from a rainy season.

Pin looked up through the branches towards the clear sky. Soon the sun would rise to its zenith and the day would swelter with tropical heat. If he wanted to get anything done before then, he would need to make a move.

A few hours later, Pin was making his way past the waterfall, dragging his second load of cane behind him when he came across the most peculiar sight.

He stopped when he heard a noise above and looked up. Expecting to see bird or beast, he was surprised to see neither, but Adam—naked as a newborn except for a pair of low hanging underwear—scaling the wide branches in search of sweet, blue fruit.

Pin dropped the cane and cupped his hands over his mouth, calling Adam's name into the trees and waiting for the boy to acknowledge him. But Adam barely waved down at the old man before twisting a swollen blue orb from its stem and letting it drop to the ground. It exploded when it hit the dirt across from Pin, covering him with sticky juice.

Angered by this, Pin yelled into the tree for Adam to, "Come down this instant and put some blasted clothes on!" But the boy was already climbing higher to harvest more fruit. "You'll break your legs if you fall!" was Pin's final word before Adam disappeared from view into the overhanging palm leaves.

Pin waited for a moment, hoping the boy would re-emerge. But, instead, another blue bomb attacked from above, splitting in two and splashing him with pulp and thick liquid as it slammed into the dirt. He groaned and wiped his face clean before picking up his lengths of cane and dragging them back towards their camp.

It was some time later that Adam emerged from the underbrush, his bare arms dyed blue and pink from carrying his wet, dripping fruit. His mouth and teeth were also colored from all he'd eaten.

Pin was digging a trench for the cane to be anchored in along the edge of the shelter when a piece of fruit was thrust into his line of sight.

"Here," Adam said as he passed Pin the large pink blob. "If you want some, you can. It's for all of us. Emma too."

Pin continued digging as he looked up at the boy. Adam could see his face was blotchy red and his forehead was dripping with sweat.

"Where is Emma?" Pin asked, breathing heavily.

Adam took a wide bite of pink pulp, chewing as he answered, "Trying to catch fish." *Chew, Chew, Chew.* "At the beach. I told her she's too slow, but she wanted to anyway."

Pin should have guessed Emma would remain at the beach. The lagoon appealed much more to her than it did to Adam. She seemed enchanted by its elegance; its stillness and calm. It was as thoughtful as she was.

Adam, on the other hand, was drawn to the wildness of the woods. It's hard for a boy to resist a world where animals always scuttled underfoot and the rocks and trees invited climbing.

"You two should stay together," Pin said sternly. "I don't want anyone getting lost. And go and put your clothes back on. It's not proper to show yourself all the time."

"But it's so hot!" Adam complained. "Plus, it's easier to climb when I don't get caught up in the branches."

"It doesn't matter about that. You just do what I say now."

"No!" Adam wailed. "I don't want to wear my stupid clothes. And you can't make me!"

With that the boy ran off towards the beach, his pile of fruit bouncing unsteadily in his arms, his bark-stained, loose-fitting undergarments flapping furiously behind him.

Pin sighed. The boy was right, he knew. Ship's clothes were made for ship dwellers. They were perfect for navigating a world of smooth walls and rounded edges—a temperature controlled world without pressure systems and terrible fluctuations in heat and humidity—but they were impractical in the jungle. Their synthetic fibers didn't breathe well with nature. They were too cold at night and too hot during the day, and they were always getting snagged on branches.

Pin's own clothes had been itching him something fierce since he'd begun working on the shelter and it wasn't until just then that he realized how hard he'd been suppressing the urge to rip them from his body and jump into the cool ocean water for relief. If he didn't have the children with him, he probably would have. Human civilization may have become all but a dream, but he still felt duty-bound to keep some decorum alive.

With that thought, Pin went back to working on the shelter. With any luck he would finish before sundown and have time to clear away some of the underbrush around its perimeter so they could set up a little camp around it.

He planned to make a hole for a fire pit and another for their waste. He would fashion a container to catch water when it rained and perhaps even a small pen for the children to keep animals for eating (when they figured out which were fit to eat).

Pin enjoyed imagining the life he would build for them all on the moon. He would teach the children how to hunt in the woods and catch fish in the ocean; how to sense danger, move with the seasons and embrace the natural world.

In a way, the responsibility made him feel young again, relevant and necessary. Like a father, he supposed.

The next morning, Pin was ready to present Adam and Emma with their new home.

Making his way from the finished shelter to the beach where they'd all spent another night, he found them already awake and draped across a smooth boulder on their bellies, exploring a shallow rock pool at the edge of the ocean.

As he ventured nearer, he saw they were extracting colorful coral, crystals and pebbles from the water and collecting them in little piles.

"That's quite a collection," Pin said as he came upon the children.

Emma flipped over and scooped up a few stones, showing them off to Pin and smiling. Then she passed him a clear blue one that was flat on one side.

"Want to see what I learned?" she asked. Pin sat down next to them and nodded yes and Emma closed one eye and lifted her own yellow stone up to the other. "It turns the world a different color," she said, scanning the beach around them.

Pin did the same and looked at the world through the prism of the clear blue stone. Their surroundings came alive in cold monochrome, like a photographic negative, certain details popping amid the forced contrast to a singular color hue.

"Very interesting," he said simply as he looked around.

"Why does it do that?" Emma asked as she opened her eyes again.

"Well, our eyes see the world using light, so when you block your eye with the stone it gets in the way of the light and makes you see it differently."

Emma looked puzzled for a moment then asked, "How do you know we see things the way they really are then? What if we're seeing it wrong and the stone is right?"

Adam turned over then and scoffed. "That's silly, Emma, of course we see it right. Just look around. If you see something in front of you it's the way it is!"

"Well, not so fast Adam," said Pin, ever the settler of arguments. "Emma might have a point here. Our eyes are very much like these stones in a way. They're stuck in our heads and much more complicated to be sure, but maybe they don't show us everything there is to see."

"See!" said Emma, sticking her tongue out.

"But I'm seeing it!" argued Adam.

"But maybe you're not seeing the truth of it. Did you think of that?" countered Pin. "For example, when you look out at the water from a distance it's blue isn't it? But right up close it's not blue anymore, but clear. The world plays all kinds of tricks on our eyes using light all the time. So how can we know what to trust?"

"The leaves are green to us, but perhaps they appear yellow to the animals here? How do we know our eyes are seeing it right and the animals are wrong?"

"But... but, how do you know the animals see them yellow?" asks Adam.

Pin could see Adam was thoroughly frustrated, so decided not to pester him with such unanswerable philosophies. Instead he jumped up and told them to bring their treasures to the woods where their new home was waiting to welcome them.

So, after bundling their individual piles in their discarded shirts, they made their way up the beach towards the jungle.

Pin made the children hold hands and shut their eyes as they drew nearer to the shelter. They giggled lightheartedly as they followed the sound of his voice to avoid the gnarled roots and rocks on the forest floor, struggling against the urge to peek.

When they finally pushed into the little clearing nestled between the two big trees, Pin stopped and told them they could open their eyes. They did so slowly, letting their lids flutter open as though not wanting to spoil the surprise with too quick a reveal.

Adam was the first to react, calling with joy and running headlong towards the tall opening of the tent and disappearing inside the large shelter.

"Come inside, Emma!" he called out. "There's lots of room and the top is so high you can't even touch it!"

Emma hesitated, looking at Pin as if for permission. The old man laughed and crouched down. "Well, what are you waiting for?" he whispered. "It's yours, isn't it?"

Emma smiled and hugged him tightly. Then she ran to join Adam. And no sooner had she entered than the two of them were jumping on the sturdy cane floor and squealing playfully.

Pin peeked inside and laughed at their revelry, enjoying the happiness his hard work had brought them. When Emma saw him she ran over and pulled him by the arm to join their fun. He obliged, and together the three of them held hands in a circle, bouncing on the cane floor and laughing together in their shelter built-for-three.

What a strange sight we must make, Pin thought as he celebrated. *Two sunbaked children and a bearded old man, jumping together in the middle of an alien jungle.*

Before it grew dark, Pin told Adam and Emma to follow him for he something very important to show them.

Leaving the camp behind, the three of them made

their way through the jungle, past the waterfall, and all the way up to the plateau of dry stone where Pin had looked out across the whole valley days earlier.

Adam jumped onto the stone table first, hollering out across the expanse of land.

"Hello!" he called, laughing when his voiced echoed endlessly across the valley.

Pin helped Emma up to join him on the rocks and hushed the boy sternly before he could yell out again.

"Don't be hollering out like that, or the Ogres may come for us," Pin said.

"Ogres?" asked Adam, his voice thick with concern.

"Ogres," started Pin, sitting low to be at the children's eye level, "are something to be feared. They are creatures we can't see that could pop out and harm us if they ever spotted us."

"Have you seen them?" Asked Emma.

"Not where we are. Not at our beach, or near our waterfall. But, as you can see, it's a vast place this moon, and we don't know the half of what's on it yet. Which means we have to be very careful."

"How do we do that?" Emma asked, while Adam listened intently.

"By staying on our side of the hill is how. We have everything we need right here: water to drink, fruit and fish to eat, a nice camp, and each other; so there's no need to go walking around in the valley, or exploring the rocks and hills. And as long as we all stay together, then I'll bet we can protect ourselves from anything that comes along."

Adam looked out across the valley then back at Pin. "I hope the Ogres don't find us, Pin," he said.

"I hope so too, Adam," Pin replied, scratching at

his beard. Then he stood up and stepped between the two children, holding a hand on each of their shoulders as the three of them stared out across the endless valley below.

14

Ever full of restless energy, it wasn't long before Adam was like a buzzing fly around an old horse, asking Pin endless questions and begging him to impart all manner of survival tricks and tasks.

For a man who wanted nothing more than to rest on the sand all day and stare at the stars at night, the boy's insensate pestering filled him with such anxiety that soon Pin had no choice but to create a schedule that would occupy them all daily.

It went something like this: In the morning when they rose, the three castaways decided on a breakfast and divided the chore of cooking it. The meal usually consisted of tangy fruits and the thick blue milk from a spiny plant that Adam had discovered growing in clumps around the rotten trunks of fallen trees.

Following breakfast, Pin set aside time for relaxing in the morning sun and listening to the waves, telling the children that, "Enjoying the world in silence is as important as carving out your place in it."

During this restful period Emma and Adam would invent a quiet game, or collect shells for necklaces and anklets from the lagoon. As long as they left him alone and stayed close to the beach, Pin didn't mind what they occupied themselves with.

Then, late in the morning, Pin would call for Adam to work with him on their first special project: a little raft made from cane and stripped bark lashed together with long vines and wrapped in fallen green palm fronds.

Adam worked hard to help Pin construct the raft, taking great pleasure in the power it gave them to conquer an obstacle set upon them by the natural world. While they worked, the boy spoke enthusiastically about the day they would venture out on the water and net the fish that swam in swirling schools where it became too deep to walk along the bottom.

While the two of them worked on the raft, Emma fetched water in two stout pieces of trunk that Pin had hollowed out and smoothed with fire and stone. They were heavy when filled, but Emma grew stronger each day and rarely spilled any on her way back through the jungle.

They all drank deeply from one of the vessels when she met them again. Emma then drained the second into a long basin that Pin had fashioned at the edge of their camp to catch the dew that trickled off the leaves like soft rain in the early mornings.

Always at some stage of working on the raft, Pin would arch his back and let out a long groan. Then, staring up into the blue sky, he'd saying something like, "That's all for today, my boy. This old back is seizing up like a rusty chain and the only cure is the cool shade of a gum tree." Then, when Adam looked disappointed, he'd lay a hand on the boy's bare back and tell him, "You should be damn proud. It's really coming together now," before moving off to a quiet place to sleep away the hot afternoon.

While Pin napped, Adam and Emma collected the evening meal. It always consisted of at least one of the large, three-clawed crabs that dotted the rocks of the lagoon like so many purple pimples on protruding chins. They were boiled in sea water and squealed horribly and snapped their claws when they hit the rolling water.

Emma refused to watch when Pin cracked their shells open with the point of a sleek black stone he'd found near their waterfall, but she absolutely cherished the meat inside. It was always bright pink and chewy, and wonderfully salty to the taste.

Finally, after dinner, Pin told stories, or let the children ask him whatever questions littered their minds (which he did his best to answer, though more often than not he relied on fictions for those, too).

This routine was virtually unchanging, and soon days turned into weeks, and weeks into months and the children forgot all about their old life beyond the moon. Emma even stopped asking after her father, and Adam never pondered the possible arrival of a rescue ship.

Pin altered the children's clothes as they grew, letting out the seams so often and refitting them again that Emma and Adam appeared to be wrapped by earthy swaths of cloth rather than tailored ship attire anymore.

To look upon them would be to assume they were native to the wild world of the moon, while Pin (bushy grey beard notwithstanding), still seemed alien to the jungle in his soiled workman's clothes.

By all accounts the three castaways had discovered the most wonderful way to live away their days free of hardship or worry, and there were many times that Pin hoped upon hope they would never be rescued, or see another human as long as they lived.

One day, when the sun hung lazy and swollen in a cloudless sky, Pin declared their raft seaworthy and ready for action.

It took some time for him and Adam to drag it from the edge of their camp and maneuver it through the trees to the beach, but before too long it sat ready to be castoff, the lather of surf licking its underbelly tantalizingly.

Though Adam was eager to venture out into the lagoon, Pin made them wait for Emma who had promised to bring some knitted nets of vine she'd made for them to catch fish with.

When the girl finally appeared, she ran down the beach towards them waving and smiling.

Pin watched her blond hair sway behind her and, for the first time, realized just how wild it had become. When he'd first met Emma in his work bay on the Tian all that time ago, her hair was well groomed and trimmed so it didn't fall too far past the point of her chin. Now it was long and thick with humidity, and creeped down her back like moss on a tree.

Recently, she'd started lining it with tiny flowers of purple and pink that poked out from all over, adding to her elemental look.

When she came up to them, she smiled and handed the nets to Pin saying, "Here you go. I hope they don't break apart in the water. It was hard to get all the knots tight."

Pin wrapped the nets over his shoulder and frowned at the girl. "I think you need a haircut," he said simply, then looked at Adam whose appearance was equally wild. "You, too. You both look like you were raised by wolves."

"So do you, Pin," laughed Adam pointing to the man's beard, now so bushy it hid the lower half of his face. "I can barely see your mouth move when you talk!"

Emma covered her mouth and laughed at this and Pin rubbed his beard thoughtfully. Then he laughed heartily along with them.

"Well, that settles it then," he boomed. "We'll clean ourselves up tonight after dinner and bring a little human civility back to this place."

With that he turned towards the raft and told Adam to climb aboard while he pushed it into the water. "Wish us luck out here, little mouse," he said to Emma as he jumped onto the craft. "Because if we are, we'll be back with a fish for dinner that might just be the size of you!"

Emma watched them paddle away from the beach and out past the edge of the lagoon. She giggled at their awkwardness in keeping the raft afloat, but, as they became smaller, she was also struck by an odd and sudden fear of being alone.

She had never imagined a life without Adam or Pin and had always assumed they would remain as they were forever. But, standing on the beach alone now, a deep doubt that lived somewhere in her gut seemed to creep up her esophagus and worm its way into her brain. She didn't know what this new and strange feeling was, but she was suddenly aware of a truth that haunted her.

She thought back to the monster that had taken their pod and disappeared into the deep. Was it still out there? Were Pin and Adam safe from its three long arms and repulsive mouth full of sharp white teeth?

With that thought, Emma gave Pin and Adam one last long look before turning away and heading back up the beach towards their camp.

Despite Emma's concerns, Adam and Pin returned to the beach that first day.

After more than three hours at sea, they brought back two sleek fish; one bright blue with white stripes and one green with a pink underbelly. And, just as Pin has promised, each was indeed much taller than Emma.

When the fish were unwrapped from the nets, Pin held each up by the tail and made the children stand next to them to judge the difference in size. Light scattered across their scaly bodies as they flexed and flopped in his hands, and the children watched as they gulped uselessly at the air until they finally went limp and stood at attention.

Emma looked up and was amazed to see the one she stood next to was even taller than Pin himself, who held the tail well above his head.

"These were two of the smallest out there, too, I'd say," said Pin. "I'd hate to come across what eats 'em in case he confuses us for dinner and swallows up the raft!"

Adam laughed, but Emma didn't find Pin's joke very funny.

"Don't say that, Pin, and don't you laugh either, Adam," she said, scolding them both equally.

"Why can't I laugh?" asked Adam dismissively. "I can laugh at a joke if I want to."

"Being eaten up is no joke," said Emma turning to Pin. "Shame on you for saying you might be eaten."

Pin laid the fish along the top of high boulder before bending down to address Emma. "You're right, Emma," he said, "it was an unfair thing to joke about. But you don't need to be upset with Adam, or I. We won't be eaten up."

"But, if you *do* get eaten up, I'll be all alone," said Emma. "What would I do then?"

Pin smiled and stood up with purpose saying, "Well, we'll just have to make some rules about taking out the raft to be sure we're all safe." He scratched at his beard, as though thinking hard, then cast a finger into the air.

"Rule number one!" he said loudly and started pacing across the camp.

Emma and Adam watched him curiously as he spoke into the air with authority.

"No fishing at night, or on cloudy days. The raft will only be used in perfect sunlight to ensure the safety of its passengers. Agreed?"

The children nodded in agreement and Pin continued.

"Rule number two! The raft must stay close to the shoreline at all times. That way, if it capsizes, one would be able to swim to shore. Agreed? Rule number three! Never, and I mean *never*, go fishing alone. In fact, all three of us will fish together as long as you two stay small enough to fit on the raft. That way, nobody will ever feel left behind or alone again."

Pin stopped pacing and looked down at Emma. "Now, do those rules suit you, Emma, or do you have your own to offer?"

Emma thought for a moment then shook her head. She was satisfied with the three rules Pin laid out and felt confident they would all be safe.

"It's settled then," said Pin moving to pick up the long fish again. "Get a fire started, Adam, while I clean these fish for our supper. Emma, you come and watch how I do it so you'll be able to do it yourself one day."

With that, the two children moved from their idle spots and got to work preparing for super.

Emma squealed and curled her fingers under her chin as she watched Pin slit the fish's bellies, their insides spilling out and hissing as they hit the hot stone. But once that was done and the head had been removed, she found she loved the feel of the smooth red flesh underneath. And the smell of it was wonderful and salty like the sea and fresh like the mid-morning winds.

After a satisfying dinner, Pin sat the children down inside their shelter and went about trimming and cleaning up their hair. Emma winced as he poured hot water across the top of her head and attempted to untangle the more matted parts of it.

"You may have to put less of these little flowers in your hair from now on, little mouse," he said as he worked through the long mess of tangles. "Your hair seems to grow around them like the jungle itself."

Once her hair was smoothed out, Pin cut at it with

the side of a jagged black stone he'd sharpened along the side of a rough bolder.

Emma watched tufts of her hair fall to the dirt and blow away on the wind. "Don't cut it too short, Pin," she said. "I like to twirl it in my fingers when I'm thinking sometimes."

Pin grunted in acknowledgement as he worked at her hair, leaving it to hang just past her shoulders. "How's that then?" he asked when he was done, stepping back to look the girl over in the firelight.

Emma stood up and twirled once, sending her hair spinning around her. Then she ran a hand down the length of it until she could finger the ends. "Perfect," she said and smiled. "Thanks, Pin."

"Definitely an improvement," said Pin before turning to Adam. "Now you, son," he said, pausing momentarily as the word passed his lips. *Son.*

Adam hopped up and took Emma's place and Pin set to work trimming the boy's blonde hair.

Over time, the three of them became expert fishermen, casting off each morning along the shoreline in search of food and returning to camp with strange new species of sea life, always colorful and thick with flavor.

Pin learned that beyond eating, fish came in handy for their oil, which—when stored in cupped-bark and waxy fronds—could be set alight in their shelter at night, or used in ointments to rub on cuts and scrapes.

To help them at their job of catching sea life, Adam fashioned spears and short knives to skewer fish and various bottom feeders. These he also used when diving in the reefs of the lagoon where they harvested large green shelled creatures that Pin called "moon clams".

After three more months of unflinchingly hot weather, a short but violent rainy season hit them hard. Its winds were so fierce that Pin was forced to rebuild their shelter four times, and, for a while, their camp was under more than two feet of rushing water at all times.

It was during this time that Adam and Emma became as comfortable in the trees as on the ground.

The lagoon was beset by such harsh winds that the beach became a danger and, for them, it was much easier to move long distances along the wide branches above than wade through the muddy jungle floor below. In fact, the two would often spend whole days together, cradled in the crooks of branches, shielded from the biting winds under tent-like foliage, playing games and sharing their secrets.

Pin, on the other hand, rarely left camp during this time. As much as he missed the company of the children at times, he was hardly nimble enough to follow them into the trees and resigned himself to a land-locked life once again. For him, the rainy days were dreary and long, and he yearned for the sun to peek out from behind the endless storm clouds and bring warmth and gladness to the moon once again.

Was it the sun, or the children he missed most? He couldn't be sure. Both seemed one-in-the-same.

Pin also found that spending so much time alone wasn't good for him. He thought too much about his past life and the many people he'd known throughout his life. These thoughts reminded him of his shortcomings and that his life had been mostly a waste. He envied the children for their empty pasts and endless possibility for happiness. This spiral of thoughts and memory turned his mind to drinking and how wonderful it would be to drink himself to sleep these wet and lonely nights.

Unlike him, when Emma and Adam ventured down from above they seemed no different than they'd ever been. Children have a stronger constitution than old men for enduring the hardships of time. Their minds and bodies were still healthy and versatile.

And so it was for months: the three would fall asleep to the sound of rain pelting the shelter and wake up to the same. Then children would vanish and Pin would be left behind to worry about them all. Their supplies dwindled over time and they were forced to leave fishing until the rains passed.

The moon was testing them, Pin realized one night as he tossed restlessly, unable to sleep. It was reminding them that paradise was only a dream. A desire destined to be left unfulfilled in old hearts.

And indeed that night, Pin dreamed of blue skies and the scent of flowers and of a woman he'd once spent a night with while on leave from his mining ship more than fifteen years earlier. He may have forgotten her name, but he still remembered the feel of her smooth, dark skin. Maybe some dreams were worth holding onto.

Part Three
Hunted by Day, Haunted by Night

15

Six weeks later, the clouds broke and the winds died to a biting breeze that swam through the world like a cold, wet eel.

Rain still sprinkled the waxy fronds, but now the wet was tempered by slivers of sun that sent puddles of light and warmth to the jungle below. The children searched for sunspots each morning, like birds rooting out worms, tracking the sky for rays of light and then journeying to find them.

Emma sat alone in such a spot, high in a tree on the edge of the valley. She sang to herself and sucked contently on a swollen blue fruit, her bare skin soaking in the subtle heat of the sun's rays.

Her hair was tied in two tight knots at either side of her head, the flowers and their green and yellow stems wound up so tightly they looked like little round cakes swirled with colorful icing.

She'd been to this particular tree many times before. It had quickly become of one of her favorite places to escape and think. It was taller than most, its top peeking out from the cover of others around and Emma loved how it allowed a wonderful view of the world in every direction.

Its tentacle-like branches were thick and venous, the bark routed out long ago by burrowing insects. As a game, she often followed a single line with her eyes to see how far she could track the bulging vein before it became lost in the mess of others.

Perhaps most importantly, her tree was the best place to watch the mysterious cave that had captured her imagination all these stormy months.

Without Pin to limit her travels during the rainy season, Emma often ventured beyond the waterfall and past the rocky cliffs that bordered the edge of the wide valley. She loved the thrill of solitary exploration and was constantly amazed at the discoveries she made, like the colony of bugs that disguised themselves as leaves, or how the swollen purple knots on trees would burst and release sweet, clear sap when pierced with sharp stone.

But her most fascinating discovery during this time was the wide mouth of a large cave that cut into the center of the tall cliffs high above the valley floor.

Since discovering it, Emma had come to the tree almost every day to watch the cave from across the valley as sheets of rain poured down around her. The more she stared into its dark opening, the more she was sure something—or someone—would emerge suddenly. But nothing ever did.

She didn't tell Adam about her tree or her cave. They were her discovery and she wanted to keep it that way. She liked having something of her own; a place to escape Adam's incessant questions and Pin's constant grumbling. A secret place she could be alone, and let her imagination wander in peace. Somewhere she could hear and feel the world around her.

She'd had such a place back on the Tian— inside the walls, where she was free to travel as she pleased. She'd loved having a place that only she could squeeze into, where she could sit and listen to the electric whirs and hums of the ship and imagine they were the heart and breath of some elegant beast floating through space to a paradise lost in time. It soothed her to imagine she was someplace else. She missed that.

Emma eyed the cave with delicious anticipation, scanning the area around it to determine how she could reach it. The only access point she could see was a thin ridge that ran along the side of the cliff no more than five feet wide, and very uneven.

At the time of its discovery, the force of the winds and the wet of the rain made scaling the cliffs to reach the ridge far too dangerous. One false step would have seen her tumbling to dash against the hard earth below. But now that the worst of the weather had passed, Emma was determined to make the journey up to the ridge and across to the lip of the cave where she would finally enter and learn what secrets it held.

Not wanting to waste any more time, she took a final bite of fruit and let the empty husk fall to the ground, stories below. Then she let herself slip to a branch beneath her where she could cross over to the next tree next over, and then onto the next, moving through the foliage until she would reach the tree line close to the edge of cliff.

She shivered suddenly as she made her way

through the branches and couldn't remember the last time she felt more anxious, or more excited.

Adam never let Emma out of his sight.

He'd promised Pin that he'd follow her months ago when, one night, neither of them could sleep for the sound of far off storms. The two of them sat perched on the edge of the shelter, watching lightning spark miles away as Emma slept, safe and dry in the shelter behind them.

"Adam, I fear for the girl," Pin said quietly as Emma's sleeping breath filled their tent. "I don't know why. She's capable, and smarter than both of us combined, but she's curious, like a dog nosing itself into a hole in the ground. The more it digs the more chance it'll find something it don't expect. I think someone should be there in case she ever finds something that aims to take a bite out of her."

"Emma's good at slipping away," said Adam with a shrug. "She likes to be on her own sometimes, I think."

"She don't need to know you're there for you to be there," said Pin with a wink.

Adam looked at him quizzically for a moment then let out a monstrous groan. "Oh, I don't want to follow Emma all around all day, staying out of sight. Why should we be so worried about her anyway? If she wants to be on her own, let her. There's nothing out here to hurt her anyway."

Pin frowned and rubbed his beard. "And what if Emma took a fall? Broke both her legs and couldn't walk? Who would hear her cries for help in storms like these? Why, she'd be left to the not-parrots, who'd peck at her until she was nothing but bones. Do you want that to happen?"

Adam thought about this for a moment and then rolled his eyes. "Fine," he relented with a huff. "I'll follow her as best I can. But I want something in return."

"And what could you need out here that you don't already have?" Pin asked, eyeing the boy quizzically.

"A spear," said Adam quickly as though he'd been waiting some time to ask. "For hunting."

"For *killing* you mean," said Pin seriously. He looked down at Adam and gave the boy a hard stare as though coaxing the truth from him.

"I guess so," Adam said, relenting. "And so? You kill fish don't you?"

"I do," Pin answered thoughtfully.

"So, there. Why can you kill fish, but I can't have a spear for hunting? I have to learn some time, don't I?"

"You do," answered Pin in the same thoughtful manner. Only this time he looked out into the storm with a grave face. "I don't mean to say you can't learn to take care of yourself, Adam. Lord knows I won't be around forever to do it for you. But you're just not ready for the responsibility of a weapon yet."

"Killing is a serious business. Probably the most serious business there is. And nobody—especially someone so young—should be forced to do it until they've got a true understanding and love for life in all its complexities."

Adam looked down, disheartened, and Pin put his arm about the boy's shoulders. He knew Adam didn't understand what he meant, and, in a sense, that was the point. The time would come when Adam would need to provide for all of them. Pin was already in his sixties and not a single day passed that his body didn't remind him of his age. But he felt too responsible for the kind of adult Adam would become to give in to his boyish blood lust just yet.

Then again, what could a boy, alone in the universe, hope to learn about life? Would he ever fall in love? Have his heart broken? Become a father? Pin realized that, out here, Adam would lead a very different life than any other boy who had ever come before him.

"I'll tell you what," Pin said finally, squeezing the side of Adam's arm. "You show me you can watch after Emma and I'll think about teaching you how to carve a spear. Maybe even show you how to use it if the blasted sun ever returns."

Adam nodded reluctantly. Then thunder crashed and they both watched the clouds flash pink and purple as electricity arched somewhere above them.

Since that night, Adam kept his promise, tracking Emma whenever she vanished into the jungle alone. He learned her routes and made sure to watch her from afar whenever she settled someplace.

Lately she'd been coming to the same tall tree, deep in the valley. Adam climbed up another tree and watched her from a distance, bored and lonely.

He couldn't help but resent Emma for wanting to be alone. It hurt him in a strange way, like she thought he wasn't good enough for her. Why would someone prefer to be alone? He didn't like being alone. It was boring.

The more Adam watcher her, the more determined he was to convince her that being with him was as good as being in her silly tree. He found he was desperate to know what she was thinking about. Did she think of him when she was alone? He didn't know why, but he hoped she did. He hoped she spent the whole day thinking of him. Maybe even missing him sometimes.

While he couldn't read Emma's thoughts, he knew she spent long periods staring out at a large cave in the cliffs, high above the jungle floor. It was so high, in fact, that it could only be seen in full from the trees. You could walk right under it and never know it was there.

Rows of jagged rocks hung down at the top so it looked like a great mouth full of teeth, ready to chew whoever entered it. It didn't seem like any place he would want to visit, so he was surprised when Emma left her tree one day and moved through the branches towards it.

She was out of her tree and out of his sight so quickly he wasn't sure where she'd gone at first. But then he caught sight of her pink skin moving among the dark green fronds and knew it was her.

Scrambling to his feet and cursing her speed, he jumped to the tree next to his and tried to keep up without losing sight of her.

"Where are you going now?" he huffed as he struggled to catch up with her. She'd never gone this way before.

He looked ahead as he moved and noticed the cave in the distance, looming larger as he left each tree behind. He was suddenly struck with a great fear.

"Oh no," he said and picked up the pace. "Of all places, not there, Emma."

Emma grimaced and set her bare foot carefully on a rock to her right. She pressed against it twice to test its stability before shifting her weight and pulling herself up with the tips of her fingers. They shook under her weight, but her footing stayed true and she managed to get one step higher on the cliff and closer to the thin ridge that lead to the cave.

The cliff was slicker than she'd anticipated and for a moment she considered giving up. But when she looked down, she was amazed at how high she'd climbed already. The ridge seemed so close now. Two more good steps upward and she would be able to touch its edge with her fingers. Maybe even pull herself up and over the side.

She squinted as the wind picked up and the rain changed direction, whipping against her face. She focused on keeping her breathing steady as she looked up at the cliff and searched for another jagged rock to hold onto. When she found one she raised herself on her toes and strained to reach it. Her fingers brushed against the rock's smooth underside, but she couldn't quite wrap them around the top. So she stretched her body as much as she could until, finally, she let out a deep groan and her fingertips folded over the edge of the rock.

She smiled and shifted to find a new foothold when her toes slipped out from under her and she felt her legs swing away. Emma screamed and dug her fingers into the rock above, her one-handed grip the only thing keeping her from falling to the ground below.

She felt her fingernails buckle and split under the strain and kicked her legs twice as though swimming against the air would be enough to push her body back against the cliff face. Looking down, she panicked, her deep, even breaths turning to thick gulps of air. She shut her eyes for a moment, overcome with fear.

Open your eyes! her mind screamed out. *Open your eyes and find a foothold, you fool!*

She ignored her mind and slowed her breathing. Then, eyes still closed, she listened to her body as it swayed back and forth. She searched for her center; that place inside where she could regain control over her movement and strength.

Her fingers screamed in pain, but she buried the feeling until it was like a dull noise in the back of her brain.

Open your eyes now, her mind said again, only this time its voice was like a whisper. *Open your eyes and find a foothold. You can do it.*

Emma opened her eyes. Scanning the cliff quickly, she saw a thin vertical crack running through the rock to her right. It had been mostly concealed by a thick red bush that grew from it in long coils of prickly branches. In one move she kicked her right leg up and stuck her toes into the center of the bush, forcing her foot through until she touched rock.

Needle-like thorns dug into her flesh but in the moment she didn't feel their sting.

With her right foot secure, she pushed herself up until she could wrap her other hand around the jagged outcropping above. Then, with both her hands as leverage, she brought her left leg up and secured it to the rock. With her body stable, she pressed herself to the stone wall and let out a long, hot scream of relief.

What are you doing?! her mind wailed, berating

her. *You should have never tried to climb. Not in the rain. You could have died!*

The pain in her fingers suddenly flashed through her body and her feet pulsed angrily. For a long time Emma didn't move. She couldn't. She just clung to the stone wall, breathing out great gasps of air in utter disbelief that she'd managed to survive.

Finally, Emma drew enough courage to look up. The stone walkway was within reach, mere feet away. She'd done it. She'd made it!

Slowly she let her right hand relax and loosen its grip on the cliff. Then, pushing up on the edge of the crack with her right foot, she caught hold of the ridge and pulled herself up and onto it. When her feet were over the side, she rolled onto her back and stared up at the sky. Rain flowed over her face, disguising the tears than ran down her cheeks.

"If you're going to visit this cave again you'll need to find another way in," she said to herself, laughing out loud.

Finally, Emma sat up. Bringing her knees up to her chest, she began picking thorny barbs from her feet; careful to find them all for fear of infection.

When she finished, she let the rain wash the blood from their tiny wounds and looked along the stone walkway to the massive opening that lead into the heart of the cliffs.

Her heart raced in anticipation. What would she find inside, she wondered. An underground lake perhaps? Maybe Pin could move their camp inside the cave to avoid the rain? She smiled at how happy it would make him to be free of the wind and wet.

With that thought to guide her, Emma got to her feet and slid along the ridge toward the cave, being extra careful to keep her back pressed against the rock for safety.

16

Emma stood in the mouth of the cave, marveling at its height. She felt like a mouse standing on the tip of a lion's tongue as she stared in at the long teeth-like stalactites hanging in rows along the ceiling.

Jungle sounds echoed around her, ricocheting off the stone entryway and disappearing into the darkness. The tiny hairs on her arms bristled with excitement.

She sucked in a breath and held it as she took her first step inside, bracing herself as though she might be transported somewhere else entirely. And, in a way, she was. The familiar sounds of the outside world vanished behind her like she had entered the vacuum of space. It was eerily quiet now that she was within the stone cavern.

But, no, that wasn't right. The cave had its own sounds. They were just smaller than the outside world's; quieter and careful in the darkness. Emma closed her eyes and let the rhythms of this new world show themselves to her: the slow drip, drip, dripping of condensation falling from the long, twisting stalactites; the fluttering of insect legs scurrying along the walls around her. The cave was indeed alive with undiscovered sounds and secrets.

Emma opened her eyes and let them adjust to the darkness before walking deeper into the cave. Thin strands of bioluminescent moss pulsed blue light along cracks in the stone walls and ceiling, lighting her way as she explored further.

She ran a finger along a line of moss lightly and it glowed brighter around her fingertips. Pointy barbs poked out in search of insects to skewer and digest, but their needles only tickled Emma's flesh before pulling away quickly.

A sound of fluttering echoed above and Emma looked up to see a large shadow flying close to the high ceiling. She tracked the dark creature until it blended in with the blackness and the sound of its wings dissipated into the distance.

The ceiling of the cave was impressively high, but Emma could see that it sloped down further ahead.

She looked back towards the cave's high opening to find it was almost out of view. She'd come so far that the moss' dim blue shine was her only source of light. She stood still for a moment to take in the light show. The way its ripples cast blue shadows on the rocks made her feel like she was underwater. Emma thought it was magical. And just like when their tiny escape pod had flooded with the blue light of the moon so long ago, her heart felt full and her stomach was fluttery with good feelings.

She turned towards a blur of motion and saw an insect as long as her arm and twice as fat skittering along the wall next to her. It moved swiftly on hundreds of spindly legs as though it had somewhere important to be. Its backside bristled with millions of microscopic hairs that lit its way in the darkness. Blue barbs erupted from the moss to grab at it, but the glowing insect was too large to be bothered by them.

Emma picked up her pace to follow it. She was curious where it was headed in such a hurry and laughed quietly as she struggled over the uneven stone floor to keep up with it.

She hadn't chased it far when the insect stopped suddenly. Its three long antennae whirled wildly on top of its narrow head as though searching for something in the darkness.

Emma moved her face closer to study its strange movements. "What are you looking for?" she said softly. "Do you sense me here with you?"

All at once, the light left the creature's bristles and it became a shadow on the dark wall. Emma heard the flapping of leathery wings and spun around to see a monstrous winged creature with glowing yellow eyes sailing towards her. She screamed and covered her face as the flying animal flew past and pulled the insect off the wall with powerful talons.

The bug exploded with color, its bioluminescence flaring under the attack. It coiled its long tubular body around the winged assailant uselessly as the larger creature torn it in two. Half its body was swallowed by the shadow-bird while the other half dangled limply, leaking glowing white blood along the stone floor.

The cave erupted with sound and Emma looked up to see a swarm of shadows descending rapidly. Hundreds of creatures flew around her, beating her face with leathery wings as they fought to grab hold of what remained of the large insect.

She flailed her arms and spun around to get away from the torrent of claws and flying bodies, but it was like she was caught in the eye of a storm whose winds were too strong to fight against.

Something sharp sliced her cheek and she panicked. Bolting and shielding her face, she screamed and ran away from the violent swarm.

She'd become so turned around she didn't even know which way she was running, but just then she didn't care. All she wanted was to get as far away from the horrible screeching of the black birds—away from their gnashing teeth and horrible yellow eyes. Away from their violence.

A moment later her right foot hit a stone edge and she tripped, tumbling forward and rolling down a passageway. Her body was pummeled by the rocky floor as she rolled down the wide chasm until, finally, she landed with a thud on smooth black stone.

For a long while, Emma lay on the cold floor, curled up and sobbing like a wounded animal. The sound of the birds was distant now, overhead and far away like a fading nightmare. She dared not look up for fear of seeing them again and kept her face buried into her folded arms.

Soon the violent call of the shadow-birds died away and the cave was nearly silent again. Slowly, the quieter sounds of the cave reemerged until Emma could hear the drip, drip, dripping of water once more.

She opened her eyes slowly and looked back to where she'd fallen. A large entryway led to slick stone steps that climbed back up to the main cave. She pushed herself to her knees and winced at a pain in her side. Looking down, she saw a wide purple bruise forming above her right hip. She pressed her thumb into it and it turned a sour yellow. Pain shot through her.

She looked back up at the steps she'd fallen down and noticed strange markings around the entryway that fanned out along the walls becoming an intricate mural of crude pictures and writing.

Amazed, Emma rose to her feet and looked around. The same blue moss streaked light along the walls and ceiling, lighting the long anti-chamber enough that she could see some ten feet in front of her.

The pictures and writing continued to adorn the walls well into the darkness. Emma stepped forward to examine them.

Depictions of great beasts, some tall with three long tentacles and angry faces were scratched into the rock. Emma traced the images with her finger. Their etched lines seemed to glow white under the moss' blue light.

She saw what looked like a flock of not-parrots drawn high above the rest. Then she noticed a series of jagged lines that seemed to form the shape of cliffs.

Are these the same cliffs that bordered the valley close to our camp?, she wondered.

She traced the cliff's lines until she noticed a section that formed a kind of face, vaguely human but for its wide features and round eyes that peered up at a massive circle higher up on the wall. The round etching dwarfed the other images below and, at first, Emma thought it must be the sun. But something about it reminded her of the giant red gas planet that was always visible in the sky, night or day. The way the figure's mouth stretched open as it watched the sky made Emma think of the wide mouth of the cave she'd just entered.

Past the cliffs Emma found etchings of the beach, their small lagoon, and the endless ocean beyond where pictured tentacles pierced crudely drawn waves.

A thought rushed through Emma's mind and she became excited. She stepped away from the wall to take the larger canvas in, holding her breath for a moment as she put it all together.

It's a map of the moon, she thought with glee and spun around to view the wonderful mural in its entirety.

She gasped at the enormity of it. The little beach and patch of jungle they called home, their waterfall, the cliffs and valley beyond, were only a fraction of the land the map depicted.

Emma walked briskly, moving further into the cave to study the endless images of land and strange animals. There were also markings that looked like writing, but she couldn't make sense of them. They were more like shapes than the letters she was used to: squares and long ovals, triangles punctuated by sudden slashes of angry single lines. She was desperate to know what they meant.

As she studied the symbols, Emma wondered what the ancient beings who wrote them might have been like, and what some future race might think about humans if they ever landed on Earth and read their languages and studied their drawings. Of course, that was assuming there would be anything left on Earth to find.

Emma remembered her father speaking of great

fires ripping through vast areas of land on Earth, destroying everything in their path.

Maybe, thought Emma, *despite all of our technology and books, all that will remain on Earth one day will be scratches in caves like these ones.*

Emma felt proud suddenly, like she'd made a most amazing discovery. It was exactly what she'd hoped for— a secret knowledge all her own. Something she could study and learn from.

With her pulse pounding, Emma continued down the long chamber, tracing the shapes of creatures and landmarks, periodically looking back at the image of her lagoon to determine how far off some of them were. The jungle went on forever, the images becoming wilder the further she got from their beach. The animals depicted became larger and the terrain seemed to rage and swirl around them. Then, at the very center of the wall, a tall peak shot up from the jungle very suddenly, dwarfing everything around it, including Emma herself.

She strained to see the top of the peak, craning her neck and following it up to where the wall curved into the ceiling. Countless thin lines streamed from the top of the tall plateau, looking something like water to her. Was it another waterfall, or something else entirely?

Emma brought her gaze back down and turned her attention to the open cave. Her eyes were finally adjusting to the dark, so the shadows that loomed further off were beginning to take shape. She thought she could actually see the chamber's end now, the smooth stone of the back wall aglow with more drawings.

But there was something else. Emma strained to

make it out, but all she could see was a shadow twice the size of a human man and wider than three Pins put together. It seemed to stand on two squat legs, broad shoulders hunched forward like it might run at her.

Her first thought was that it was a man standing at the far end of the cave, watching her from the darkness. She stiffened and her heart began to race. She almost turned to run but when, after a moment, the shadow didn't move she relaxed again.

She slid along the stone floor slowly, focusing her eyes on the figure at the end of the chamber until it began to take shape.

A great skull rested on its top. It towered over her, large, open eye sockets leering out across the room menacingly. Its long mouth hung open to show rows of sharp teeth. It was vaguely bird-like, but too big to be a not-parrot

Clusters of smaller skulls and bones ran down either side of the shape from there, forming the rest of the figure. It looked like a statue. Folded arms constructed of varying sizes of bones and skulls crossed at the chest, their crude hands grasping something. Emma moved closer to see the object— a long, silver bar made of what looked like metal. It seemed out of place in the rocky cave, surrounded by smooth, bleached bones.

Emma noticed something familiar suddenly. Each of the figure's hands was made of two skulls distinctly unlike the rest. She tracked back up to examine the features of the other skulls. There were hundreds, piled in a mass to form the terrifying statue before her. Or was it a suit of some kind?

Little care seemed to have been given to their

placement, and many had similar animal features. Why then, were these two rounder, medium-sized skulls given such specific placement?

The two skulls on the backs of the towering figure's hands reminded Emma of the one she'd found when they first arrive, the one that had scared Pin so that he—

Emma heard the shuffling of quick steps behind her and froze. Something grabbed her shoulder roughly and she screamed as she was spun around by a strong arm.

"What are you doing in here?" Pin asked in a hoarse, angry whisper. He gazed past Emma and scanned the great figure made of bones. Then, looking at her worriedly he said, "We're leaving," and pulled at her to follow.

"But—" Emma began to protest.

"Now!" Pin said as he pulled her back towards the stone doorway.

Emma continued to argue as they moved through the entrance, up the stone stairway and into the high cave.

"Did you see the drawings?" she asked quickly. "It must be a map of the moon. And the big statue, did you see it? And there was writing, I think. And, oh Pin, don't you want to learn more about where we are? Don't you want to know about the ancient people who lived here long ago?"

Pin stopped suddenly and put his hand over Emma's mouth to quiet her. Together they listened, Emma wondering what for, but the cave was silent save for the ever constant dripping of water.

Pin whistled a short, high-pitched whistle. The sound of it bounced off the stone walls until it hit the mouth of the cave. It was quickly met with another whistle and Pin urged them forward.

"What's going on?" Emma asked as they made their way back towards the cave's opening.

"The ancient race you discovered," Pin started sternly, "are not so ancient."

"You mean..." Emma began, her face falling as a wave of fear ran through her.

"They're coming," Pin finished. Then he picked her up and quickened his pace.

17

Emma saw Adam's shadowy silhouette as she and Pin approached the mouth of the cave. She knew him well enough to know his body language suggested nervousness. The way his arms moved constantly at his sides and how he was checking over his shoulder told Emma he was scared of something.

As he came into focus, Adam waved them forward anxiously. Pin paused when he reached the mouth of cave, pressing the children against the wall gently and peering out into the distance.

"We've still got time, thank goodness," he whispered to himself. Then, turning to the children, he waved them forward saying, "They're moving slowly. Looks like a whole tribe in tow."

The children stepped forward and Pin led them out into the open air. From the rocky ledge, Emma stared across the valley to see what had spooked Adam and Pin. At first she saw nothing out of the ordinary. But then Adam pointed slightly east of her gaze and further into the jungle and she saw hints of movement in the valley below.

Trees swayed when there was no wind, and every so often trails of black smoke escaped the thick foliage. And while she couldn't quite see what was moving along the jungle floor, she could make out flashes of figures between the cracks in the foliage and heard a low, steady rumble as though a great wave was rolling ever closer.

"What is it?" she asked Pin, as the three of them inched their way along the ledge.

"Not what, but who," answered Pin thoughtfully. "I don't know for certain, but a place as full of life as this may have a sentient species. Adam spotted them first, so we owe him our thanks, I'd say." He looked down at Emma then and asked, "You say you saw drawings on the walls of the cave? Could be you found their home."

"But, why have we never seen them until now?" Emma asked.

"Perhaps they're returning since the storms have passed," said Pin, his eyes trained on the coming horde of creatures. "Perhaps they're nomads following a migrating herd. Could be they're only passing by this way, on their way to somewhere else entirely. Either way, we'll need to climb back up the cliff and get to camp. With you two keeping watch from the trees, we should be safe enough to pack up and move. With any luck, they'll keep to the valley and leave the cliffs between us."

"*Up* the cliff?" Emma asked suddenly, thinking about her arduous climb to the ledge. "Don't you mean down?"

Adam looked at her and shook his head. "There are big ladders carved into the rock this way," he said, pointing away from the cave. "They're not far." His voice turned cold suddenly as he continued. "It was really stupid of you to climb up how you did, Emma. You could have killed yourself. And if I hadn't been here to tell Pin, you could have been trapped in that cave."

Adam's anger confused Emma. She'd never imagined that her journey into the cave would affect anyone else. She was about to apologize when she realized something that bothered her.

"Wait, how did you know I climbed up at all? Were you following me?" she asked angrily.

"Yeah, and you're lucky I was!" Adam yelled back, facing her. "You obviously can't take care of yourself."

Pin shushed them both harshly. "I asked Adam to keep an eye on you, Emma," he said urging them onward. "To keep you safe."

Emma shot Pin an angry look and said, "I don't need anyone to keep me safe." Then she turned to Adam and said, "And you stop following me. You can come along when you want anyway. You just have to ask me."

Adam looked away and the three continued along the wall in silence until they reached a large section of carved holes in the rock that lead to the edge of the cliff. It was the ladder Adam had mentioned, but carved by whom, none of them knew.

One after the other, they climbed up to the top of the rocky plateau where they could survey the valley at a safe distance.

For a while they watched the migration of the horde from behind a squat boulder. The mass of figures was still mostly obscured by trees, but as they drew closer they became easier to examine.

They marched in a formation of two long lines. Their naked bodies were tall and tanned with rounded shoulders and three long, muscular arms. Thick, mossy colored hair hung wild on top of their wide-browed heads.

They walked slowly and with a gait that suggested tortured joints in agony. Most of them looked towards the dirt, carrying packs across their shoulders, or dragging long bamboo sleds filled with slick purple meat, or crying children behind them. A few beat drums languidly, while a small group in front chopped away the thick underbrush with long, silver poles that glinted in the sun with every strike.

Emma looked up at Pin who was squinting and had a look of both curiosity and concern. She looked back down towards the coming horde again and a sickness filled her belly. She thought had never seen such wretchedness and wished she could look away.

To her, the moon had always seemed like a paradise—a playground for her and the living things around her. But the way these creatures worked against it—cutting the jungle away as they moved—presented an angry kind of conflict she wasn't used to seeing. It was as though they were more alien to this world than she was.

Before Emma could voice any of these thoughts, Pin had them by the arms and was pulling them back down the hill towards their camp. He kept his voice low as he urged them forward and looked around as if watching out for something constantly.

When they got back to camp, Pin motioned upwards and told the children to climb into the trees.

"You two keep up and out of sight until I come

back," he said quickly as he lifted Adam up to grab hold of a low-hanging branch. "If you see anyone approach, you stay still and quiet. Do you understand?"

The children nodded and scrambled into the trees and out of sight. Pin watched their little bodies disappear into the foliage then went to work knocking down their shelter and throwing the fronds away in as random a fashion as he could in a hurry.

He dragged the poles of cane into the trees in all directions and kicked dirt over their fire pit. Then he dumped out their water stores and buried the dried fish they'd been keeping in the shade.

When he was finally satisfied that the area looked like it had never been inhabited, Pin picked up any clothing that was scattered about and bundled it under his arm. He saw Emma's little wooden box under her favorite tree and stuffed it into his pocket before leaving the campsite behind and walking briskly towards the beach where their raft would be waiting at the edge of the lagoon.

Throwing what little supplies they had onto it, Pin pushed the craft into the crystal water and rowed it along the coast.

He watched the beach disappear as he rounded the land and sighed deeply, cursing the appearance of the moon's natives and the uncertainty they brought with them. After being marooned for so long he had grown content living as they were. He had the children for company, enough fruit and fish to eat. His days were lazy and his nights were open to deep thoughts about his new and past life. The only thing that could have made him happier was alcohol at his elbow, but even his want of drink had waned over time.

This new event had destroyed all of this in a single moment. Now he would need to be diligent and ever watchful. Until he learned the movements of this tribe of moon men, he would feel hunted by day and haunted by night.

When Pin had rowed the raft a few hundred yards down the coast, he eased it up onto the overgrown shore and hid it under a pile of waxy fronds. Then he began his long walk back to camp through the wilderness.

They spent that night huddled and shivering, far away from their old camp in the densest patch of jungle they could find.

Pin was restless, his sleep disturbed by Emma's anxious twitching and his own dark thoughts. It seemed that whenever he drifted into dreaming he was met with violent images of broken men attacking him and carrying off the children. And when he was awake, every sound conjured images of hunters stalking them in the trees.

Eventually, Pin rose. Careful not to disturb the children, he covered them with fronds and walked out into the night.

It was quiet. Despite his fears, no one met him in the trees with murderous intent. He felt the only thing to ease his mind would be to venture out and check on the actions of the tribe.

If it weren't for the children he would have walked all night until he reached the cliffs. But this reconnaissance would need to wait until morning. Instead, Pin took a tour of the area. Again, all seemed quiet; the only sound was the buzzing of light-bugs the size of his fists. And so, satisfied, he walked back to the children and lay down beside them again.

It had been some time since Pin had been so distressed about their safety. Wild animals had always posed a threat on the moon, but at least animals could be counted upon to act according to their nature. They were predictable, mostly fearful and easily avoided. If these beings had evolved to be anything like Earth's humans then Pin knew they were not only unpredictable, but would be most likely to kill the three of them for being so very different than take the time to understand how they came to be there.

If we are to live on this moon, thought Pin, *then we'll need to be worthy enough to our claim.*

As much as it hurt him to admit to it, Pin knew what needed doing.

When Adam awoke the next morning, Pin had already fashioned two long spears. Both were plunged deep into the earth, their ends having been sharpened to fine points using obsidian.

The old man was sitting on a flat rock, working on the third, stripping away rough bark from the sides and doing his best to straighten out the long piece of wood in the process.

Emma sat beside him, quietly making a wreath of large blue flowers. She was humming contently, seemingly uninterested in Pin's work.

Adam got to his feet as she pulled the last knot tight. She looked up and smiled as she placed the colorful crown on her head. For a moment Adam thought the dark blue of the flowers made her lighter eyes glow slightly and she became a vision to him in the early morning sun.

Intrigued by what Pin was doing, he turned his attention away from Emma and towards the long wooden stakes in the ground. He ran his hand along one of them. It was smooth and dark red. He was tempted to pull it out, but didn't dare do so without Pin's permission.

Without looking up from his work, Pin addressed the boy brusquely. "Don't think I'm going back on what I told you now," he said before looking up to eye the boy. "But in light of our recent visitors I think it's only wise for the three of us to have some protection around."

He finished smoothing the last spear and stood up to look it over. Emma walked up and stood beside Adam, the two of them watching as Pin tested the weight and strength of the weapon, thrusting it out in front of him then holding it tightly across his chest. When he was satisfied that the spear would do for a weapon, he looked down at the children who were still watching him wide-eyed.

His heart broke to see them, their innocent eyes burning with a curiosity wasted on what he was about to teach them. He would have preferred them to be off discovering new natural wonders and exploring the moon to being stuck in a cramped patch of jungle studying the art of war.

"I hope we'll never need to use these," he said gravely. "But, to be safe, I'll show you how to hold a spear with confidence, and how to make and block a blow."

With that, Pin walked away from the rock he'd been sitting on and stood at the center of their makeshift camp. He spread his legs slightly, bent his knees and held the spear across his body diagonally.

"Just the sight of a weapon can be enough to stop violence before it even begins in most cases. If you look fierce, like you're not afraid, an attacker might just decide to walk the other way."

Pin nodded to the two spears sticking out of the earth and told the children to take one each. Adam pulled his out quickly, dark earth puffing up around the thick wooden shaft. He spun it so the sharp end pointed towards the sky. It was taller than him by a head and he looked it up and down with excited reverence.

Emma, on the other hand, took hers in both hands gingerly, pulling the spear from the ground and making a determined face as though willing herself to play along out of duty to Pin.

"Watch me closely and do as I do," the old man said as the lesson began. "See how I'm standing, with my legs bent and my spear crossing my body?"

Adam and Emma nodded and mimicked his stance, bending their legs and bringing their spears to their chests.

"This is a defensive position," Pin continued. "With your weapon like this you can protect your body from an attack. But you're also ready to move quickly if you have to run or fight back."

Pin stood up straight again and twisted his hips, bringing his spear back and pointing the sharp end down slightly. The children followed suit, moving their bodies awkwardly as they tried to copy their teacher.

"A powerful thrust doesn't come from your arms, it flows from your shoulders," he said then stabbed the spear into the earth with a great twist of his body. He let go and the wood remained upright. "Let your whole body power the blow and you'll inflict a deeper wound."

Adam tried first, yelling out as he threw his arms forward and struck the ground with his spear. His hand lost hold of the weapon when it hit the earth and he fell forward, falling onto his knees. The spear fell from the earth and landed on top of him.

Emma laughed as Pin moved to help the boy up. Adam shot her an angry look before taking the spear back from Pin.

"You need to find your balance," Pin said and held his spear perpendicular to the ground. "Every spear has a balance point, a spot along the shaft where you can keep hold of it without gripping it too tightly. Hold yours up and see if you can find it."

The children did as they were instructed and held their weapons up in front of themselves, trying to balance them in one hand. More than a few times they dropped their spears to the ground, but eventually Emma found she could balance the spear in her palm if she held it just the right place near the center.

"I did it!" she called out proudly, her eyes never leaving the spear for fear of dropping it.

"That's good, Emma," said Pin enthusiastically. "That's your sweet spot. Grip it loosely there and move your hips and shoulders around into an attack pose."

Emma did so slowly, her body flowing gracefully into this new position.

"Now, let your shoulders do the work. And remember, you're not driving the spear forward with your hands. Imagine you're throwing it, like you would a rock, only a very short distance. Over time, the feeling of holding a spear should fade away entirely. It will seem like just another part of your body."

Emma nodded and held her stance, waiting for the feel of the weapon to fade away like Pin had said it would. She relaxed her grip and focused on her shoulders, shifting her sense of energy to them instead of in her arms. Then she trained her eyes on a spot on the ground and threw herself forward, letting her whole body move as she drove the end of the spear into the earth.

She didn't stumble when its sharp end pierced the top layer of jungle dirt, but remained steady on her feet. She let go and straightened. Her spear didn't waver. She had plunged it deep into the ground.

"Very good!" Pin said proudly.

Adam looked on with a twinge of jealousy. He would have liked to have mastered the move first.

"We'll keep practicing lunges and then move onto throwing," Pin went on. "But remember, the most important thing is to avoid conflict. Only use force if you are left with no choice."

"What about hunting?" Adam asked.

"We won't be doing any hunting until you're good with a spear," Pin said quickly. "An animal faced with the sharp end of a weapon is as dangerous as anything else. I still don't think you fully understand how dangerous it is out here. Could be it's my fault. Maybe I've sheltered you. Heaven knows we've had an easy time of it hidden away with the ocean at our backs. I fear it's only a matter of time before we learn the true nature of life on this moon."

Unsatisfied, Adam nodded but didn't protest. Instead he found the balance point of his spear and set about practicing, determined to master the weapon.

18

The appearance of the tribe changed much for the three castaways. The general sense of freedom they'd once enjoyed to live and roam as they wished had all but vanished.

Forced to stay close together, their little patch of jungle felt like a prison at times and—to make matters worse for Emma—Pin would only fish at dawn and he refused to take her with him anymore. This contradiction of the rules they'd all agreed upon upset her, and she told him as much one morning as he was making to leave.

"You're breaking a promise, you know," she said, sulking in the branches above his head. Adam was still asleep next to her, lying on his belly, his arms dangling from the branches.

Pin looked up and rubbed sleep from his eyes. "How long have you been waiting for me up there?" he asked as she scaled down and stood in front of him.

He was suddenly surprised how tall she had

become, her head reaching nearly to his chest. The little girl he'd once met on The Tian seemed to have been replaced entirely by the spritely figure before him.

"You said we would always fish together," Emma continued. "For safety, remember? You promised you'd never leave us alone. You can't break a rule like that, because, well, it's the rules."

Pin smiled and knelt down to her level. "I know it feels like I'm breaking a rule, Emma, but I'm doing it to keep you both safe. If I'm caught out there, I'll be happier knowing you two are back here in your trees, safe as can be."

Emma frowned. "But then no one will be there to help you. Me and Adam, we're getting good with our spears now. If ogres try to grab you we can help you get away."

"Hard to argue that logic," said Pin with a grin. "And your skills with a spear are coming along, that's true. I'm very proud of you both. But you're just not ready yet. I'm sorry, little mouse, but I have to be firm about this. Maybe when it gets darker I can spy on the tribe and see if they've stayed in one place or moved on altogether. If they're gone, maybe life can get back to normal again. Wouldn't that be a nice thing? Until then, wait here. We'll have a nice breakfast when I get back, okay?"

Emma refused to answer and turned her back to him. Pin rose and frowned. He hated to see her upset, but he knew it was for the best.

Without another word, he picked up his fishing spear and the nets Emma had made him and left the small camp.

After he'd walked a few yards through the trees he

looked back, but the girl was gone. *Already up in the trees no doubt*, he thought and continued to where their raft was hidden and waiting.

As soon as Pin left her sight, Emma tied her spear across her back and stormed away from camp. She didn't need to be sheltered or protected.

I'm almost ten years old! she thought angrily as she pushed though the dense underbrush. *I'm not a kid. I can take care of myself!*

She just needed to get away for an hour, get to the waterfall and cool off. Pin wouldn't be back for that long anyway, so he wouldn't even know she was gone. And Adam would sleep all morning as usual.

Emma looked up as she moved, catching the first light of the rising sun as it crested the tree tops. She loved the way it lit the jungle in sharp beams and showered her in warmth. It almost made her feel better and she picked up her pace, looking forward to stripping down and escaping into the cool water.

Recently, she'd taken to bathing alone. She felt increasingly private about it and didn't always want to play the boisterous games Adam did. Sometimes she just wanted space to think, or make up stories in her head.

She liked to dream up tales of the Royal Twins and their life ruling from the silver tower. Secretly, she'd decided that the prince had set out to rescue his sister from her captors across the mountains. And when he stormed their stronghold, his magic filled it with such brilliant light that they were blinded, and the twins escaped hand-in-hand.

She didn't share this with Pin, of course. She liked the way this ending to the story made her feel and didn't want it ruined by his usual questions that were impossible to answer.

Emma heard the burbling of water then and knew she was getting close to the waterfall. She'd grown accustomed to picking out its soft tones from the rest of the jungle noises.

But, as she approached, she was met with another sound. It was strange, like a low humming that floated on the wind like a song. She stopped to listen. It wasn't like any sound she'd heard in the jungle before. It wasn't an animal, or a bird. (She had learned to distinguish the sound of their songs). This reminded her more of how her nanny sang to her back on the Tian.

Emma thought about turning back, remembering what Pin had said about being grabbed. But her curiosity got the better of her and, looking up, she decided to climb into the trees to look out over the water from a safe height.

Moving quickly and quietly, Emma scaled the trunk next to her until she reached the interlocking branches above. Then, moving stealthily on all fours, she made her way from tree to tree until she could look down on the waterfall from on-high.

There—wading naked in the water—was an ogre.

It seemed to Emma to be a female, but it was hard to tell for certain by its alien features. This one had white lines drawn across its forehead and down its neck. Dark green and brown hair grew long down its back and dipped into the water. But the thing that made it seem more woman than man was that it cradled a baby in its lower, third arm, keeping it close to her stomach as it washed it with its two others.

The baby had short hair, a similar shade as its mother's, but its skin was different. Instead of a rich tan, its skin was marbled in three different shades of black, dark green, and pink. Emma thought it looked beautiful; strange and special.

Emma watched as the mother bathed the child, gently singing to it in the same low humming she'd heard earlier. She hadn't realized how large the creatures were when she'd studied them from the cliffs days ago. This one was twice as large as Pin and its arms were thick with muscles. And yet, it treated the fragile baby with impossible delicacy and care.

Emma wondered if her own mother had held her as close, then realized she had almost no memory of her at all anymore save for the hologram. She closed her eyes for a time and tried to conjure a memory of being with her mother, but nothing came. It was as though time had erased her from existence.

Emma's thoughts were disturbed by a commotion and she opened her eyes to see two hulking figures barreling through the trees on the opposite side of the waterfall. They were ogres, male, and much larger than the mother in the water.

They stepped onto the wet black stone along the edge of the pool and barked in their alien language, pointing at her aggressively and waving her towards them. She refused to come at first, howling back and using her three arms to shield the child in a way that made Emma nervous for it.

One of the males was in the water in an instant, wading towards her, the two of them batting at each other as he moved in close. The mother tried to move away, but his thick fingers grabbed her long hair and he pulled her back towards him roughly.

She spun around and battered him with her two larger arms as she held the child behind her back with her lower third. But her strength was no match for his, and she was easily overpowered. Holding her arms up over her head, he used his third hand to rip the child from her grasp. Its wailing pierced the jungle and its mother cried out helplessly.

Emma covered her mouth and muffled a cry, confused by what was happening and overwhelmed by the mother's sadness. Why would they take her child? She had an urge to jump down and help, and realized she was already holding ~~the~~ her spear, ready to attack.

A hand touched her then and she turned with a start. It was Adam. He'd come up behind her silently, his spear strapped to his bare back with thick vines. He opened his mouth to speak, but Emma pressed her hand over it and pointed below. Adam glanced down and his eyes grew wider as he took in the conflict.

The tall creature with the child was leaving the waterfall now, the other male striding close behind him. The mother remained at the edge of the pool, weeping, her face planted in the palms of her two large palms.

"What's happening?" Adam mouthed silently.

Emma pointed to the next tree over and they both clamored through the thick red branches until they were a safe enough distance away to speak freely.

When they stopped, Adam reached up and pulled a blue fruit from the branch above. Then he sat down cross-legged and bit into it, speaking as he chewed.

"Pin said we're not allowed to leave camp," he said flatly. "You shouldn't break the rules, Emma. Not after what happened at the cave. Not with ogres around."

Emma was too angry to sit. She looked down at Adam and pointed a finger in his face saying, "Pin's not our father, Adam, he can't tell us what to do. My father's dead, yours is dead, too, and that's all there is to it."

Adam stood up quickly and pressed his face close to hers. "You don't know that! Don't say that!" he said angrily.

"Just because you don't want to think about it doesn't mean it's not true," Emma said and crossed her arms. "We're all that's left and..." Emma sat down suddenly and pressed her hands to her face. Tears poured down her cheeks.

Adam sighed and let his half-eaten fruit drop to the ground. Then he sat down next to her.

"Hey, what's gotten into you, anyway?" he asked. "Why have you been so weird lately?"

Emma shrugged without looking at him. Then she pulled her hands away from her face and sighed deeply.

"You didn't see it, the map in the cave. This world is so big, and we're so small." She turned to him and their eyes locked. "And we're never going home again, Adam. I never really thought about it until just now, but we're never leaving this place. I hate it here. I want to go home."

Adam didn't answer as they sat in silence for a long moment. *Home*, he thought. *Where is that?* He was space-born, raised on ports his whole life. The blue moon—with Emma and Pin—was the first place that felt like home to him.

Adam watched Emma as she looked off into the distance and wished she felt the same, wished he could bring her thoughts back to happier things. She was always so distracted and moody lately. He missed how easily happy they used to be.

"They took that little baby from its mother," Emma said suddenly, looking down at her palms in disbelief, as though something she was holding had vanished. "They ripped it right from her hands. Why do you suppose they did that? The baby, what will they do with it?"

Adam put his arm around her shoulders and pulled her close. "Cheer up, Emma," he said. "Pin said the ogres will be gone soon and everything will go back to normal. The way it was before. You'll see."

Emma turned back towards him and smiled thinly. She wished he understood what she was feeling but liked that he was there to comfort her all the same.

"Now, come on," Adam said and pulled her to her feet. "We'd better get back before Pin does, or we'll never hear the end of it. You know how he gets. He'll yell until he's all red in face and that big blue line appears on his forehead."

Adam puffed out his cheeks and held his breath until his face turned a bright shade of red. Emma laughed at his imitation, which in turn made him laugh. He blew out a large breath and began to feel dizzy. The sound of Emma's laughter mixed with the sensation made him elated.

As they travelled back to camp, Emma took time to look down at the waterfall as they passed it, checking for the mother ogre. But the pool at the bottom of the falls was empty and the water was still, save for the ripples caused by the steady downpour.

When Pin returned to camp, he and the children set

about preparing breakfast. They ate in silence, none of them feeling much like talking.

Emma still thought of what she'd seen, wondering what would become of the child, so innocent and small. Adam could tell she was still upset and wondered what he could do to help set her mind at ease. And Pin—who had no knowledge of her experience at the waterfall—still thought Emma was upset with him and decided it was best to not disturb her further.

So, huddled together and eating a meagre meal in silence, they made a most depressing sight.

When night fell and they all lay down to sleep, Adam was restless. Emma had been quiet all day, preferring to keep to herself even more than usual. He knew she was still troubled by thoughts of the Ogres and was worried she would never be at ease until she knew the fate of the baby once and for all.

If there was only a way I could learn what happened to it, he thought as he stared up at the red gas planet in the sky. *Maybe if she knew it was alive and well, she would go back to being the old, happy Emma?*

Suddenly, Adam was struck by an exciting idea, and—waiting until he could hear the heavy breathing of his two companions—he grabbed his spear, crept out of camp, and ran back through the jungle to spy on the ogres.

It was easy to stay hidden in the cover of night. Even if he was spotted by unwanted eyes, he knew his small size and shape would register him as an animal in the tress.

So he flew through the branches with grace and

confidence towards the cliffs where he would be able to peer down on the tribe.

His mind set to his task, he arrived at his destination quickly. His heart pounded as he left the tree line and stepped onto the rough stone. Even in the cool night it felt hot on his bare feet.

The cave was still a ways east, but he could already hear the loud rejoicing and hollering of creatures in the valley below. And, as he slunk along the edge of the cliff face, he began to make out the glow of bonfires burning violently.

When he reached the spot above the cave, Adam crawled to the edge of the cliff, careful to stay in the shadows. Too nervous to look over the side, he took in a breath and let his nerves settle until he found the courage to peer over the rock face and down into the valley.

Truly, he was overwhelmed by what he saw.

The ogres had set up an elaborate camp directly under the gapping mouth of the giant cave. Large tents—constructed of dark red logs and draped with multicolored animal hides—formed a perimeter. Small fires dotted the landscape, figures hunched around them, eating strong smelling meat and drinking from swollen animal bladders. All of them were speaking loudly all at once.

Most of the tribe, however, was massed in celebration around a single fire that raged in the center of their camp. A complex structure made of hundreds of thick wooden logs, the bonfire towered over them, sending inky smoke into the dark night. The fire was so large Adam's brow began to moisten as he watched wide-eyed from the top of the cliff.

He let his gaze wander around the camp, looking

for a sign of a marble-skin baby. But—while he saw many young ogres sitting together in clumps off to the side, passing drinking bladders back and forth—he didn't see any babies in the crowd.

As he continued to scan the area, something large and set to the side of the bonfire caught his attention. The curious object sat atop a twelve foot tower made of thick wooden beams and was unlike anything he'd seen in the jungle before.

It was perfectly round and black and had a number of long silver spikes jutting out from all around it. As Adam inspected the strange object, he began to notice the ogres acting just as strangely towards it.

Their frantic dancing and wailing song seemed to all be directed towards the spherical monolith. They waved their hands at it, gyrated wildly and ran on the spot. Some even fell to their knees, raising their three arms towards the red gas planet looming over the scene and calling out as if appealing to some unseen god.

All this went on for some time, until the celebration reached an ecstatic climax of drumming, chanting and dancing and then everything stopped suddenly.

Adam crouched lower, unnerved by the deafening silence. He backed up and lay on his belly for fear of being spotted. Then, as though the entire tribe had read his mind, each of them turned towards the cliff and looked up at the very spot he was watching them from.

Adrenaline shot through him and his heart pounded in his chest. *They see me!* he thought, expecting ogres to burst from the trees and grab him at any moment.

He was about to get up and bolt back to camp when a single deep voice boomed from the valley below. It spoke slowly and clearly, and with an air of authority, though Adam could not understand the words. He listened as the voice continued for another moment and then the entire tribe called back in a single voice.

"Chara!" the voices of many cried at once.

"Daa!" boomed the single voice in response.

"Chara! Chara!" the tribe wailed madly.

Adam peered over the edge of the cliff again to see what was happening below.

The entire tribe was on their knees now, staring at a single ogre standing in front of the tower, the mouth of the cave directly above him. Covered in bones and holding a long silver object in his hand, he addressed the tribe like a pastor would a congregation. Adam had seen small church ceremonies on space ports, but never anything on this scale before.

He watched as the ogre in bones held the silver spike over his head and faced the red gas planet overhead. The tribe did the same.

"Daa-du!" he called loudly. "Daa-du! Daa-tu!"

"Chara!" the tribe answered.

A silence fell over the camp then and the tall ogre brought his metal spike down again. He pointed it away from the crowd and towards a tent at the edge of the camp saying, "Taa-tura," solemnly.

Two figures rose and drew open the colorful tent flaps, their scaly texture sparkling slightly in the firelight.

A hush fell over the crowd and Adam sucked in a breath.

A figure emerged from the tent—a female, clothed in colorful hides, her hair tied lavishly in vines and she cradled something wrapped in skins.

Adam squinted, trying to make out exactly what was happening.

The female walked slowly towards the ogre in bones. The crowd parted as she passed, some of them whispering inaudibly. When she reached the tall tower, she peered up at the round object that rested at its top.

"Daa-du!" said the ogre in bones.

"Chara," the female replied softly.

"Chara!" boomed the tribe in a single voice.

With that, the ogre took his silver spike into his lower arm and reached out towards the female with both his others.

Nobody moved. It seemed to Adam that nobody even breathed.

The female glanced over her shoulder quickly, her eyes wild, as though pleading for someone to help her. When no one moved she turned back and stared at the ogre in bones who remained unmoving. Then she looked up at the red planet overhead and let out a piercing scream that cut through the silence like an explosion. She screamed a second time, but the anger in her voice was gone. This time it was a cry of pure sadness.

When all her breath was gone, she looked down mournfully at the package in her hands and unfolded its wrappings. She leaned her face down and kissed the little marble-skinned baby inside it before closing her eyes and passing it to the massive ogre in front of her.

The ogre in bones took it from her and cradled it

in his upper arms. Then he shook his upper body slowly so the bones he wore began to rattle.

"Chara! Chara! Chara!" the tribe chanted.

As he rattled his bones faster, they slapped their knees and shook their heads as they repeated the word, until a thunderous vibration echoed across the valley.

As the sound reached a fever pitch, the ogre in bones lifted his third arm, bringing up the long silver spike and turning to look at the round black object on top of the tower. The crowd continued chanting, "Chara! Chara!", and his bones rattled as he pressed the end of it against the child's chest.

Adam covered his mouth and turned away quickly as the ogre thrust it downwards.

The baby never made a sound. The chanting stopped. There were no more cheers below. There were no more songs.

Adam didn't look down on the tribe again. Instead, he scrambled across the rock until he reached the tree line and vomited into the grass.

He remained hidden in the shadows for a few minutes more, heaving and sobbing. He would never tell Emma what he had seen. He would never tell her what happened to the marble skinned baby. He wished he hadn't seen it. He wished he'd never come to the cliffs.

Adam pulled himself to his feet and leaned against a tree, trying to find the strength to climb it. But his will to move had vanished, as though it was swallowed by a black hole. Something inside him suddenly felt dead.

A noise somewhere in the darkness made him jump and he finally moved, more out of instinct than anything else. He scaled the tree and ran back to camp under cover of darkness as quickly as he possibly could.

19

The next morning, Adam didn't help prepare breakfast. He didn't follow Pin through his morning tasks, asking endless questions as was his ritual. Instead, he remained high in the branches, claiming illness when Emma called up for him to come eat with them.

He watched her shrug and turn back to the small fire where fish sat smoking, ready to eat. It was a mere flicker compared to the ritual blaze he'd seen the previous night— a sight he couldn't shake from his mind; the flames licking the darkness, filling the valley with an acrid haze. He could still taste the smoke on his tongue. It stung his lungs and itched his eyes even hours later.

He hadn't lied to Emma. He *did* feel sick.

Adam watched Pin and Emma eating from above. They sat across from one another, the fire between them, engaged in idle chatter. Emma laughed at something Pin said, obviously no longer angry or upset. They seemed happy in a way he felt he never could be again.

Adam sat up and leaned against the dark red tree trunk. He closed his eyes and tried to clear his mind, but the wicked images of the night before were not so easy to erase: the ogre in bones, his deafening death rattle, the baby with marbled skin and its mother's piercing screams still lingered in his mind. They were a part of him now, the scene playing out like on a loop in the back of his mind.

He opened his eyes to see a lime green hopper with a transparent carapace scamper across his bare foot. It tickled his toes as it moved across his skin, then jumped off and landed on a branch high above his head.

They were in danger, Adam knew. Maybe he didn't understand everything he'd seen the night before, but that much he did know. He needed to warn Pin, get them all as far away from the ogre camp as possible. Maybe then the chanting would leave his mind.

Chara! Chara! Chara! The word rang in his ears like a ringing death knell.

His mind made up, Adam plucked his spear from its resting place beside him and threw the strap over his shoulders. Then, with simian agility, he gripped the trunk and slid down to the dirt below. It felt cool against his feet, becoming gradually warmer as he approached the breakfast fire.

Emma looked up as he sat down next to her, but said nothing. Pin nodded towards a slab of purple fish, halved and steaming on a flat warming rock next to the fire. But Adam didn't feel like eating.

Pin eyed him for a moment before saying, "And where were you so late last night?"

Adam looked up, surprised. "How did you—" he started.

"Saw you creeping into camp just before sunrise," Pin replied before Adam could finish the question. "Unlucky for you, my old bladder gets me up early."

Pin ripped a hunk of fish away from its bendy spine and stuffed it into his mouth. "Even if you can't sleep, you have to stay close to camp. You know this."

Adam hung his head, overcome. He was bursting with thoughts and feelings, yet didn't know how to get any of them out. Instead he started crying. Softly at first, then, before he knew it, he was sobbing.

Emma looked at Pin, shocked. Adam rarely showed emotions openly.

Pin dropped the fish he was holding and moved to sit beside him. The boy crumpled into his lap as soon as he sat down. Pin held his hands up in surprise, unsure of how to comfort the boy at first. Then he lay his hands over Adam's head, letting him weep uncontrollably in a type of close seclusion.

He didn't know what could be troubling the boy so much, but for now he needed protection. Adam being who he was, Pin knew he would talk soon enough.

And sure enough, later that morning, Pin and Emma listened intently to Adam's story of the ogres, their raging bonfires, wild dancing, and cries to the red planet above.

While he told them everything he'd seen, he kept the fate of the child to himself. He did this for Emma's sake, but also because he couldn't bring himself to speak of it.

Pin scratched at his beard thoughtfully as Adam

spoke, raising his right eyebrow and grunting to himself as certain details emerged.

Then, when the boy began describing the large black sphere that sat atop the tall wooden tower, Pin's fingers froze and his eyes opened wider. He leaned forward and motioned with his hand as though urging the boy to provide more detail.

"This object," he said seriously, "how big was it?"

"Bigger than me," Adam replied. "Bigger than you, too. And round like a big black boulder."

"And you say it had spikes on it?" Pin went on. "How many? How long were they? And were they thin, or thick?"

"I don't remember, exactly. Maybe six, or even ten spikes where on it. It looked like some had been ripped off and some were broken. I think the ogre wearing all those bones was holding one of them. He pointed it at the sky, up at the red planet as he spoke. I remember that."

Pin rose and kicked dirt over the fire. It hissed out of existence.

"Follow me, children," he said calmly, picking up his spear. Adam and Emma got to their feet quickly and grabbed their own spears, slinging them across their backs.

"Where are we going?" Emma asked.

"Far away from here, I hope," said Adam.

"Keep your spears close and your eyes open for danger," said Pin gravely. "We're going back to the cliffs, to where Adam was last night."

"What?" Adam huffed angrily. "We can't. Please, we need to get as far away from there as we can."

"We will," answered Pin. "But first I need to get a look at this black object you say you saw last night."

"But why?" Adam asked, letting his shoulders slump in disappointment. This was not the course of action he thought they would take.

"Because if it's what I think it is," said Pin, "then it could very well get us off this moon."

When they were close to the cliffs, Pin told Emma to get in the trees and signal them if she saw anything approaching. She nodded without a word and scampered into the branches, pressing on ahead of Adam and Pin below.

"We'll stay in the tree line until we reach the cave," Pin said as they kept moving. "Then, if Emma says it's clear, we'll move out and you can point out the probe below."

"Probe?" Adam asked, stopping a moment to take in the new word. "What's that?"

"Years ago, when I was a boy about your age, there was a scientist named Sophia Le Guin. She was in charge of finding a new Earth, a new planet for humans to move to. They called it Eden Star, gave it a name before they even found it. Maybe a bad idea in retrospect."

"Why?" asked Adam, curious to hear more.

"Because they never found it. Spent millions of dollars sending hundreds of probes out into space to search out new planets and moons, but none of them returned any information about a planet that could support life."

"I suppose the folks in charge eventually figured it was a better idea to spend money on getting us into space and onto ports than on a dream. Earth was making too many people sick by then."

"But if there's a probe here on this moon, why didn't they all come here?" asked Adam. "Everyone could have lived here."

"I'm curious about the same thing," said Pin. "Maybe the electric storms on the surface of the gas planet disrupt its signal somehow. Hell, maybe it just broke plain and simple. But, if it *is* a probe and we can turn it on then, well, my boy, there just might still be someone listening on the other end."

"Why do the ogres have it?" Adam asked, ducking under a low hanging branch covered in bright yellow vines.

"They must have found it," Pin said, then stopped. He held his hand up to block the sun as he looked up towards the sky. "Can you imagine their wonder at hearing it break atmosphere, then looking up to see it hurtling towards them in flames? Imagine their surprise at discovering its manmade oddness? In a natural world like this, with nothing remotely resembling technology, it would have seemed like magic to them. Like a gift from their gods."

Pin paused to wipe sweat from his brow then said, "Or a curse." He looked down at Adam, who was looking up, intrigued. "It probably scared the hell out of them. And like you described, drove them to ritual. Or worse."

"We'll have to get it away from them," said Adam as though he'd just realized the challenge in that himself.

"That we will," replied Pin gravely.

"It's very big."

"That it is."

A soft whistle rang out from above and the two of them looked up. Emma had come back with news.

"Is it all clear?" Pin asked in a whisper.

"Come and see," replied Emma.

"What is it? What did you see? Did you see the camp?" Adam asked nervously.

"Just come and see for yourself," she said, waving them onwards before disappearing into the foliage again.

When she had gone, Pin and Adam looked at each other. Pin could tell the boy was scared. He walked beside him and patted his back comfortingly as the two of them moved to break the tree line together.

"Don't worry, my boy," Pin said softly. "You're not on your own anymore. You don't need to be scared. Whatever happens, I'll be right here beside you."

20

Adam's shoulders slumped and his grip loosened around his spear. His mouth hung open in complete disbelief.

Standing next to Pin and Emma, looking out across the valley, he was shocked to see it was completely barren. Save for the scorched remains of the bonfire, everything he'd seen the night before seemed to have vanished.

The colorful tents made of scaly animal hides, the black probe on the tower, and the hundreds of three-armed ogres were all gone like night-time shadows erased by the light of a new dawn.

"Damn," Pin said with a huff, scanning the horizon for a sign of the ogres. "We're too late."

"But—" Adam stammered. "They were all right here. The valley was stuffed with them, I swear! Shelters and fires... They were eating and drinking and dancing. I don't understand."

"Maybe you dreamed it all," said Emma flatly.

"I didn't dream it!" Adam shot back. "I know what

I saw with my own eyes."

Pin cast his eyes towards the red planet hanging above them. It had become much larger and more oppressive in the weeks leading up to this moment. Most likely due to the rotation of the moon in its orbit, he thought, then turned his gaze back down to the valley below.

"I think they came here for one purpose," he said finally. "A pilgrimage to a sacred place. They came to speak to their god. That done, they've moved on." He scratched at his beard for a moment then threw his spear across his back, continuing, "With so many, they should be easy enough to track."

He moved along the edge of the cliff towards where the ladders were carved into the rock face. "The question is: do we follow them for the probe? Or do we cut our loses, be thankful we went unnoticed?"

Adam watched Emma slip her spear across her shoulder and look out across the endless expanse of wilderness. He could see a longing in her gaze and thought back to her outburst the day before. He knew she wanted to leave. Her desire to escape the moon must be taunting her now. She didn't need to speak to make her feelings known. She wanted to follow the tribe.

But with everything he'd seen, he knew it was too dangerous. Torn between Emma's wishes and his own fear, he felt conflicted and confused.

"Let's get a closer look," came Pin's voice, interrupting his thoughts. "I'd like to learn as much about these creatures as I can before making a decision. What a culture discards can tell you a lot about who they are, their habits, and what they value.

Who knows, we may even find something useful—tools, maybe. Or food."

Emma let her thoughts of home linger a moment longer before turning towards him and following. She didn't look back, but heard Adam take his place at the end of the line behind her. *For all his bragging*, she thought, *he can be a real scaredy sometimes.*

She watched Pin ease himself over the cliff's edge and grab hold of the jagged rungs of the ladder. For the first time in a long while, she was glad he was there with them, to be brave and keep them safe. She shuddered suddenly at the thought of a life without Pin. A life with only Adam to turn to if she was in trouble.

"Go on," Adam's voice urged from behind. "Hurry up, Emma. If we're going to go down, let's hurry and be done with it."

Emma didn't respond. She just sighed and crouched, and eased herself over the side of the cliff.

———◆———

The valley air stung Pin's nostrils, and each breath burned his lungs as he took his first steps around the deserted camp. Dense blue smoke hung like a sheet of toxic mist and lines of black ash snaked up the cliff face.

He reached down and tore a length of fabric from along the bottom of his shirt and ripped it into three swatches. Pressing one over his nose and mouth, he passed the others to Emma and Adam as they jumped down from the cliff and onto the valley floor.

"Protect your lungs, children," he said as they each took a piece and hid the bottom half of their faces with it.

The three of them moved out into the open. It was difficult to see through the smoke, which still drifted up off burnt black logs, so Adam and Emma began searching the area close to them, methodically overturning rocks and rooting around great logs that had been cut down by the tribe and used as seating around the fires.

They weren't sure what they were looking for exactly, but Pin had told them, *You'll know it's odd when you see it.*

Pin stayed close to the cliff at first, sifting through the mountain of grey ash under the bonfire with a stick. Adam watched as he examined the remains of the fire, suddenly worried he'd uncover the tiny body of the child. But after a few moments Pin moved away and began studying the ground where the ogres' great tents had been staked in the ground.

Adam turned back towards Emma to see she had moved away from the open area and was walking into the tree-line. He didn't follow her, but sat down on a log. He didn't know what they were looking for and didn't care. His mind told him to leave as soon as possible and that no good could ever come from being in such a cursed place.

"Pin!" Emma's voice called from trees.

Pin rose quickly and called back towards her. "What is it, girl?"

"I think I've found something!"

"Well, what is it?" Adam asked getting to his feet.

"I don't know," Emma answered after a moment. "But it smells awful!"

Pin began walking across the camp just as the girl emerged with her hands cupped together. She was looking down in concentration, as though trying to balance something in her palms. A strong, sour odor hit his senses as he met her at the edge of the camp. It was strange, yet familiar for some reason. Emma held her hands out and he saw she held a pool of dark brown liquid.

"What is it?" Emma asked.

Pin scratched his beard for a moment, studying the substance. He took the cloth away from his nose and bent over to sniff it. The smell of it bit his nostrils and sent a sharp spike through his sinuses. His heart began to race suddenly.

"Could it be?" he whispered before dipping his index finger into the strange liquid.

Adam pushed in to get a closer look, then jumped back when he caught a whiff of the stuff.

"Yuck!" he said, covering his mouth and nose with the fabric again. "Don't touch it!" he yelled as Pin went to taste the thick liquid. "It's poison!"

Pin licked the substance off the tip of his finger. A wonderful, familiar heat moved across his tongue and ignited his taste buds. He closed his eyes for a moment, enjoying a singular sensation he never thought he'd know again. When he opened them again, he saw that Emma had let the liquid drop to the ground where it was already seeping into the dusty earth.

"Where did you find it, girl?" he asked her, urgently. "Where is it? Is there more?"

"There's great big bags of it next to a tree back there," Emma replied, pointing to where she'd been searching in the underbrush. "I pulled off the tops to see what was inside and this funny stuff poured out."

Pin held his hand to his forehead and moved towards the spot quickly. "Did you put the tops back on?" he called back, worry in his voice.

"Of course I did," Emma said, following after him. "What's wrong? What is it, Pin, did I do something wrong?"

Pin pushed into the tree line and through the underbrush, casting his eyes around wildly. Finally, he saw them: three large bladders made of multicolored animal hides, each the size of a small child, piled against the trunk of a tree.

He got to his knees and picked one of them up. It was heavy and difficult to hold steady as its contents sloshed around inside. He checked the top and saw a crude wooden stopper plugging the pour spout. He sighed deeply and fell to his knees, letting the bladder heap cross his lap.

"Are you okay, Pin?" Emma asked as she and Adam approached from behind. "Did it make you sick?"

"I told you not to put it in your mouth," said Adam gravely. "I tried to say that, but you didn't listen."

Pin looked back at them and a smile came to his face. "I'm not sick, children, and I'm not angry. Quite the opposite, actually. I'm overwhelmed. I feel as though I've been granted two wishes in one morning. Not only have the ogres left us once again to peace and paradise, but they've left me the most wonderful gift."

Pin packed the bladders on top of one another and heaved them over his shoulder as he got to his feet. Adam and Emma exchanged a look of confusion.

"But, what is it, Pin?" Emma asked again.

"It's booze, girl!" Pin exclaimed. "Liquor! Alcohol!" He chuckled as he moved past them and out into the open again. "I suppose you could call it moonshine!"

The children exchanged another flustered look before following. Pin seemed to have forgotten what they had come for and was making his way back towards their camp.

"Can't climb up holding these, so we'll have to take the long way back," he said loudly. "At least I'll have a stiff drink at the end of the journey."

"Aren't we going to follow after the ogres?" Emma asked, picking up speed to catch him. Adam followed behind her, his eyes darting all around. He still couldn't believe they were truly safe from danger.

"Why look for trouble, I say," Pin answered. "Perhaps it's a sign to leave well enough alone and get back to enjoying life. Why, I wouldn't be surprised if we never saw another ogre at all."

"But what about the probe?" argued Emma. "You said it could get us home. You said it could get us off the moon once and for all."

Pin patted the swollen bladders on his shoulders, thick with brown liquor and looked down at the girl. "Maybe life here isn't so bad after all. And more people would just bring more trouble and more problems for us all anyhow. They always do. No, my girl, I think the three of us are just fine as we are. We'll set our camp up on the beach tonight and sleep under the stars once again. Won't that be nice?"

Emma looked away from Pin, disappointed and irritated at losing the opportunity to learn more about the moon and get back to where they'd come from.

She looked up at the sun to track its position. It was almost done its journey west, so they didn't have much sunlight left. She knew it wouldn't be safe to follow the tribe on her own, but maybe she could determine the direction they'd traveled in tomorrow.

Emma relaxed at the thought of taking matters into her own hands. Maybe she didn't need Pin's help or approval. And it would be nice to finally escape their cramped, hidden camp and move out onto the spacious beach. If it stayed warm, she could even swim while Pin cooked dinner. It had been so long since she'd sat on the rocks and looked out at the sun setting over the ocean.

"That does sound nice for a change," she admitted finally, to which Pin smiled and nodded.

"Come along, Adam! Don't dally!" he called over his shoulder as he picked up his pace. "It's a long way around and back to the beach. And I don't want to waste a moment of daylight."

Adam waved smoke away from his face and took one last look across the barren, scorched camp under the cave. He wondered if so much vile darkness could ever truly be gone from their lives now that it had infected it. He wasn't so sure.

He looked down to see his right hand was trembling. He let his grip go from his spear and swung it over his shoulder. Then he examined his palm. It was red and puffy from holding onto the wood so tightly. He hadn't realized how nervous he'd been the whole time they were down in the valley.

When he looked back up, Emma and Pin had already disappeared into the trees. The sudden call of a not-parrot urged him forward and he ran to catch up with them.

21

The change in Pin's disposition came swiftly and much to the joy of the children.

It began early when they returned from the valley and were enjoying a warm night on the beach. Pin cooked dinner on the sand while the children played in the surf, all the while sipping brown liquor from a long, pearly shell Emma had fished out of the sea for him.

The shift in his behaviour was subtle at first. Watching him from afar as he worked, he seemed to have been injected with youthful energy, bobbing and swaying, almost dancing as he prepared food.

Emma could hear him singing over the sound of the waves, his voice hoarse and broken, the tempo upbeat and full of life.

Emma didn't attribute this show of happiness to the power of the strange drink— in fact she didn't question where it sprang from at all. She was merely happy for Pin, who had been so prone to being quiet and demanding quiet from her and Adam. Seeing Pin acting this way made her feel like they were all having a celebration together.

When the fish was cooked, Pin lumbered down to the edge of the water and called for the children to, "Come and get it before the not-parrots pick it to the bones!"

Laughing at Pin's enthusiasm, Emma and Adam ran up the beach and sat in front of the fire. They shivered as the night breeze brushed against their wet skin, but the fire dried them quickly.

They watched Pin brush sand off their long flat carving stone before laying the charred pink body of a fish across it.

He poured a shell-full of brown liquor and slurped half of it out before dragging a sharp-edged stone across the fish's scales. They flaked off easily, sparkling like a silver snowfall in the firelight as they flew up and landed on the sand.

Once scaled, Pin cut three large hunks of meat and passed them around. Then he sipped the rest of his drink and poured himself another before setting to work on his food.

To the children's delight Pin was full of conversation that night. He pointed to the stars and told them stories of Earth, about cities made of glass and steel so vast they spread from coast to coast, some even plunging under the waves.

"Some folks," he said slowly, "lived their whole lives in underwater townships, never once venturing to the land or seeing the sky. Kelp and krill farmers made a point of it, I remember. Odd lot, people used to say."

Pin stopped and looked around as though seeing if anyone was watching before leaning in closer and saying, "Some people said they'd lived under the waves so long they'd grown gills and were turning into fish people."

Emma and Adam shot each other the same disbelieving look before yelling, "Pin!" and laughing heartily.

"That's impossible," said Adam with a dismissive wave.

Pin raised both his hands and made an innocent face saying, "It's just what they said, Adam, I don't claim to know if it's true or false. But I will say that strange things were happening on Earth by the time I left it. Poison smog, acid rainstorms. The environment was changing people in all kinds of ways. Making them sick. Fish people under the waves would not have surprise me in the least"

"Where did *you* live, Pin?" asked Emma suddenly.

"Yes," Adam chimed in. "Tell us more about Earth. Tell us about life when you were a boy."

Pin refilled his shell and scratched at his beard. "The details are foggy, it was so long ago. Memories of my youth are more like feelings now, but I'll do my best to recall what I can."

"We lived in government housing like most everyone else. The mega towers housed thousands of families stacked one on top of another other like cans of tuna. It seemed as though life for my parents was hard, but my memories of being a child are mostly fond."

"I lived with my mother and father and my two sisters. Then my grandparents moved in with us when I was about ten years old—not much older than you two in fact. They brought our four cousins with them due to the fact that my aunt and uncle had been killed during a robbery of some kind or another. Can you imagine all of us living together in a two-room dorm not much larger than our old escape pod? It must have been absolute madness..."

Pin trailed off and Emma lay down on her back. She wanted to watch the stars as Pin recalled his old life on Earth, a place that seemed so far away at that moment.

"Now where was I?" Pin said, suddenly snapping back to reality.

"What was your father like?" Emma asked, her thoughts turning to her own father.

"I think he always dreamed of a place like this, Emma," Pin answered her. "I remember he'd always say he'd *get us to the top floor one day*. Everyone said dorms on the top level had more space and even skylights so you could see blue sky above the smog. Everyone wanted to live up there, but no one seemed to know how to make it happen."

"Did you get to the top floor, Pin?" Adam asked.

"No, Adam, I'm sorry to say we never did. And I think my father probably felt like a failure most of his life because of it. Imagine it: here was a man who wanted more for his family as the world crumbled around him. It must have killed him a little bit each day. So he drank. Everyone drank."

Pin raised his shell as if about to give a toast before announcing, "Life's a struggle, children! Humanity's great curse is restlessness and a desire for something else. Something better. Something to bring us peace of mind. Nature made it impossible for us to be happy, so we made ourselves a cure."

With that he gulped back the rest of his drink and moved to pour himself another. Before doing so however, he stumbled forward as though losing his balance and fell face first into the sand.

He looked up at the children and laughed drunkenly, spitting sand out of his mouth as he struggled to sit back up. Then, looking at Emma and Adam he said, "Having said that, don't drink, children. Stuff'll turn you inside out in the end."

Pin laughed heartily again at his own words and poured himself another drink. Then he plugged the stopper back into the bladder, raised his shell and started sing a funny song about eggs and bacon.

He sang low and huffy, his voice craggy and his face turning a dark shade of red from the drink.

Emma and Adam laughed and clapped along and Pin got to his feet. He danced on the spot, balancing his drink and kicking up sand as he raised his feet one after the other in a slow, awkward kind of way.

It wasn't long before the children were up and dancing too, the three of them cutting a comical image as they raised their knees and bobbed back and forth in the firelight.

When Emma grew tired, she dropped back down on the sand and watched Adam and Pin as they took up lumbering around the fire together, singing and dancing the funny dance. She laughed at how silly they looked and realized it had been so long since they'd all laughed together. A feeling swelled within her and she realized she was quite pleased that she'd found the smelly moonshine for Pin to enjoy. For, not only did it fill him with song and stories, but it had brought joy to them that night. And that was something they'd all desperately needed.

Later, when the fire had died to cinders and the air had grown cold from the wind coming in off the water, Pin covered the children's sleeping brown bodies with green fronds. Emma stirred, but did not wake.

Though his head was swimming with alcohol, Pin wasn't ready to lie down for the night. Instead, he dragged a heavy bladder through the sand towards the rocks where he could lose himself in the sound of the ocean and sing if he wanted without disturbing the children.

Once he set himself upon the rocks, Pin poured himself another drink and looked out across the water. The light from the red planet above gave it a stunning pink glow that made him think of the lost sunsets of earth.

Speaking about his family and thinking back to his childhood made him feel profoundly small and far away from everything, and everyone. Like a spec of dust in a great sand dune blowing across an endless desert, Pin felt helpless against the pressures of time and space.

His heart ached terribly. He'd lied to the children that night. He hadn't told them his father had killed himself before he was thirteen years old. That was a truth for him to wrestle with. And now, knowing what it is to have children in your care, Pin cursed him even more for leaving him all alone in the world at such a young age.

He also didn't tell the children that after his father died his family were forced to move to the lower floors of the tower where the lowest income residents lived in shared slum space. Or how his mother became sick and his sisters had come to—by necessity—rely on the value of their natural commodities as they grew. Or how he was unable to help them off the planet when he'd finally gotten his first off-world mining job.

Indeed, he never saw any of them again, and speaking about it now made his heart burn with regret.

Why, with all my impotence and failure, do I deserve to end up here in splendor and comfort when so many I know suffer?

Pin threw the shell into the water, watching it skip across the pink surface and sink into oblivion. Then, picking up the heavy bladder of strong, alien liquor, he pulled the stopper and gulped deeply from it. The liquid burned his insides, but he didn't care. He welcomed the pain.

When his stomach wouldn't hold any more, he sputtered and closed it up again. The world spun wildly as powerful and dangerous drugs swam into his bloodstream. For a moment he thought he might throw-up, but managed to bring about focus by staring at a single spot on the beach—their raft sitting at the edge of the lagoon.

Seeing the raft there, he was suddenly struck by the most wonderful idea of escape and slid off the rock and onto the sand.

Grabbing the bladder and grunting hoarsely as he heaved it across his shoulders, Pin staggered drunkenly towards the raft, swaying and tripping over his feet a few times before he reached it. When he did, he placed the bladder upon it and looked back towards the children asleep on the beach.

They'll be fine alone for a while, he thought and he pushed the raft into the ocean and got on it. *I just want to drift alone amid the pink light for a little while.*

And so, with a heavy heart, Paddington Pin drifted out to sea alone.

He watched the stars and marveled at the red gas planet. He felt small, a spec of dust in an endless galaxy.

Nobody saw him drink. Nobody heard him sing, or comforted him as he cried. Nobody watched over him as he closed his eyes and fell asleep, and no one noticed his raft disappear into the darkness.

Or saw three tentacles rise from the darkness and pull him under the waves. Or heard the sounds of his body breaking.

The tempest of his end—like his beginning—fell upon the deaf ears of a heartless universe. As he had always suspected, it was the uncaring way of things.

22

Emma dreamed about her nanny.

She was back on the Tian, tucked into her bunk. Nanny was singing to her and Adam and brushing their hair behind their ears to soothe them into sleep. The tune she sang was hollow and far off, the words inaudible. Emma thought her voice sounded like water lapping off stone.

She looked up and her nanny smiled and stroked her cheek with the back of her hand. "You are safe," she whispered. "You are loved."

Emma stirred and woke then. The sun was still down and she was back on the beach. Her nanny was gone, yet she could still feel a hand brushing her cheek softly, like a phantom sensation still present in her mind's eye.

She let herself relax and sink back into a light slumber until something wet and cold touched her lips. She wiped it away, whatever it was, and the feeling vanished. Then, in a moment, it returned. Only this time it tickled her nose and the tops of her cheek bones.

She opened her eyes and narrowed her focus. A small creature covered in purple fur was perched on her chin, licking her around the mouth with its long, thin tongue.

She shifted onto her elbows and the creature sucked the appendage back into its mouth and stood at attention. Its round yellow eyes opened wide to focus on her face in the early morning darkness. Then it cocked its head slightly and made a harsh little clicking sound with its mouth that sounded like, *Koko*.

"Shoo," whispered Emma, waving away the animal.

It hopped off her chin and onto the sand, but didn't run away as she'd expected. Instead it scurried under her palm frond covering, its minuscule claws tickling her legs and thighs as it clung to her skin.

Emma screeched and shot to her feet, kicking away the frond and shaking her limbs like she was having a fit. Adam woke with a start and settled a quizzical stare upon her as though unsure whether to help her or enjoy the wild display.

"Help!" Emma yelped as a flash of purple crossed her tummy, ran up her back and disappeared beneath her long, flowered hair. It clung to the nape of her neck and stopped and Emma yelled as she tried to grab it. "It's on me! Adam, it's stuck to me!"

Adam hopped up and laughed despite his concern. Emma didn't seem to be in any real harm. Coming up behind her, he lifted her hair to reveal the thing clinging to the back of her neck. It looked at Adam with wide yellow eyes and he could see it was frightened.

"Oh, it's just a little thing, Emma," he chided. "Here, let me pull it off." Adam dug his fingers into the creature's purple fur and it made another series of harsh clicking sounds.

Ko-ko, Ko-ko, it clacked quickly and Adam let it go, startled. Then he laughed at himself for being so easily scared off and made a move to grab it again.

"Hey, come here!" he yelled as the creature scurried from Emma's neck and onto her left shoulder.

Emma stood frozen, peeking at it from the corner of her eye. "What's it doing now?" she whispered.

"Nothing," Adam answered curiously. "It's just sitting there, sort of looking around."

"Well, get it off," Emma said hotly. But, as Adam walked around her, the animal ran to her right shoulder and clacked at them again.

"I think it likes you," Adam laughed. "Maybe it's hungry. Here, I'll get it some fruit."

With that, Adam ran from the beach and into the underbrush in search of fallen fruit, leaving Emma and the creature alone.

They looked at each other for a moment before it ran back across her body and onto her left shoulder. Emma bristled as its tiny claws nicked her skin as it moved.

"Are you lost?" she asked it finally. The creature turned towards her, it's yellow eyes widening. "Well, you can eat some food, but then you have to shoo, okay? I'm very busy and I can't look after you. Do you understand?"

As far as she could tell the thing did *not* understand. Instead it lay on its belly, draping its body over her shoulder and closing its eyes.

Adam returned then, a small blue fruit for each of them balanced in his hands. "What happened?" he asked when he saw the creature.

"I think it fell asleep," Emma sighed.
Adam's face scrunched and he looked around the beach as though suddenly remembering something.

"Hey, where's Pin?" he said finally. "I'm hungry."

Emma scanned the beach as well. It was strange for Pin to leave them alone for long. "The raft's gone," she said flatly. "Maybe he's fishing. I'm sure he'll be back soon."

"Well, he'd better be," said Adam taking a bite of his fruit, "or we'll have to eat without him, like it or not." Then, turning his attention back to the purple creature dozing on Emma's shoulder, he said, "So what will we call it?"

"We're not calling it anything, because it's not staying," said Emma sternly. "After it sleeps and after it eats it can go back to wherever it came from."

"We could call it KoKo for the sound it makes," said Adam, ignoring her. "I like it."

"Well you can have it," Emma said and sat down with a huff.

Adam sat next to her and passed her a fruit. She took a quiet bite and the creature opened its eyes suddenly and stood at attention. Opening its mouth, it shot its thin tongue at the spot where Emma had bitten and began licking it all over with quick little flicks.

Emma lost her appetite immediately. "Here," she said to the creature and dropped the fruit to the sand. "You can have it."

It clicked excitedly and hopped off her shoulder

to chew frantically at the fruit.

Adam laughed at the way it moved, excitedly rolling the fruit along the beach as it gnawed at it. It wasn't long until the purple thing had burrowed its way into the fruit's core entirely, its thin pink tail the only part of it still visible. A few moments later its furry head poked out the other side, the hollow rind covering its middle like a soggy blue coat.

Emma laughed despite herself as the animal tried to free itself from the fruit's blue skin. She sighed and shook her head, then reached down to pick it up.

The creature calmed down immediately when she scooped it up and pulled it free.

"Silly KoKo," she said soothingly, petting the fur along its back. "You really are lost, aren't you? Just like us."

KoKo clacked, *Ko-ko ko-ko*, then ran up her arm. She winced as its needle-thin claws pricked at her bare skin until it lay down on her shoulder again.

Adam's expression turned serious then and he rose to his feet. "Well, we can't sit here all morning without a decent breakfast. Pin always says morning meals are most important and I intent to see us fed."

"But, what will we eat?" Emma asked.

"Pin keeps extra fish buried in the shade just there," Adam said and pointed to where Pin liked to lie to escape the hot sun. "He says they stay fresh longer if they're cool. We'll just have to finish those ones off without him."

"Who will make the fire?" asked Emma.

"I can do it," said Adam confidently. "I've watched Pin do it many times, and he showed me how to do it once. We just need the right kind of rocks to hit together and a lot of little sticks and brush for the flame. You'll see, Emma, I can do it."

Emma looked up at Adam, surprised at his determination. His quick thinking and resourcefulness put her at ease and she felt her shoulders relax a little. She hadn't even realized how tense she'd become since waking. Adam had always been a companion to her, but she never considered him someone to provide or protect.

"Help me gather wood first, then I'll dig up the fish," Adam continued. "I'll get the big pieces and you get brush and tinder... that's the small sticks."

"I know what tinder is," said Emma, sticking out her tongue. "I've heard Pin say it plenty of times."

"Well, good then," said Adam. "If we hurry, we can have a fire going before Pin comes back. What a funny trick that would be."

So Adam and Emma parted ways, each going off to gather what they needed to build a fire.

Adam moved quickly, stacking as many long branches as he could across his arms. When he couldn't carry any more he brought them to the beach and laid them on the sand. From there he leaned them together to build a tent-like structure. For a moment, it reminded him of the ogre's large bonfire in the valley and he brushed the thought aside.

Emma emerged holding handfuls of dried moss and bark. KoKo was perched on her shoulder looking around curiously. When she reached Adam, she passed him the tinder and he placed it carefully underneath the structure.

"There," he said, standing up and brushing dirt off his knees. "Now to find some rocks. Pin always used one big black one, and hit it with a white one with pink crystals inside it. The black ones are everywhere, but the white ones are harder to find because they're part of those boulders along the beach. You have to search the water to find pieces that have broken off."

"Let's split up," said Emma. Then she pointed to one side of the lagoon saying, "You look over on that side and I'll look over on the other."

Adam nodded and jogged away towards the far side of the lagoon. Emma looked after him, please with how well they were working as a team. Seeing him like this changed him in her mind. He seemed older and—even though she hated to admit she'd thought the opposite many times—smarter as well.

She watched him scamper up a large boulder along the shore and survey the pools of water below. His silhouette stood lean and tall in the morning sun. Then he jumped down off the rock and disappeared from view.

"Come on, KoKo," she said, turning away and skipping towards the opposite side of the lagoon. She was suddenly determined to be the first to find the perfect white stone to both impress and show Adam up.

It was fun playing like grown ups with him and she suddenly hoped Pin didn't return to the beach until they had cooked and finished their breakfast together.

When she reached the shoreline, she planted a bare foot onto a slippery, wet boulder and climbed onto it. Sun glinted off the shallow pools of water between the rocks, making it hard to see what lay on their bottoms so, sliding onto her belly, she reached down and let her fingers sift through the sand and barnacles until they felt something large enough to be a fire stone.

Pulling it out of the water, Emma examined it. It was smooth and white with two pink crystal spires poking off one side. She smiled broadly and shot to her feet.

"I found one first!" she called out across the beach to where Adam was searching. "I found a white rock!"

She saw Adam standing erect close to the shore, but he didn't turn towards her when she called out. Raising a hand to her forehead to block the sun, he came into focus. He was standing on a tall rock and peering out across the water.

KoKo clicked excitedly and dug claws into her shoulder to remain steady as Emma jumped down from the rock. Curious, she jogged across the beach to join Adam and see what he was looking at.

He didn't turn right away when she climbed up beside him, so she attempted to show him the rock she'd found.

"Look," she said holding it up on a flattened palm.

"What's that?" Adam asked, his eyes still locked on the ocean.

"A white fire rock," she answered.

"What?" he asked absently then turned towards her. Seeing the rock, he shook his head and pointed out across the water. "No, what's *that*?"

Emma squinted as she peered out across the water, scanning for whatever Adam had seen. At first she saw nothing, but then an object slowly came into focus; something bobbing up and down with the waves.

"I can't tell what it is," she said, "but I think it's

coming closer with the tide."

Adam brushed past her and jumped off the rock. She followed, confused by his keen interest, and they both walked to the edge of the water where the tide was rapidly rising.

They watched the object bobbing in the waves for a moment longer before Emma turned to Adam. "It will be a while before it reaches the shore, and I'm getting hungry. Why don't we start a fire and eat? When we're done, we'll know what it is."

Adam hesitated. He had a vile feeling in the pit of his stomach and didn't know why. Maybe if he ate it would go away. Finally he turned to Emma saying, "Okay, come on then. Give me the stone and I'll start the fire."

Emma did, their fingers touching momentarily as the stone passed from hers to his. The moment they met, she sensed his anxiety. The sensation surged through her like a thunderbolt and—while she didn't know to what the feeling was due—like him, she realized something wasn't right.

Letting the feeling subside, she followed after Adam as he marched back up the beach to where their fire structure lay under the fronds of overhanging trees.

Adam fetched a glassy black rock from the underbrush then knelt down low to strike the rocks together near the tinder.

Emma got down beside him, ready to blow gently if a spark caught and became a tiny flame. Neither of them spoke as Adam struck the white stone against the larger rock again and again. They were uncharacteristically patient, as though prolonging this morning's breakfast might even spare them a dreaded chore to follow.

Eventually, after some minutes, sparks began to fly from between the two rocks more regularly until ignition was finally made and a small, hot flame began eating the tinder.

Emma leaned in and blew lightly to help it spread and grow. Adam did the same until the flame had consumed the tinder and grass and was nipping at the larger logs.

"Come on, come on," whispered Adam as the fire danced around the logs.

"I'll get some more grass," said Emma and she ran to the underbrush.

"Hurry!" called Adam when he saw the fire was beginning to die.

Emma rushed back, hands heaping with brush and sticks, and passed it to Adam. He parceled it out slowly, careful not to suffocate the fire under too much cover. The flame rose in fits as the new tinder caught alight. He repeated this several times until, finally, one of the larger sticks began to glow and a flame climbed it slowly.

Adam fed the newborn fire with tinder and it spread quickly. He pulled another stick from the fire and held it to the heat until it caught on fire also.

Emma did the same and it wasn't long before the fire raged large and hot in front of them.

They both cheered and laughed, overjoyed at their accomplishment. KoKo clacked along with them, running back and forth across Emma's shoulders.

Emma squeezed Adam's arm and smiled and he squeezed hers back. Then he got up and ran to Pin's favorite gum tree to dig up the fish as quickly as he could. They would need washing and some prep before they could be cooked, so Emma stayed behind to keep the fire alive.

He looked out across the water as he washed a handful of small purple fish in the surf. The dark object was still bobbing on the waves, though it seemed no closer than before. It might be hours before it was close enough to identify.

He looked back up the beach towards Emma—who was standing now, holding her hands over the fire for warmth—and felt glad for having her with him. Pin would be back soon, he was sure, but in the meantime it was fun taking care of important things themselves. It made him feel, well, like Pin must feel all the time; smart and skilled and like a grown-up.

When the fish were washed of dirt and clay, Adam ran back to the fire and joined Emma. They planted the slick bodies on long sticks sharpened on one end and let them hang over the fire until their scales were black and crispy and oil bubbled from around their eyes. Then they took them off and tore them open to enjoy the steaming pink meat inside.

They screamed and laughed as hot oil fell against their skin, brushing it away quickly, red streaks left behind. Then, when they were finished, they fell on their backs and stared up and the clouds, pointing out the shapes they made. Adam always saw monsters where Emma saw plainer things from the world around them.

For Adam, the whole morning was a much needed escape from his mounting worries of ogres and the recent mystery of Pin's whereabouts.

For Emma, it brought her thoughts and interests back from space and Earth to the moon where she realized she had so much to be happy about.

"Adam?" said Emma.

"Hmmm," answered Adam, his thoughts far off.

"Do you think we will we be married one day?"

Adam raised himself on his elbows and looked at her, confused. He gazed out at the ocean for a long moment. Finally he turned back to her and said, "I supposed we'll have to be married one day. How will we know when we're married?"

Emma sat up and shrugged. "I don't know. My father gave my mother a ring and she gave him a ring back. But they said most people don't do that anymore."

"Okay. I guess we'll wait until we're grown-ups and see then. When we're married I think we'll know and we can give each other a present. I don't know if I want an old ring though."

"Okay," said Emma and she lay back down. "Something else, maybe."

"Okay then," said Adam and he did the same. Then, with their bellies full, they fell asleep on the sand for some time.

When Adam awoke the tide was finally in and the surf lapped against his toes. He raised a cheek off the sand and brushed it clean.

Emma was still asleep beside him, KoKo hiding under her hair and nibbling at a fish carcass.

He could hear the surf crashing against the rocks, but there was something else also; a rhythmic knocking accompanying each wave.

Adam eased himself up from the sand and got to his feet. Without waking Emma, he moved down the beach to the shoreline and climbed up the rocks.

Looking down at the water he saw wreckage from their raft clipping the barnacled rocks as each pulse of surf pushed it forward then pulled it away again.

Carefully, he moved along the rocks until he reached the edge of the water. Then, sliding down slowly, he dipped into the water beside the broken craft.

Grabbing hold of the side, he saw that more than half of it was gone. Mostly, it had become rods of cane held together haphazardly by frayed vines. Why he felt compelled to salvage it at all, he couldn't say. He just knew was it wasn't right to leave it to the mercy of the waves until it broke apart and drifted away forever. He was determined to rescue what he could of it.

Since there was no way to heave it up and onto the rocks, Adam moved around them, wading through the waves towards the beach, letting the raft float behind him. It was hard work fighting against the current, and the raft seemed strangely heavy, perhaps due to its pieces floating every which way. But eventually the bottom grew shallow and the waves calmed and he was able to pull the first of the raft's remains onto shore.

The pieces of cane revealed themselves one at a time as they slid up onto the wet sand. Oddly, even as the last of them exited the water, the wreckage still felt weighed down as though something had snagged itself to the end of it.

Seaweed perhaps, Adam thought. The ocean was lousy with it, multicolored and briny. Bunches of it had affixed to the raft during fishing trips many times before.

Letting his grip go from the vines, he ran down the beach to get closer to where the last of the raft remained stuck under the water. He picked up a rod of cane with both hands and pulled at it with all his might until the final pieces of raft rose from the surf and climbed onto the shore in a swell of frothy bubbles.

Adam dropped the cane he was holding and starred at the monster caught up in the tangle of vines, cane, and what looked like Pin's old ship's clothes. Watery, red liquid poured from all sides of it, turning the sand a light shade of crimson.

He crept closer to examine the remains of the creature, careful not to let his bare feet step into the streams of blood.

Emma jogged up behind him and asked what he was doing from a safe distance away. He turned to her sharply and waved at her to keep back before leaning over to see what horrible thing the wreckage had dragged in with it from the open ocean. That's when he saw it— Pin's mining barcode, the lines separated along rows of shredded flesh on his left arm. His right arm was gone altogether as was most of the old man's lower body.

Adam stood up and looked away, holding a hand across his mouth tightly for fear of screaming. Then he turned abruptly as Emma's shrill cries rang out behind him. She had ventured closer and looked down just as a small purple crab pushed its way from Pin's mouth and scuttled up his face and through what remained of his matted wet hair.

Adam caught her around the middle when her legs gave out from under her, holding her limp body up as she cried.

"Pin!" Emma sobbed, then looked up at him. "What's happened to him?"

Adam shook his head, unable to speak. "I don't know, Emma," was all he could say. "I don't know."

They held each other for a long while, neither of them able to look upon what remained of their dear friend and protector, Paddington Pin; neither of them able to contemplate the dangerous predicament he'd left them in.

"It's okay, Emma. I'll take care of us." Adam repeated the words over and over, and yet Emma's conscious mind never once picked them up.

Eventually, they moved arm-in-arm up the beach and into the trees, out of sight of the sand and the lagoon that had once brought them so much joy.

They spent the night in the trees, curled up together against the red trunk of the tallest one they could find. Though neither of them spoke of it, they both shared the fear that if they dared looked down they'd see Pin's broken body roaming the underbrush in search of them. With no concept of the finality of death, the terrifying prospect seemed wholly likely.

The next morning, Emma insisted they move away from the lagoon and the beach and never return again. Adam agreed without knowing where they'd go, what dangers may await them, or even realizing an important first part of their life had come to a violent end. He just knew Emma was right. They couldn't stay in a place where such a thing had happened.

So, with no knowledge of ritual or religion, they left Pin's remains heaped at the edge of the water, gathered what they could carry, and moved inland, abandoning the life they knew in favour of the unknown and unexpected.

Part Four
Love Awakens

23

Emma's eyes burst open and she sat up.

Her mid-morning sleep had been interrupted, though she didn't know by what. She pushed away her golden coverings made of tightly woven sweet grass and scanned the large hut for any unwanted guests that may have wormed onto their homestead looking for an easy meal. But it was empty and the alarms outside weren't ringing.

KoKo emerged from her sleeping basket in the corner and stood at attention. Her ears perked up and she twitched her head like she did when she hunted for bugs at dusk. Whatever the disturbance was, she sensed it too.

Emma pulled her hair back and tied it into a ponytail before rising and looking back at the animal. She was still amazed at how large her spirit companion had become. Despite her initial rejection of KoKo all those years ago, they'd grown up together and become inseparable. And while she was far too big to sit comfortably on Emma's shoulders anymore, KoKo still traveled curled around her neck, her body stretched across both.

A thought occurred to Emma suddenly and she said, "Where's Adam, KoKo?"

KoKo cocked her head inquisitively then jumped up at a human cry that rang out from somewhere in the jungle.

Instinctively, Emma got to her feet and ran for the entrance, grabbing her spear and bursting outside in a single blur of motion.

KoKo took chase, struggling to keep up as Emma ran through the homestead, past the flapper pens and water troughs, and through rows of planted red crisp and sweet root until, finally, she could climb a tree at the edge of the jungle and sail down onto the girl's shoulders.

Together they raced into the dense jungle in search of Adam, Emma whipping past trees and bounding over roots and rocks as KoKo scanned the horizon with her large yellow eyes.

Coming to the edge of a sharp bank, Emma held her spear above her head and yelled, "hold on!", as she sat and slid down, not caring if the dirt and sharp brush tore at her slender bare legs.

KoKo dug her nails into Emma's skin and flattened on her shoulders as they descended, but the girl hardly noticed. If she'd learned one thing in ten years of living in the heart of the moon, it was to endure the inflictions nature set upon the body and push forward when on the hunt (or the escape).

She reached the bottom of the hill and skipped effortlessly to her feet as another cry echoed through the trees to the east. Without slowing, Emma shifted direction towards the sound. Adam wasn't far off now, she could tell.

Based on the direction and level of his cries, he was close to the base of the great mountain where the waterfall drove hard and deep into the rocky lake at its base.

Emma saw two massive slider tentacles through the trees as she rounded a large red trunk. She cursed and grit her teeth, but didn't slow. The monstrous limbs were raised in the air and waving wildly in a display of aggression. Before she saw the rest of the monster, a hollow tone filled the air as the beast bellowed.

Emma knew that sound. The slider was aiming to kill.

She pushed through the tree line and leaped onto the smooth stones that surrounded the base of the great mountain. The slider was there, up on its bulbous lower limbs, barbed tentacles flailing and lips peeled back to reveal rows of bony teeth. Its translucent skin showed a tempest of rivers underneath, yellow blood pumping through veins as the slider's black and yellow heart beat furiously.

Emma thanked the red planet it was a yellow slider and not a red one. Yellows were the smallest of the species, standing roughly three times her height. They were easily angered and very dangerous, but small enough to best. They also tasted wonderful if you could actually get close enough to kill one.

Sliding to a halt, she stood back to avoid the attack she knew was imminent. Her gaze wandered instinctively upwards to where the mountain's peak touched the clouds. It was a colossal natural wonder that dwarfed everything else on the moon, so it was hard to train the eye away when you approached it.

Its size was what drew them to their final settlement and—even though she'd walked in its shadow hundreds of times—its scale never failed to stop her cold. In fact the entire jungle seemed to grow out from under it.

Another cry rang out then and Emma turned, crouching low. It was Adam, perched, legs apart and spear out, standing on a tall, narrow boulder that sprang from the mountain lake like an ancient pillar.

Mist from the great waterfall swirled around him as he challenged and taunted the slider to attack.

"Go on, you yellow slime sucker!" he yelled from the rock, waving his spear back and forth. "What are you waiting for? Eat me!"

Staying low, Emma held her spear tightly. KoKo clacked, urging her forward, but they were too late. There was nothing she could do but watch the slider send two tentacles shooting towards Adam, bellowing another cry and bringing its teeth together in an ear-splitting *crack*.

Adam ducked as the first tentacle swung towards him. It missed and sailed over his head, but the monster had time to adjust the second one that followed close behind. It came at Adam low, and was about to sweep him off the rock when the boy spun around once, sliding his feet backwards to avoid the tentacle. Then he lifted his spear and drove the end of it into the slow moving appendage as its sharp barbs scraped across the stone.

The slider sent a deep, agonizing wave of sound across the rocks that blew Emma's ponytail up into the air. The force of it was so strong it actually pushed her back and it was all she could do to stay standing.

Adam pulled his spear out of the tentacle and drove it in again quickly. Dark yellow puss spilled out from the wound and covered the rock.

The Slider bellowed and sent its third tentacle lumbering towards him. The fleshy mass fell fast and heavy like a stone through water and slammed into Adam with a sickening thud. His feet slipped on the slick stone and the blow sent him backwards off the rock, his limbs hanging like a rag doll.

Emma screamed as she lost sight of him behind the boulder then stood tall on the balls of her feet. Pouncing like a tree stalker she charged for the slider while its attention was elsewhere, spear at her side and driven by a savage instinct to avenge and protect.

The animal's black round eyes rotated in their sockets and locked onto her as she ran underneath it and weaved between its three lower tendrils.

KoKo jumped from her shoulder and bounded from one flailing tentacle to the other until she rounded over the slider's body, attempting to distract it away from Emma.

The slider raised itself up and slid backwards to find Emma, but not before the girl drove the sharp end of her long spear up and into its fleshy underside. It made a loud, sickened sound before its heavy, gelatinous body began to fall back down.

Emma dropped and rolled to the side, avoiding the monster as it flattened out on the wet rock bed, the spear shooting up and into its insides, piercing its giant heart.

Staying low and at the ready, she watched the slider writhe for another minute before its heart stopped pumping and turned a dark shade of black. Only when she was sure it was dead did she draw a relieved breath.

KoKo emerged from behind the fallen creature and bounded towards her, but Emma was already up and racing for the waterfall.

She veered around the tall stone that Adam had fallen from and scanned the water for any sign of him.

"Adam!" she called frantically and—half expecting to find his body broken along the rocks—was almost relieved to find he wasn't there.

She picked carefully down to the water's edge and peered into the crystal water to see if he was trapped along the bottom. The sound of the waterfall swirled around her in a deafening roar.

She thought she caught sight of him under the waves and leaned in, straining to make out the wavering shape of a figure under the ripples.

"Watch out!" cried a voice and two hands pushed her from behind.

Emma's eyes flared open as she flew headfirst towards the water, plunging under the cold surface. She flailed underwater and turned herself around quickly to find the surface again. Looking up she saw a familiar figure standing on the shore, hands on his hips and laughing heartily.

Swimming up quickly, she broke the surface and scowled. "Adam, you bug brain!" she yelled up at him, treading water. "You scared me!"

Adam laughed harder and pointed down at her. "You should have seen your face, Emma," he said, imitating her surprise at being pushed into the water.

"Stop that right now and help me out of here," Emma said sternly as she swam toward the water's edge.

Adam rolled his eyes and skipped down the rocks. He reached out and waited for Emma to put her hand in his. When she did, she held his tightly and kicked her legs hard, pulling him forward. Adam's eyes widened as he fell, hitting the water on his belly, the bare skin sending a hearty *flop* ricocheting across the water.

He broke the surface, angered at having been caught off guard. "Hey, that's not fair!" he said as Emma swam towards him, taunting him with little splashes to the face as she laughed. "Come on, Emma, I mean it, stop that right now."

Emma frowned mockingly then swam past him towards the shore. She pulled herself onto the warm rocks and flipped over. Then, propping herself onto her elbows, she watched Adam climb out of the water behind her.

At nineteen, he had grown very tall, at least a foot taller than her. His hair was a messy mop of wet blond curls that stood in stark contrast to his tanned, muscular body. Still doe-eyed with fine young features, he cut a curious blend of innocence and savagery as he slicked his hair back and fished his spear from the water. Diluted yellow blood dripped down it, pooling on the dark stone.

"So, you killed it I suppose," Adam said flatly, almost disappointed. "You didn't have to. I was just having fun with it. We never have any fun anymore."

"Fun?" Emma scoffed. "Are you sun sick or something? You could have been killed! I though you were dead when the slider got you."

Adam waved dismissively and straightened, boasting, "Takes more than that to hurt me. Didn't you see how I was playing with it? Poor thing didn't stand a chance once I lured it down here. You know sliders are useless on wet stone, Emma."

"*Lured* it?!" Emma yelled, stunned. "Adam, I thought I'd lost you and you say you *wanted* it to attack you? What might have happened if I hadn't killed it for you?"

"You think I couldn't win?" Adam replied indignantly. "Is that what you're saying? Because I could kill any old slider and you know it! Next time just stay out of the way and you'll see. Why did you even come down here? I don't need your help with everything you know."

"Fine!" Emma yelled, getting to her feet. "Come on KoKo, let's go."

KoKo climbed up her leg and settled on her shoulder before Emma turned and marched away.

"Good! Go! I'll just harvest it on my own then," Adam called after her. "Maybe I'll eat it all myself, too!"

"Fine! You don't want any help, remember?" Emma said hotly without looking back.

"That's right, I don't!" Adam yelled as Emma slipped out of sight and into the trees, leaving him alone at the base of the mountain.

Adam looked across the rocks at the slider's souring mass of translucent flesh and suddenly wished he'd asked her to bring him a pull sled and black blade to help with the harvest. Sliders looked soft, but their skin was rubbery and tough to slice.

I'll just have to come back, he thought with a mournful sigh as he slung his spear across his back and trudged along the rocks towards the trees.

24

Adam's leg pinched angrily as he moved through the jungle. Stopping to inspect it, he noticed a bony slider was barb sticking out of his thigh.

He bent over and twisting it, pulling it from his flesh. A thin line of blood ran down his leg and made a trail along a stop of sun-bleached rock bed as he limped along.

He threw the barb away and sighed. He was disappointed. It had taken him all morning to hunt that slider and he'd looked forward to killing it himself. His wounded leg hurt twice as much without the satisfaction of a good kill.

As he parted the tangled branches and moved into the jungle, he tried to bury his dissatisfaction along with the nagging pain in his leg by turning his thoughts to his fight with Emma. It was just one of many silly outbursts they'd had recently. Something was changing in her, but he couldn't put his finger on what.

For one thing, she was always *helping*. She worried about him all the time and seemed to be just around every corner. She never wanted him to hunt alone anymore, or travel to the shore to fish.

Adam winced as his foot slipped out from under him on a mossy rock. He decided to rest and eased himself onto a thick, tall root that protruded from the ground like a miniature archway. The pressure left his wounded leg immediately and he blew out of relieved breath.

Something called from above and he looked up into the tangled branches. When nothing caught his gaze, he looked back towards the jungle floor and his thoughts returned to Emma once again, no doubt back at the homestead by now and stewing about their argument. He felt badly about tricking her into thinking he was dead. Maybe it wasn't too late to make amends and get her help after all.

I'll gather some rock nuts on the way back and she'll forgive me, he thought. Emma loved rock nuts, but they were difficult to harvest because they grew deep in the ground and only under a very specific sort of boulder—one that was silver-streaked and extremely rare. They were also heavier than you'd expect from their size and hard to roll over as they were always stuck oddly deep into the earth. Then, if you could move one and find the nuts underneath, there was the chore of cracking them open, which was time consuming. But once the hard mineral shell was cracked, the flavor of the translucent jelly inside was divine enough to make the work worth it.

A single bite brought bumps to the flesh and a soft buzzing under the skin. Too often they'd eaten more than they should and drifted off to sleep in each other's arms for hours during the day, only to wake in the evening confused and thirsty.

Adam imagined walking into camp and seeing Emma lying in her favorite sun spot, weaving a basket or blanket. Or maybe she'd be tending to the flappers.

He imagined sneaking up behind her and surprising her with a handful of cracked rock nuts. Oh, she would reject his advances at first; playfully pretending she was still mad. But eventually she'd smile and give in, and they'd enjoy the soft fruit together, growing tingly all over and laying in the shade of the giant gum tree that sat behind their hut and spread its limbs across the homestead.

The inevitability of their reconciliation made Adam smile and he found he had the energy to stand up again. Limping slowly onwards, he searched the ground for dark boulders with silver streaks he knew were somewhere along the jungle floor.

25

Back at the homestead, Emma stormed angrily into their hut. She stopped abruptly and stomped her feet, dust erupting from the cane floor, forming small clouds around her bare feet that evaporated in an instant.

KoKo jumped from her shoulders and skipped towards her sleeping basket as soon as she hit the floor. Emma watched her disappear inside it then let out a therapeutic lungful of air before turning her attention to her surroundings.

She loved their hut. It was round and large with cane walls and a thick roof of weaved palm fronds. And while it would look like a plain abode to anyone unaccustomed to life on a jungle moon, to Emma it was pure opulence compared to the shelters she'd grown up with. And, in a way, it had become the first true home she'd ever known.

She thought back to her childhood life with Adam before they'd settled close to the great mountain. Without knowledge of how to build anything—or the strength to even try—they'd lived in the trees for many years, relying on their massive limbs and fronds for safety and shelter from the harsh elements.

For months after Pin died, they scavenged in vain for food during the days, hurrying back to the branches before the sun went down and night creatures ventured out. On a good day they might have a sweet root to share between them, or a few handfuls of edible blue rock moss. It was a hard and tiresome life without the stability that Pin had established for them.

At merely ten and eleven years of age, migrating inland while learning how to survive took its toll on them quickly.

Within six months they were skinny and all but starved owing to a lack of fish or fruit-baring trees deep within the moon. Without water for bathing they were often filthy, their lips and the skin between their fingers and toes splitting from dehydration.

Their hair grew wild and tangled, and before long their ship's clothes turned to tatters, pieces shedding from their emaciated bodies like old skin from an aging lizard. After all their clothes had eroded they wrapped themselves in whatever coverings nature provided, truly becoming creatures of the jungle.

Within a year, the usefulness of language had all but eroded and they barely spoke to one another. They became no different than the native animals of the moon. Not that they lost the ability to speak, but silence was essential to survival in the jungle's interior, where a vast array of previously unseen and dangerous monsters lived and bred.

Sliders were the deadliest— land octopods as

quick on the ground as they were in the trees, their barbed tentacles like grappling hooks, chopping into the bark to help them slide through the branches after their prey. Many times in the early days of their travels, Emma had found herself cornered by a red or blue slider, whip-fast appendages lashing around branches in chase, desperate to pull her into their round maws.

Luckily, her years on the moon had made her fast, and Adam was never too far off to help at her call. For all the dangers of the jungle, they'd been lucky. The worst injury Emma had experienced from a confrontation was the odd slider barb in the arm, or leg. Barbs pierced deep and hurt like hell, but the wounds healed within days if carefully treated and bandaged.

Eventually, as the years strengthened them and experience increased their daring, they became more comfortable living a life on the ground. They learned the routines of nature and the movements of the animals around them and exploited those rhythms.

They speared mud mice in the early morning when the nocturnal rodents were sleepy and slow. They gathered sweet roots in the afternoons, which, when mashed together with the bitter red leaves of a common shrub, made a tart, earthy chew that helped them stay alert and energetic during the hottest times of the day.

The only downside of the natural stimulant was that it also made them incredibly thirsty, and water was always challenging to find when on the move. With no camp to set up rain basins, finding small rivers or jungle streams was left entirely to chance and mostly they survived on morning dew by licking it off fronds.

After years of roaming free and living from one meal to the next, Emma finally admitted to herself that they couldn't go on living as they had. They needed to find somewhere to settle or the moon would claim them like it had Pin. But in a dark world of endless jungle where everything posed a deadly threat, where could they go? What had happened at the ocean—the violence and loss she'd experienced—had devastated her so profoundly that the thought of traveling back was impossible to fathom. No, they had to push forward. She just hoped something better was waiting for them somewhere.

It was four months into her thirteenth year when Emma glimpsed the great mountain, shrouded in cloud and peeking out from the tops of the trees.

It was a typical morning. The wide red limbs of the trees were cool and slippery with evening sweat and she had struck off to hunt alone before the sun rose.

KoKo was on her shoulder, half dozing. Adam rarely woke before the dawn forced his eyes to accept a new day, but she'd learned that early mornings were the best time to gather eggs and snatch young not-parrots from their nests. Watchful mothers were usually off searching for insects and sluggers at this time.

It wasn't long before Emma's efforts paid off and she heard the high-pitched wine of a baby not-parrot somewhere above her.

She looked up to see a mess of sticks and ground flora and recognized it was a nest. She climbed higher until she could peer into it and survey its contents. One newborn and three smooth, brown eggs not yet hatched lay inside.

The baby not-parrot became excited when she reached a hand in to snatch the eggs, bobbing its head up and opening its mouth expecting food from its mother. After wrapping the eggs carefully in a frond, tying it up with a vine and sticking the package inside what remained of her shirt for safe-keeping, Emma looked back at the animal, still calling for food.

If it wasn't for the hunger pains in her own stomach, Emma might have felt sorry for the animal's confusion. In this case, however, she took advantage and snatched the not-parrot up without much thought.

She held the animal close to her face and examined it for signs of skin rot. She smiled as she scanned its scales, brightly colored and shiny in the dawn's light. They'd learned over time that dull scales or marbled underbellies were an early sign of flesh disease, but this young one appeared healthy and safe to consume. It was a lucky find.

Emma was about to twist its neck to snap it when the not-parrot's head shot forward and pecked her cheek twice swiftly. Its needle-thin beak broke her skin and she dropped it in surprise.

"Oh, you little monster!" she yelled, wiping away a line of blood.

KoKo jumped at her outcry and stood at attention on her shoulders, wondering what was happening.

Emma looked at the red smudge on her fingers for a moment then moved to grab the not-parrot from the nest. It jumped away and fluttered to a higher branch. KoKo clacked excitedly and Emma scowled as she watched the creature chirping down at her, almost taunting.

"So, you can fly already," she said as she readied herself to chase after it. "This should be fun."

Pressing the balls of her feet against the red wood, Emma leapt up and grabbed the branch above her head with both hands. KoKo dug her claws into her shoulder as she swung hard, kicking both her legs up and spinning into a balanced crouch on the upper limb.

The not-parrot hopped backwards swiftly as Emma leaned forward to snatch it again and she just missed, almost losing her balance in the process. Looking away to grab hold of a vine, she steadied herself before turning back to search for the animal. But the not-parrot was already gone.

"Now where did you go?" Emma whispered as she scanned the branches. Not one to give up—especially on a hunt—she was determined to see the animal caught and roasted over an open flame for her breakfast if it took her all morning.

Fronds shuffled slightly overhead and she looked up to see the not-parrot disappear even higher into the branches. Emma was after it in a moment, climbing with simian agility until she was once more within reaching distance. A lightning-quick swipe of her hand and she pinched its leathery wing between her nails. The not-parrot chirped and flailed, but it wasn't strong enough to escape now that she finally had it.

Emma turned and leaned her back against the trunk. She closed a hand around the not-parrot and pressed its wings to its side. Reaching up, she tore a thin vine off the closest branch to her and, holding the not-parrot tightly, she began wrapping its legs quickly and efficiently. It was a task she had performed so many times before, she barely looked as she wound the vine, instead taking a moment to look at the view from the tree. That's when she saw it— a massive red monolith of stone rising from the sea of trees.

For a moment, Emma was stunned by what she saw. The great mountain's body dwarfed everything around it, red stone breaking from the sea of trees like a monstrous beast breaking the ocean waves. Its bottom was miles wide, hidden by foliage, while its top disappeared into the clouds giving it the impression of an infinite structure. The only movement she detected was the thin line of a waterfall on one side. She couldn't hear it from where she was, but she was mesmerized by the brilliant light reflecting wildly from its far away stream.

Emma's grip loosed around the not-parrot and the animal wriggled free of her and flew away. KoKo chirped wildly in warning, but Emma barely noticed she was so taken with the mountain's presence. The moment she saw it called to her and she knew immediately it was where they needed to go.

Snapping back to the moment, Emma double checked that the not-parrot eggs were still wrapped up safely before scaling back down the tree. Her body tingled with excitement. For the first time in years, she felt like she had a purpose, a *plan*, and a final destination. She could already imagine a better life waiting for her and Adam if they could just get to the mountain.

As she touched down on the jungle floor, she imagined climbing all the way to the mountain's top, into the clouds, and looking out across the whole of the moon, watching the animals roam far below as though she was their ruler. She began to run, desperate to tell Adam about what she'd seen and to convince him of their destiny.

When she found Adam again, he was awake and brushing a long procession of bark mites from his bare legs. He winced as their tiny pincers nipped at his skin, but they were no more than a nuisance.

"This tree is dying," he said matter of factly when he saw Emma push into view. He didn't notice the marveled look still lingering in her eyes. "It seems that more and more of them are. Or they're sick or something. Have you noticed that? We should be moving on. And be careful where we bed tonight."

He flicked the last of the mites off his leg and stood up. "I don't want to wake up one morning with a nest of mites in my ear."

He stopped talking when Emma moved in close and grabbed both his hands unexpectedly. Her chest heaved with excitement and pushed against his, which sent a warmth up his body and through to his cheeks.

"What's gotten into you?" he asked, the smallest hint of suspicion arcing through his words.

"I've seen it," she said, her voice soft and breath hot in the morning air. "Adam, it's enough to light a fire in my heart."

"Seen what? What is it?" he asked in a whisper, seeing her arms ripple with goose pimples. He ran the tips of his fingers across the bumps gently saying, "You're trembling. Emma, what is it?"

"Our future," she said looking deep into his dark blue eyes. "Adam, I've found our home."

26

Unable to do the sight justice using mere words, Emma led Adam through the trees so he could see the mountain for himself.

It took no more than an hour for the two of them to arrive at the broad-limbed tree that had offered her a view into the distance and she buzzed with excitement as she lead him higher into its branches. She passed the not-parrot nest—barely looking to see if the feisty baby that had put up such a fight had returned—and made her way to the same spot she'd stood earlier.

When she finally arrived at the spot, she looked down and flashed Adam a brilliant smile. Then, when Adam had climbed up to share the branch with her, she pulled away a bunch of sagging fronds now limp from the heat to reveal the view in full.

She looked out, surprisingly relieved to see the mountain was still there. The bright red of its stone radiated in the midday sun and, when she squinted, she could see black specs on the horizon. Flying creatures soared in and around the smooth, bulbous rock formations that seemed to roll like water drops down its sides to the jungle below. After allowing herself this brief moment to take in the view she turned to Adam, her eyes wild with anticipation.

She could tell Adam, who was looking over her shoulder, was as taken with the view as she was, but the look on his face puzzled her. It was contemplative rather than joyous and, indeed, the more he looked out at the mountain, the more his expression seemed to sour. Her heart sank.

"Isn't it marvelous?" she asked, desperate to know his thoughts. "With the rock at our backs, we would be sheltered from attacks. We wouldn't be looking over our shoulders all the time." She pointed towards the endless waterfall running down one side saying, "There's fresh water, which means animals will come to *us*. And if we find enough space we could even trap some of them somehow so we wouldn't need to hunt anymore. Wouldn't that be—"

"Stop," said Adam, cutting her off and turning away from the view. "Just stop. It doesn't makes sense and you know it."

"What do you mean? It's perfect," Emma replied, not angrily, but firmly, careful not to let the conversation turn into yet another argument.

"What have we learned all these years? The only way to stay alive is to keep moving," said Adam. "As soon as we slow down, we're slider food. Or worse." As he finished he started to turn away as though about to climb down, but Emma grabbed his shoulder and spun him back towards her.

"You're wrong," she said, keeping a firm grip on his arm. "I think we've never found the right place to settle is all. I don't understand why you won't give this a chance."

"We don't know anything about that place!" said Adam quickly, raising his voice. "*They* could be from there."

"They?" asked Emma, letting him go and looking at him, confused.

"You really don't remember? Has it been so long? Well I do. Not a day goes by that I don't see their twisted faces in my dreams, or smell their fires. Smell their *moonshine* that Pin drank before he..." Adam's eyes moistened and he turned away. He sniffed and rubbed his nose, but didn't turn back.

"You're talking about... ogres." Emma whispered the word. "I do remember them. Of course I remember. They were the only things could turn Pin scared. They took everything from us; our beach, our family, our safety— everything. But we haven't seen them for years. Not once since leaving the beach. In fact, it's been so long, they seem almost like a dream to me now. Or ghosts, like they were never here at all."

Adam turned to face her and she could see he was shaken, as though mere talk of ogres was enough to fill him with dread.

She studied his eyes and could see there was more to his feelings, something he wasn't saying.

"What is it?" she asked slowly. "What's making you so scared."

After a short pause, Adam blinked and waved his hand dismissively. "It's nothing, I'm not scared," he said coldly. "I just don't think it's worth the risk. We're doing fine out here, we don't need anything different."

"I do." Emma's voice was steadfast. "I can't go on living like this. We can't go on like this. This isn't even living, Adam, it's, I don't know, dying slowly. I can't explain it other than to say even a not-parrot makes a nest and stays there long enough to hatch her eggs in it. I miss having a place of our own. I miss how it used to be for us so badly that it hurts my insides."

Emma stopped speaking and lowered her gaze, letting her words live on in silence. Perhaps she had said too much in her excitement. Even if she was within her right being honest about her feelings, it didn't mean Adam was wrong. They'd stayed safe for this long, why risk a hard journey towards an uncertain future.

Adam moved past her without speaking and pushed away the fronds to look out at the mountain in the distance.

"It will take a long time to get there," he said after a long silence.

Emma looked up and turned around, stepping forward until she was standing next to him.

"More days than we've ever traveled. Forty maybe, if we're fast," he went on.

"And the rains are coming, I know," Emma added before reaching her hand down and sinking her fingers into his. She squeezed his hand in a silent acknowledgement of his agreement.

Adam faced her, his expression serious in a way she'd seen many time before when he was determined to accomplish something. "And this would make you happy?" he asked simply.

Emma nodded once and he leaned down and pressed his forehead to hers. She rose onto her toes to meet his eyes, feeling their lashes entwine as they came together. He cupped the back of her slender neck and let his fingers wander down between her shoulder blades. Then he tugged her even closer, feeling them poke out as he said, "Where you go, I go."

"Adam—" Emma began, overwhelmed, but he stopped her.

"We leave at dusk," he said.

"We can bundle food, carry what we can on our backs, to keep moving," she added. "We can make it before the rains come, I know it."

Adam nodded in agreement and pushed away from her, their bare, moist bellies making a slight *sucking* sound as they parted.

Emma felt the jungle air caressed the area where they'd been joined, sensing her sweat grow cool.

Adam walked past and began to climb down the tree, but she didn't move to follow. Instead she lingered a moment and pressed her hand to her abdomen and closed her eyes. Her heart raced as she applied pressure to reclaim the feeling of his body against hers. Noting the excitement of it was a new sensation and, for some reason, Adam seemed new as well.

She opened her eyes again and saw the mountain, now mostly obscured by a thin sheet of cloud cover. It called to her in a way she couldn't describe with words, like it was somewhere she was meant to go. She only hoped she was right to trust her instincts and that Adam wouldn't come to regret the decision to trust them also.

The call of a not-parrot drew her attention away from the view and she looked down to see her leathery foe from earlier that morning, flapping its wings and hopping back and forth on a branch some feet below. She crouched and watched with interest as it jumped away from the tree and took to the air for the first time, rolling and arching awkwardly as it flew in the direction of the red mountain hundreds of miles away.

Emma was elated as she watched it fly off, joining clusters of other young not-parrots bursting from the tree tops. For the first time she felt a kinship to them in some meaningful way, like she was also about to take a leap of faith and journey into an unknown future.

Emma watched the not-birds until they became specks in the distance then started to climb down to search for Adam. They would need to pack quickly if they were going to leave by dusk. And it would be a very long journey.

27

Looking down at the waxy floor boards of their hut, Emma spread her arms and stepped gingerly along a single piece of cane. Then, pretending she was balancing on the limb of a tree, she closed her eyes and recalled her old life hidden high among fronds and flying creatures, before they'd settled at the foot of the mountain and built the homestead.

Thinking back, she could barely remember why she'd longed to leave it behind in the first place. *Isn't time funny?* she thought. *Hardships from long ago seem to fade, while warmer memories take deeper root.*

She stumbled slightly after a few feet, her right foot slipping off its mark. Opening her eyes she sighed softly and slumped her shoulders. If she *had* been in a tree, she would have just fallen to her death. Though she was healthy, strong and capable, she knew that living a comfortable life on the homestead had taken away some of her agility and animal instinct.

Moving to the wall of the hut, Emma spun around

and pressed her back against it. Then she closed her eyes and listened to the sounds outside.

Flappers cooed and squabbled in the pens and zappers buzzed in the midday heat. What she didn't hear was what she was hoping to most— Adam's footsteps coming up the path and the tapping of sticks on boulders as he checked the security alarms they'd set up along the edges of camp.

After years sharing a life together, she felt like she knew his every routine and movements. For example, each day he left her in the late morning after they'd shared a meal of sweet roots and flapper eggs. When he left he never let her know or told her when he would return, just picked a spear from his growing collection and marched off into the trees in search of game.

There was a time early on when they arrived at the mountain that they would hunt together, but after a while Emma preferred to stay close to the homestead. Caring for it was a lot of work and she took pleasure in seeing it expand and flourish around them.

Each day before it got too hot she fed the flappers a mixture of dead tree crawlers and bits of dried sweet root, gathering up any of the light green eggs that were laid during the night.

When that was done, she fixed any pens that were coming apart, cleaned out the rain basins and checked the traps (both on the ground and up in the trees). If any birds or ground animals were caught she would kill them and prepare them for eating, wrapping the skinned bodies in fronds and burying them under the floor of the hut to keep them cool and away from predators.

Sometimes she played with KoKo, the two of

them chasing each other around the hut, one trying to steal a stick away from the other. Other times they napped away the hottest part of the day, curled up in the shade of the hut, waking just as the sun was setting.

That's when Adam would usually return, his bare feet patting in slurred rhythm as he trudged tiredly onto the homestead after a long day out in the jungle.

She would listen, lying on her back in the darkening hut as he came closer. If she heard him drop something heavy on the black carving stone at the edge of their fire pit she would smile, for it meant he'd had a successful hunt. It also meant he would be in good spirits. Adam was always happiest when he felt accomplished (and had a full belly).

When she heard him moving about outside, Emma rarely ran out to meet him. She didn't call to him either. Rather, she preferred Adam to come to her. Even if he whistled and called her name, she would wait. Perhaps it was silly—a childish game—but she loved to listen as he fussed outside, prepared the evening fire, cleaned his spears, and washed himself in the bathing trough.

She imagined his dirty tanned face coming clean as he pressed his wet hands to his cheeks and forehead, the water running down his neck and beading off his strong chest. She also, admittedly, wanted him to miss her enough to find her, and to rouse her when he did. And inevitably, when he was finished his rounds, the sound of his feet would begin to draw closer.

When she sensed him approaching the hut she would close her eyes and pretend to be sleeping before he had a chance to pass through the hanging vines that covered the entryway. When he entered he always whispered her name and crept closer until he leaned over her. Sometimes he tickled her ear or plucked at her eyelashes playfully to wake her, while other times he was tender, tickling the underside of her arm or blowing on her neck.

If he had grown tired he might lie next to her and wait until his presence was enough to cause her to stir. In those cases she would shift and turn her head, pretending to peer at him through bleary, sleep filled eyes. Then she would turn over fully to face him and he would whisper excitedly about his day, boasting about his hunting success and showing off any new wounds he may have endured— a gash along his palm from a blood viper perhaps, or, one time, a fat purple bruise that colored his lower back and down to the top of his buttocks.

Adam embellished his adventures and Emma enjoyed their drama, and sometimes they'd lie for hours just talking of nothing in particular but the details of their day apart, or the adventures they'd shared over the years. With no concept or care of time, or need to consider its tyrannical momentum, they might drift off and sleep, waking during the peak of night to start a cooking fire, eat supper, and enjoy the warmth together.

Of all the time they spent together, this was Emma's favorite. The jungle was wonderfully still at night, alert and alive as always, but peaceful as well, as though an unspoken truce stayed all the natural dangers of world until the start of a new day.

Emma opened her eyes. She was back in the present, her back pressed against the wall of the hut, her bare chest moist with midday heat. She wiped away the wetness with the back of her tanned hand

and the spot felt cool for a moment. Reaching up, she untied her hair, letting it unfurl down her shoulders and fall over her small breasts, the ends nipping at the top of her hip bones.

As was usual these days, her feelings concerning Adam were confusing her. Sometimes he made her so mad she couldn't stand to look at him. And yet, when he was away, she couldn't stop thinking about him, worrying for his safety and looking forward to his return.

He had become important to her in ways she couldn't comprehend, let alone explain to him. He now seemed much more than a childhood companion, but what exactly she couldn't say.

And then there was his love of killing. Lately it had been worrying her greatly. What had started as the need to hunt for food and security had turned into something all too pleasurable for him, gleeful in a way she found uncomfortably sinister. He seemed to enjoy killing for its own sake, the incident with the slider being the most recent example of his making sport of it.

Once, when they were working quietly on the homestead—Emma weaving a basket for gathering fruit while Adam carved another long spear with deadly points at each end—she'd tried asking him why he enjoyed killing things so much. The words had slipped almost unconsciously from her mouth as though her lips had read her mind aloud.

Adam stopped carving and let the end of his spear droop towards the ground while he gave the question a moment's thought. Then he replied, "I don't know," in a low and taciturn grumble and went back to working on the weapon.

She had been slightly taken aback by his response at first, for it seemed as though her question was unworthy of consideration. But she decided not to press him further, satisfied that his answer came from a place of truth. Because, of all the things in life to consider, *why* was a concept that was completely foreign to them.

Why did anything happen as it did? *Why* did the sun disappear over the horizon at the end of the day? *Why* did sliders kill and *why* did the great mountain rise up from the center of the jungle?

Everywhere, the moon was full of whys that defied answers. *Why* did thinking about Adam make her stomach jump sometimes and why had he taken to staring at her, glassy-eyed like a flying buzzer caught in place by the sight of a flickering flame? This boy who she had considered such a nuisance when they were children?

Indeed, life on the moon was full of whys and the only answer that seemed fitting to most was, "I don't know."

The unknowing of things made Emma miss Pin all the more. He had known things, had *answers*, and even when she could tell he was making something up, or talking in circles to avoid her questions, his assuredness had a way of putting her mind at ease. As the years moved on, even surrounded by all the beauty and splendor of nature, her mind was rarely at ease anymore.

Emma's thoughts were racing. She needed to clear her head.

She rose, deciding she couldn't just wait around for Adam to return anymore. Suddenly, she longed to be somewhere more secluded where the emotions and history of the homestead wouldn't influence her feelings about everything. And there was only one place she knew of to visit if she wanted to feel like stepping into another world.

She whistled for KoKo as she made for the exit, but the animal didn't emerge from its sleeping basket. The battle with the slider had worn it out, poor thing, so Emma crept silently through the exit, careful not to wake her up.

Though the day was coming to a close, it was still incredibly hot and the fading light stung Emma's eyes as she stepped out of the hut and into their camp.

She ran her gaze across the homestead, hoping to catch sight of Adam. Perhaps he was there and she just hadn't heard him. But no— the only greeting she received was from a flapper that rushed to the edge of their pen, honking and hopping to receive a meal.

Emma ignored its calls, instead grabbing her spear from the side of the hut. Then, tying it over her shoulders and swinging it onto her back, she jogged past the perimeter, away from the homestead, and towards her favorite place to be alone.

28

Adam was still scanning the jungle floor for silver streaked rocks when he noticed the light beginning to fade.

Looking up he saw the sun was already half-eaten by the horizon. It wasn't safe to be deep in the jungle at night, so he decided to give up the search and head back to the homestead with what little rock nuts he'd been able to root up.

Harvesting the slider could wait until morning, though he didn't relish seeing Emma's smug look when he returned empty handed.

He looked down at the strange fruit in his hands—six perfectly round orbs in all. Rubbing moist dirt off one of them with his thumb, he examined its husk, rich brown, the texture of leather. The rare fruit underneath would be worth the time it took to cut it open. They tasted sweeter than any tree fruit and the sensation they brought to the body and mind was something like floating on the waves in the early morning sun.

Adam decided to let his feet rest a moment and sat down on a long crooked root that protruded from the ground like the arm of a monster attempting to pull itself up from the center of the moon.

The balls of his feet pulsed quickly as he relieved them of his weight and his bare legs itched from being on the move all day. Reaching up, he pulled a frond away from a low hanging branch. Then, tearing it in half, he packaged the rock nuts tightly on top and folded the frond over them once before tying the small bundle together with vine and then to his spear. When that was done, he blew out a long sigh and rested his spear against the edge of the root.

The night world was beginning to wake, new sounds emerging around him as the day died away. He'd learned over the years that night sounds were shy and strange compared to daytime ones. They hummed at a lower frequency as though the creatures that made them were trying to stay quiet in the darkness. Everything evened out in a dangerously soothing way that could lull you into thinking you were safer than you were. There were certainly as many monsters in the dark as in the light.

A rustling sound along the ground made him perk up and grab hold of his spear. Looking into the brush he saw two mud mice emerge from a hole at the base of a tree and begin to root blindly for bugs. He shifted his weight and they froze. While blind, their other senses were still acute.

Adam rose to his feet slowly and they scurried off into the jungle. The way they moved reminded him of KoKo, the two of them together were like he and Emma. All they had was each other.

Suddenly, he longed to be home with Emma and the strangest feeling of shame washed over him as he realized he wasn't mad at her anymore. In fact, he could barely recall what they had fought about in the first place. And, as the world grew darker around him, Adam knew Emma was right to worry about losing him in his battle with the slider, because the thought of being alone on the wild and massive jungle moon felt suddenly unbearable to him.

How awful it would be to be all alone day-in and day-out. How scary and dreadfully lonely to be the only one of your kind.

Suddenly Adam wanted nothing more than to be with Emma; to see her face and feel her close and watch her weave flowered necklaces and tussle with KoKo until they all fell asleep in a heap.

He moved with haste through the jungle towards the homestead, his sore feet and the wound in his leg no longer causing him any pain.

Adam raced towards the hut when he reached the homestead, ignoring the traps, the hungry honks of the flappers and the cold fire pit. They could wait. Right now, he wanted Emma. He wanted to wake her if she was sleeping and tell her how silly he'd been.

Stopping just outside the hut, he leaned his spear against the wall and untied the small package of rock nuts. Then, pulling them behind his back as a surprise, he peeled back the hanging vines and stepped in through the entryway.

The air in the hut was sweet and Adam recognized the scent as Emma's immediately. She had always carried a distinct and pleasant aroma, as though her skin radiated with the pollen from the thousands of flowers she'd worn and weaved through her hair and clothing over the years. Mixed with the day's perspiration, it was a powerful and alluring potion. But while her scent lingered in the air, the girl was not inside.

Adam's heart sank. Bending down he peeked under KoKo's covered sleeping basket to find the animal resting peacefully. Emma and the creature were usually inseparable, so maybe she hadn't gone far. Maybe she was just gathering fruit for the evening meal and would return in a moment?

Adam decided that made sense and sat on their bed to wait for her. Placing the rock nuts on the floor next to Emma's side, he lay down and stared at the ceiling restlessly.

How long would he need to wait? What if it was all night?

Adam huffed in frustration and sat up again. It was no good. He couldn't wait. He had to find her immediately. So, leaving the package of rock nuts next to the bed, Adam ran from the hut and out into the cooling air of the homestead.

Stopping just outside the hut, he leaned close to the ground and looked for fresh tracks, signs of any recent disruption to the plants or flowers littering the area.

He found a bunch of young reeds that appeared to have been flattened by a footstep and gauged a possible direction from there. Once he discovered the general direction she'd gone, Emma would be easy to find. It was an old hunting trick they'd used many times before.

Adam grinned as he moved more quickly, tracing Emma's footsteps through the homestead and into trees. As much as he loved hunting game, he was struck by how quickly his heart raced as he worked to find her. He could think of nothing in the world more satisfying at that moment than seeing her floating amid the trees, wild and free and unaware he was approaching. He relished the idea of surprising her, could almost see her smile as she turned to see he'd found her.

He began to ache for her as he walked ever quicker, his body crying out as though having lost some integral piece of itself. It was like, without her, he might die.

29

Ancient faces, deeply lined and radiating the wisdom of ten thousand seasons, looked on from the side of the mountain as Emma slid her feet across the slick ledge.

Spray from the waterfall pelted her face as she approached it slowly, careful not to slip off the slick blue moss that spread out over the red rock face. If an onlooker would have spied her from a distance she would have barely seemed a speck climbing under the faces' massive scale. Each was as large as a small island, their disinterested eyes peering off into the horizon; at what, no living creature would be able to say with any degree of certainty for none was alive at the time of their sculpting.

Emma called these figures "the stone men", and she dared never look at them whenever she made the climb up to the small cave tucked in behind the waterfall. They seemed to stand guard over it in a way that made her fearful, like they might just strike her down if they felt taunted by her presumption to enter their sacred chamber. Plus, the way they looked out across the world made her think they could see and hear all things, perhaps even her own unspoken thoughts. In that way, it seemed to Emma, they might know her better than she knew herself, and so they filled her with awe and fear and made her sad, for she also knew they would outlive her and every living thing on the moon.

The hard spray pricked at her supple skin as she reached the great waterfall. With her back against the rock, she tucked herself behind the downpour and into the stone cave set deep into the mountain.

Once Emma passed through the curtain of water, its thunderous roar evened out to a steady thrumming that didn't bother her ears much.

Removing her spear from around her shoulders, she leaned it against the stone entryway before wiping water from her face and flicking it to the ground. The drops made a subtle patting sound off the stone which turned into a constant dripping as tiny drops fell one after the other from the ends of her hair.

Reaching back, she balled it up in her hands, giving a single squeeze and sending a torrent of water splattering to the floor. Then she moved further into the cave.

Set into one of the back corners was a thick cushion of moss and dried brush. She'd carried the materials in small bunches over the years since discovering the hidden cave. It created a comfortable space large enough for her to lie down and stare at the reflections on the ceiling. Sometimes she slept there if the afternoon was particularly hot.

Emma didn't think she'd be able to sleep today.

Her mind was still racing. She didn't know exactly why, but she felt as though a restless spirit was trapped inside of her, fighting to burst out.

She lay down, letting out a deep sigh before plucking the wet ends of her hair and twirling them between her fingers. Then, staring up at reflections dancing along the ceiling, she tried to make sense of the random shapes that formed as they moved. Four waving lines turned into a star then burst apart like a spark jumping from a fire in the night sky. Another set of lines floated over the uneven rock ceiling like ripples on a crystal lake.

Was there meaning to these morphing forms? She couldn't help but wonder this whenever she found herself fascinated by the movements and spectrums of the world around her. Was a higher power attempting to speak with her through the dazzling shapes and colors of the world?

She became mesmerized by the reflections and lost in a deep reverie as they danced and spoke to her soul in their secret language. Then, ever so slowly, the real world and the world of sleep became one, her mind's eye blinded by the charm and magic of the natural world as she slipped into unconsciousness.

Emma was so lost in utter tranquility that she didn't hear the sound of wet feet quietly patting against the stone floor towards her. She didn't feel drops of water tapping against her cheeks as a figure leaned over her slick, tanned body lying on the bed of brush and grass; didn't notice eyes studying her lustfully as she lay, half asleep, half awake.

Finally, when a drop of water ran down her forehead and over the lid of her right eye, she opened it and looked up.

At first she saw Adam looking down at her, a wide smile spreading across his face as he leaned in closer. But when she wiped the water from her eye she saw it wasn't him, and her sharp, horrible scream pierced the tranquil silence of the cave.

Adam was nearing the tree line when a strange sound caught his attention. He crouched low in an instant and pulled the long spear from around his shoulders, listening to identify what the sound was and the direction it came from.

SH-SH-SH-SH

He tightened his grip around his spear as he listened. The sound was rhythmic and sharp, unlike anything he'd heard in the night before. It seemed to come from the direction of the waterfall and he pressed on despite a sense of fear, driven by curiosity and concern equally.

The world had grown dark since he left the homestead so he needed to be careful as he approached. Whatever was out there, he needed to find Emma before it found her.

SH-SH-SH-SH

Adam followed the sound until he reached the edge of the tree line. Crouching low, he peered out across the smooth black rock surrounding the great pool at the mountain's base.

The dead slider was still there, only now it was separated into many pieces, its foul bile and blood spreading out across the stone.

Four Ogres, three male and one female, were slicing its flesh with sharp tools, strange blades singing out unnaturally in the night and they slid them back and forth across the creature's rubbery skin.

SH-SH-SH-SH

As they tore each piece from the slider's body, they moved the meat onto a large sled made of cane and vine.

Adam cursed his bad luck. That slider would have fed them until the rains came. But his frustration didn't linger long. He had a bigger problem— ogres were back.

Adam slunk through the tree line away from where the four ogres continued their work harvesting the slider. There would be more of them close by, Adam knew. He didn't know if the entire tribe was back or not, but he and Emma needed to leave regardless. He needed to find her quickly.

He froze suddenly, his muscles tensing when he heard a sound behind him. Narrowing his eyes Adam spun around quickly, taking an offensive stance with his spear out, ready to lunge. But there was nothing there.

He remained still and ready for a long moment, scanning the jungle for a sign of movement. His body shook as adrenaline pulsed through his veins. Without knowing how many ogres were around, he didn't know whether to stay or run.

Better to run, he thought and was about to flee when something fell from above and landed on his outstretched spear. The thing chirped at him sharply and he heaved a sigh of relief.

"KoKo!" Adam whispered sharply, shaking his spear to get the creature off. "You silly bug, you scared the breath out of me!"

The animal ran up the spear and sat on Adam's shoulders, chirping intently at the boy.

"Be quiet," Adam replied. "I don't know where Emma is, but we can't stay here. It's too dangerous. ogres are back."

KoKo grabbed a clump of Adam's hair in her mouth and yanked at it hard. He winced and tried to shoo the creature away, but she seemed intent to keep his attention.

"Ouch! What's gotten into you?" Adam huffed, confused. KoKo yanked his hair again and Adam took a step forward. "Are you trying to tell me something? Do you know where Emma is, KoKo?"

KoKo chirped and hopped on top of Adam's head, pulling at his hair until he took another step.

"The mountain? Is Emma up the mountain? But Koko, we can't go there now, it's too dangerous with ogres— OUCH!" KoKo pulled his hair so hard that a clump came out in her mouth. "Okay, okay. You don't have to rip my hair out. Show me the way then. You know how to stay hidden better than anyone. Just keep quiet, would you?"

Sensing that Adam understood, KoKo jumped off his shoulders and bounded ahead through the underbrush.

A small blur in the darkness, Adam did his best to keep up with the animal as she led him around the other side of the lake, towards the massive mountain and the cave she knew Emma liked to go.

30

Adam's heart was racing.

His intuition had become acute enough over the years to know that something was terribly wrong.

Treading carefully over the smooth black stone surrounding the mountain lake, Adam trailed KoKo towards the rock face until they reached a narrow crag tucked just out of sight. No sooner had he stopped to take a breath than KoKo chirped and disappeared between jagged boulders, vanishing from view.

Sucking in a deep breath, Adam stood tall, making himself as thin as possible in order to push between the sharp rocks and into a tight tunnel beyond the opening.

The tunnel was so narrow that he had to crouch low, and the rough walls scraped against the smooth skin of his shoulders and elbows and the top of his head as he shimmied forward in the dark.

After years of living by the mountain and exploring much of its north face, he was surprised that both he and Emma had missed the passageway altogether. He didn't know where KoKo was leading him, but just then he felt he had no choice but to follow.

"KoKo?" he whispered as he pushed forward blindly in the dark. "KoKo, where are you? Where are you taking me? Where does this tunnel go? KoKo, are you there?"

He stopped dead and strained to listen. If KoKo was too far gone he would have to turn back. If he became lost in the mountain's dark passageways, he may never find his way out of them again.

"Where is that blasted creature?" Adam said and leaned against the cold stone wall.

He had never cared for KoKo the way Emma had over the years. The truth was he found the animal something of a pest most of the time and Emma's devotion to her irked him something fierce. He couldn't understand why she doted on the animal when doing so took time away from other fun things they could do together.

Taking care of things the way Emma did wasn't a notion that came to him often, but it seemed like an indelible part of what made her who she was. Maybe if he had been better about that—thought to take care of her better—she wouldn't be lost to him now. His drive was to protect, sure, but perhaps *caring* was something altogether different.

Adam decided to keep moving and quickened his pace through the tunnels. He realized how grateful he was now for the bond that KoKo and Emma had forged over the years. Without it, the animal wouldn't be leading him now, and he was ready to put all his trust in the belief that she knew where Emma was.

A chirp echoed from somewhere up ahead and

his gaze darted towards the sound. His eyes were adjusting somewhat to the darkness and he could actually make out a few feet of tunnel ahead now.

KoKo was still out of sight, but he kept moving through the darkness, guided by the animal's distant chirps and whistles.

After some time, the rock above his head grew higher and he was able to stand upright again. He arched his back, relishing the relief it gave him, as he quickened his pace forward. The deeper he dove into the mountain, the more its subterranean sounds began to surround him until he found it difficult to distinguish the tones of dripping water and insects from KoKo's noises. A few steps later he stopped, fearful he'd lost her again.

"KoKo!" he whispered harshly. "I can't hear you. Come back you little—"

Something landed on his shoulder then and he jumped in the dark. Thinking is was KoKo, he turned his head towards whatever it was, but instead came face-to-face with a large three-legged insect with long, sharp mandibles and hundreds of microscopic glowing eyes.

The thing scuttled up his neck and burrowed into his thick hair faster than he could react and he jumped around spastically, writhing and pulling at it in desperate attempt to get the nasty thing of him. A pain ran down his spine as the thing bit him on the back of the neck and he yelled out.

His knees weakened and he noticed a thousand more yellow eyes coming out of the darkness.

As the creatures materialized in his line of sight he tried to bat them away with his spear, but found he was losing dexterity in his fingers. A clatter rang out as he let it go and his weapon fell to the stone floor.

"Koko!" he rasped, realizing he was also losing his voice, his throat constricting as venom pulsed through him. It was so quick, he could feel it sting as it travelled through his veins.

He fell against the wall, trying desperately to stay upright as a dozen ugly spider-things ran onto him and nipped at his tender body.

"KoKo..." Adam could barely push the sound from his lips.

He collapsed to the rock floor and the spider-things clamored over his entire body. He became numb, and his limbs convulsed erratically as he lay helpless. The last thing he saw before his eyes closed was the mandible of a spider-thing carving a slice of flesh away from his side and stuffing it into its grotesque maw.

Emma struggled furiously against her bonds, but couldn't lift her head off the cane sled to see where the ogres were dragging her. Fear and adrenaline surged through her and she cursed herself for being so careless as to be found alone and captured so easily.

She could hear the two large ogres making strange noises ahead as they trudged along the narrow mountain passageway. It sounded like they were speaking to one another in a series of guttural sounds and whoops, but if the language had meaning it was lost on her, and her head was so tightly secured to the cane sled that she couldn't see anything around her except the rocky ceiling above.

Though she was silent now, she had called out

and screamed for some time for the ogres to let her go. But they never answered her.

They'd travelled so long through the mountain passageways that it wasn't long before Emma gave up all hope of Adam ever finding her again. How could he when neither of them had even known about the tunnels under the mountain?

She noticed the rock above her head was beginning to slant upwards, slowly rising until it became a high, domed cavern covered in stalactites. Large flying creatures with translucent wings hung between the long rocks, or flew around squawking. A few of them shot down towards the ogres as they broke into the open, swooping overhead to see if they might be something to eat. But those that got too close were met with the hard blow of an ogre fist and flew back up towards the ceiling with a deafening screech.

A new sound arose as they continued through the cavern, and Emma was suddenly truck with an icy fear that made the hairs on her arms and the back of her neck stand at attention. The grunts and chatter of more ogres - *many more* - grew unmistakable until it became a deafening roar all around her.

Finally, the ogres brought the sled to a stop, dropping the thick vine ropes before moving into her sightline. Their breath blew hot as they both leaned down towards her and, for the first time, she was close enough to the moon's sentient inhabitants to get a good look at them.

Their skin was as thick as leather with deep weathered lines crisscrossing their cheeks and forehead. Black, sooty paint was streaked underneath their jaws and around their eyes and Emma wondered if these two were warriors or hunters—an explanation perhaps of how they found her in the first place (though she imagined the truth of how they lived and moved around the moon would never truly be known to her).

Their hair was long and rope-thick and shimmered oddly, resembling the multicolored mosses that grew on the sides of the moon's trees. They tied it in knots to keep it out of their faces.

They seemed to be so a part of the moon's environment that Emma wouldn't have been surprised to see more of them sprout from the earth and grab her right there.

Reaching their thick, calloused hands under the sled they heaved it upright. Finally, Emma could see where she was. And as they dragged the sled forward, her mouth hung agape, as she took in the sights before her.

The two ogres had taken her to the heart of the mountain where hundreds more were assembled in a massive cavern. The rock ceiling hung more than fifty feet overhead and the area was so large, Emma couldn't see where its walls were. She felt like she was floating in a sea as waves of activity and sounds swirled around her.

Lengths of colorful animal hides hung from the ceiling creating opulent draping that surrounded a tall throne made of bones in the center of everything. And sitting on the throne was the largest ogre Emma had seen yet; a male with fierce red eyes who wore a suit of bones and held animal bone spear in his lower hand with a slider bard tied to the end of it.

The hunter closest to Emma bellowed a call towards the throne and a hush spread over the crowd like the hissing of millions of insects. A moment later it was so quiet that Emma could hear every beat of her heart as it pounded in her chest.

Slowly, methodically, the ogre in bones stood tall and stepped away from his throne. Marching towards her, his suit rattled with every step, sending a chill down Emma's spine.

Unable to speak for the fear she felt, her eyes looked around the cavern wildly, looking for an exit, a weapon, a friendly face— *anything*!

But while no help presented itself, she noticed a strange object on top of a high tower of logs that sat next to the throne. It was black and smooth, lined with chrome, and round, the size of a large boulder. It was clearly manmade, long metal spikes sticking out from all around it. It looked otherworldly to Emma, surrounded by the rock and natural chaos of the mountain cavern as it was.

The moment she saw it she knew it was the probe that Pin had told them about, the one that had come from Earth but had never sent its message back home. She wanted to run to it, find a way to turn it on and get out of this horrible place once and for all.

Surrounded as she was now by hordes of ogres, she hated the moon more than anything. Any moments of gentle kindness it had shown her in the past were wiped from her mind when she turned away from the probe to see the ogre in bones looming over her.

Emma found her voice then and screamed. She screamed so loud that the whole crowd of ogres ducked as if escaping a creature that had suddenly dove upon them from above. And indeed, screeches rang out along the ceiling as flying creatures returned what they deemed to be a scream of an animal somewhere below them in the cave.

Taken aback by the force of Emma's scream, the ogre in bones took a single step back . He stood tall as though reassessing her. Then he leaned in cautiously, pressing his huge face close to Emma's.

His breath, putrid and hot, washed over her as he examined her. She winced and closed her eyes tight, but he forced her lids back open with his thick fingers and peered into her light blue eyes for a long time, as though searching for something supernatural within them. Following that, he forced Emma's mouth open and examined her teeth, which, compared to his, were blunt and small.

When he was finished, the ogre in bones stood tall again and turned to the silent crowd assembled behind him.

"Ti-ta!" he bellowed, his voice echoing through the cavern.

The crowd of ogres muttered in low, muted voices. Some nodded, some cowered, but all watched their king intently as he lifted his great spear and pointed it towards the probe next to his throne.

"Ti-ta! Chara!" the words spat from his mouth like he was jettisoning a piece of rotten food. He shook his suit and the death rattle of bones ricocheted around the cavern. He continued to bellow in the strange language Emma couldn't understand and point to the probe, yelling, "Ti-ta! Charra! Ti-ta! Ti-*tu*!"

The crowd screamed out in horror and the ogre in bones turned towards Emma again, gripping the top of her head and forcing her gaze towards the probe.

"Ti-tu!" he yelled at her. "Ti-tu! Ti-tu!"

"I don't know what you want," Emma whimpered under the pressure of his grip.

"Charra! Ti-tu!" the ogre in bones bellowed back in response.

"I don't know what you're saying!" Emma screamed.

This made the ogre in bones even angrier and he wrapped his thick fingers around her throat. It was nothing more than a thin branch in his massive hand, and Emma thought, *How easy it would be for him to snap it in an instant.*

The ogre in bones spoke low and serious, waving his staff towards the assembly of ogres before them. Then he pointed it towards the probe.

Emma strained her thoughts, desperate to understand him. The fact that he hadn't killed her yet made her think there must be something he was trying to communicate to her, some connection he was trying to make between her and the probe.

He waved his staff towards the assembly once more and Emma let her eyes wander over them. Suppressing her fear, she began to notice how retched many of them seemed—not menacing, but weary, bent and broken, their camp at the center of the mountain less a violent stronghold than a place of retreat. They seemed like animals hiding from a predator stalking somewhere outside. Emma didn't know what could make such formidable creatures cower in fear, but it seemed like *something* had driven them underground.

Despite her realization, Emma was still rendered mute, unable to understand her captors and what they wanted from her.

What was it about this probe that made them both worship it and fear it at the same time? Emma understood enough to know the creatures associated the probe with her, but exactly why, she couldn't decipher.

One thing the moon had taught her over the years, however, is that when creatures are scared they can become dangerous. Fear drives all animals to attack. In that regard, her life was in real jeopardy here.

Disturbing her thoughts, the ogre in bones suddenly thrust his spear into the air and barked some kind of order.

Emma watched perplexed as the crowd of ogres parted to make way for a bamboo palanquin draped in the dried slider flesh. It was carried on the backs of four ogres who trudged forward, backs bent in agony. Emma could make out the figure inside, completely wrapped in green and gold animal hides only were visible. Even in the firelight, the scales covering the hides sparkled brilliantly.

A hush fell over the crowd and some ogres bowed low as the figure drew closer. Emma's flesh bristled with goose pimples and her mind raced to understand who it was and what was happening and what it had to do with her.

When the figure on the palanquin reached the ogre in bones, he lowered himself onto one knee and bowed his head. Upon doing so, the figure swung its legs over the side of the palanquin and stepped onto his shoulders, using his body to climb down like a step stool.

Once on the ground, the covered figure glided towards Emma, swaying gracefully, betraying a sense of the feminine hidden underneath its coverings. The figure came close. Its eyes studied her. They were bloodshot and piercing, almost panicked as they scanned Emma's face and half-naked body.

The ogre in bones rose from the ground and stepped in tall behind the figure. Then, reaching around with his strong three arms, he pulled away the colorful hides to reveal the figure underneath.

She was female as Emma had suspected. Her thick, ropey hair was tied back tightly and lined with precious stones and the teeth and bones of different animals.

She must be a queen, Emma thought.

She was mostly naked, covered only by a sparse covering of hides so Emma could see her skin and how different it appeared to be from the other ogres assembled.

Her skin was marbled with large white blotches, and angry looking red lines—like sores—crisscrossed her arms and chest. It looked like something was eating away at her flash and suddenly Emma realized that, whatever was causing it, must be afflicting the tribe. The female grabbed Emma by the arm roughly and ran a finger along her skin.

"Mu-ah," she said quietly, her voice ragged and sickly. "Mu-ah, ti-tu."

Dropping Emma's arm, she turned and pointed to the probe behind them. When she turned back she had fire in her eyes and sneered angrily.

"Mu-ah, TI-TU!" she yelled, pressing her face close to Emma's.

Emma shuddered under her anger and began to cry.

"I don't know what you want!" she said hopelessly. "You're sick? I don't know why! I can't help you—"

"Charra!" the female screamed, her breath blowing hot across Emma's face.

Everything happened all at once then. The crowd became active, ogres moving in every direction as though responding to an order.

Emma watched, panicked, as they tore down tents, packed sacks, and prepared long bamboo sleds with supplies. It seemed to Emma that they were setting to leave the cavern.

While the horde was occupied, Emma watched the ogre in bones wrap the queen back up in her animal coverings and lead her to her bamboo palanquin. At the same time, the two ogres that had dragged her through the mountain lowered the sled to the ground again and began pulling her away.

"Wait!" cried Emma. "Where are you going? Let me go!"

Her cries went unanswered as the sound of commotion swirled unseen around her and she was dragged off into the crowd.

31

Adam awoke to the sound of running water and the warmth of the sun on his face.

I'm dead, he thought in a sudden fit of awareness. *Like Pin, my body has been dashed. But my thoughts are floating along the ocean of forever.*

Ten hours earlier he was on the floor of the mountain tunnel, eyes rolling wildly and teeth grinding painfully as his mind fought the powerful darkness that tried to consume him. He was a horror of retching and shivering; of barely breathing as the spider things took their fill from his flesh.

The spiders' poison was strong, but after nearly eleven years of bites and scrapes, his body had become a formidable opponent to the moon's natural aggressions. If it weren't for that, the subterranean world would have claimed him forever.

Adam struggled to open his eyes, but no matter how hard he tried he couldn't find the strength. He attempted to call out, but his throat was dry and unable to form sounds.

Something touched his lips then. It was cool and wet and dribbled into his mouth. *Water.* He sucked at the drops greedily, letting the liquid soothe his throat and slowly fill him with life again. He became aware of why he was unable to see. Something covered his eyes.

Bringing his hands to his face, he tried to determine what it was. It felt like some of kind of rough animals hide was wrapped around his head. He pulled the hide away from his right eye and light flooded it making him wince and shut it tightly again.

"Chi-tu. Un-aha," came a voice from somewhere unseen. The words came slow and husky and were followed by a strong hand that reapplied the bandage over Adam's eyes.

Adam's skin bristled at the sound of the alien voice. He knew that language, had heard it spoken once before during the violent ritual back at the cliffs. Adrenaline shot through him and he sat up. The ogres had him!

Ripping the bandages from his eyes, Adam shuffled backwards in a lame attempt to escape blindly. Waving his arms defensively at the blurry world, his back eventually hit stone and he knew there was nowhere to go.

The sound of hearty laughing surprised him then. It wasn't malicious, but a kind of warm chuckle that reminded him of Pin when he used to laugh so hard it seemed to come from the middle of his belly.

"Where are you?" asked Adam, continuing to grope the air wildly. "Why are you laughing?"

The laughter became louder then and Adam wondered if the ogre that had him wasn't a little crazy, like that time their flappers escaped their pen and eaten a whole harvest of rock nuts making then unable to walk straight. Adam remembered how they'd tripped around each other in circles for hours after, making the oddest sounds chuckling. He and Emma had absolutely bowled over laughing as they watched them circling the yard, no more able to escape than walk in a straight line.

Emma!

The moment Adam saw her face in his mind he knew he couldn't stay blind if he ever wanted to find her. He strained to open his eyes, letting the lids up as much as he could stand. Light flooded in but with some effort he found he could keep them open.

The world came into focus slowly until he could make sense of where he was. He was in a small cave, open to the air. A small fire burned at his feet. It was night out and Adam realized the heat he felt when he awoke wasn't the sun, but the fire next to him.

Across the cave, kneeling next to the stone wall and scraping it with a large stone, was an ogre. Adam let his eyes set on his captor until the ogre came into focus. It was a female. She looked ancient with thick white hair that coiled all around her like vines growing around the trunk of a tree. Even though she was twice his size, she seemed small hunched where she was against the wall scraping away at the stone.

As soon as his vision was clear enough to run, Adam jumped up to escape through the cave's opening. But he skidded to a halt when he saw it was a dead drop down hundreds of feet to the ground below. He waved his arms to keep his balance and just barely stopped himself from falling over the cave's edge.

Cackling laughter echoed off the stone walls and

he turned around. The old ogre was looking over her shoulder at him, snickering. Finally, she motioned to the fire as though inviting him to sit, and for the first time he noticed there was a large stone pot perched atop the hot flame. A crude serving spoon made of wood stuck out from it. Adam hesitated, unsure, but the ogre turned away and focused again on her task without so much as another word.

Studying her movements for a moment, Adam finally noticed what it was she was doing to the wall. Spread across the length of the stone wall, and far above her head, were pictures; images that she had carved. Adam looked in wonder at the crude pictures, and driven by curiosity he stepped forward to get a closer look despite his fear.

Pictures of plants and animals, fierce creatures and rolling hills met his gaze as he tried to take it all in the firelight. The more he looked, the more the images began to look familiar. At the farthest edges he saw the ocean, their old beach and lagoon, and the cliffs. He saw the dense jungle and cane fields, and the places he and Emma learned were too full of danger to tread. And at the center, towering above the ogre's head—and over the entire moon like a monolith—was the mountain.

"It's a map," whispered Adam in awe, a memory coming to him suddenly of something Emma had told him long ago when they were children. Something about a map in the caves of the cliffs close to their beach. Adam wondered if this ancient ogre was the one who had etched those, too.

The ogre turned towards him and urged him to sit once again. She moved her hand to her mouth and mimed taking a bite of food, showing her long, rotten teeth in the process.

Realizing that she meant him no harm, Adam did as she bade, sitting next to the small fire.

"If you saved me, thank you, but ... I can't stay here," he said as the ogre turned back to her work. "Emma, my friend, she's out there somewhere. I need to go back into the mountain to find her."

When his words were met with no reply, he sighed deeply. It was no use. He may as well eat before striking out on his own and again. He'd need his strength.

Reaching out, he grabbed the tip of the wooded spoon that jostled in the pot as whatever inside boiled away. He gave the hearty broth a stir and thick steam broke the surface. He sniffed and, to his delight, it smelled fine, earthy and hearty and his appetite swelled.

Moving closer to the pot, Adam scooped a spoonful of the brew close to his mouth and blew. It was then that he noticed yellow eyes staring up at him. They were the same eyes as the spider things.

He pulled the spoon away and saw it was piled with dissected parts of the spider things— bristly legs, pieces of abdomen and even faces with the fangs cut out. Adam's stomach lurched and he dropped the spoon back into the pot.

He stood up tall and addressed the ogre once more out of respect. "I'm leaving," he said defiantly. "Thanks again for helping me. You don't seem bad for an ogre, but Emma might be in danger. I have to find her. Can you show me how to get back into the mountain?"

The ogre turned and looked at him blankly.

"*Pass-age-way* into *moun-tain*," he said slowly,

enunciating each word as if it might help her understand.

"Chi-aura," the ogre hissed thoughtfully.

Into the *mountain*," Adam said pointing towards the back of the cave. He was getting frustrated. "You know, where you found me?"

The old ogre stood up slowly. She appeared so ancient, her joints cracked and popped like branches breaking. Without addressing him, she waved her arms across the expansive map on the wall. Landing on the tall mountain above her head, she pressed a boney finger against it and spoke.

"Chi-wa-way," she said slowly.

"The mountain, that's what I said, yes," Adam said, excitement in his voice. She seemed to understand him, which was a good sign.

"Ta-tu, chi-wa-way," the ogre said and slid her finger away from the mountain, letting it travel away from the mountain and across the depicted terrain. "Ti-tu. Chi-wa-way... Cha," she finished as her finger landed on the image of the cliffs.

A sudden realization hit Adam and his heart sank. "What are you saying? They took her away from here? They're taking her to the cliffs? But that means..."

Looking at the map again he noticed a large half circle etched into the stone above the cliff's location. It was a depiction of the red gas planet that hung in the sky above them at all times.

"They're going to kill her!" Adam spat, his knees almost buckling.

The old ogre poked her chest with a bony finger again and again, and began to laugh slowly until the sound became a maniacal cackling that echoed through the cave and sent a shiver down Adam's spine.

He ran.

The laughter continued, following him as he ran deep into the cave and found a tunnel to retreat into. And he swore he could heard the laughter on his heels as he felt his way along the inside of the mountain, looking for an exit that would bring him under the sky once more and closer to Emma.

He just hoped it wasn't too late.

32

Emma steadied herself in the bamboo cage as it rocked over the rough jungle terrain. It was fashioned to a wide sled—constructed twenty-six chutes across—that was being dragged by a strange, lumbering beast the likes of which Emma had never seen before. An underground dweller perhaps?

The thing walked low to the ground on five crooked legs, its two front ones rippling with muscles under grey, scaly flesh, while its back three seemed to steady it over the uneven ground. Its head was oddly small for the scale of its body with a low hanging jaw that was home to vicious incisors so long they nearly dragged through the dirt. It breathed great burdened breaths as it struggled to drag the heavy sled behind itself, bellowing out in pain when the ogres struck its haunches with their thick wooden spears.

All variety of wild animals were drawn to the marching horde as it cut its way through the dense jungle. Like parasites, smaller creatures like mud mice scurried underfoot searching for leavings of food or beast excrement, while not-parrots and other flying animals circled overhead, doing the same from the air. A few perched on the top of Emma's cage and she had to constantly wave them away or become covered in their droppings.

The cage that held Emma wasn't much larger than herself and left her no ~~for her~~ room to stretch her legs. For more than two days she'd been forced to kneel or sit with her knees tucked under her chin and had developed a terrible cramp because of it. She doubted she could run very far even if she could escape because of it.

Not that escape was likely. She'd tried for hours to tear at the rope vines that held the cage together but her soft, human nails were no match for the moon's hearty fauna, designed to fend off tougher attacks than she could ever muster.

Not surprisingly, it had proven useless to yell out or appeal to the ogres around her for food or water. Most of them had barely looked her way during the journey, almost as if they were afraid to.

Once a group of ogre children had approached the cage and poked at her curiously with sticks. She'd tried to ask them for help amid their jabs, desperately offering them colored stones from her hair in return for some water, but no sooner has they arrived than they were beaten fiercely and dragged off by her adult captors. She hadn't seen them—or any children—again since. In fact, there were hardly any children at all, which surprised Emma considering the tribe was in its many hundreds.

So Emma had resigned herself to simply sit and wait to see where they were going, and learn why her presence had driven them to mobilize their entire tribe on such an arduous march.

At the end of the second day, when night began to loom over the jungle and the moon rose full and bright, the deep bleating of horns sounded from somewhere at the head of the procession. At their command, the horde halted their march and began the busy activity of setting up camp.

Emma watched as fires were lit and crude tents draped in red, gold, and green animal hides were erected all around her. Female ogres knelt in groups over stone pots cooking strange smelling stews and speaking together quietly while the larger males chewed mouthfuls of dried meats as they pounded wooden stakes into the earth, and cut away the underbrush.

Once this work was done and food was prepared, the ogres huddled into small groups of five or six to eat heartily in front of fires, and drink deeply from long bladders spilling over with rank smelling dark liquid.

Emma recognized the sour smell immediately. It was the same moonshine Pin had drunk so much of before they found his body broken on the beach. At the memory of such a horrible thing she turned her back to the ogres as the night went on, trying to get comfortable despite the cramped cage that held her.

Deep into the night their voice grew louder and they became rowdy, cheering and calling out. Some fought violently and females screamed, and, in all her life, Emma never thought such wretchedness could exist in the universe. It troubled her so much she could barely stand to look upon them.

After a while, her eyes grew heavy and sleep took hold of her despite her anxiety. At once, she fell into a wrestles dream.

In it, the sun shone warm and lovely and she was a young girl again. She lay stretched out on the sand and the ocean was a constant din of crashing waves that enveloped her. Something tapped her forehead lightly and she opened to her eyes. Adam stood over her, a devilish smile on his face.

"Bet you can't catch me," he whispered, his voice sounding far away. He ran off laughing and Emma jumped up and chased him down the beach, a feeling of pure joy a freedom filling her in a way she hadn't felt in years. She gained on him, sand kicking up behind her as his body grew larger in her field of vision.

"I'm coming to get you, Adam!" she cried joyfully as she approached. "You know I'm faster than you!"

Laughter rang out ahead of her and then Adam vanished. Emma stopped and looked around. "Adam?" she called across the beach. "Adam, is this a trick?"

Emma shivered as clouds rolled in and cold rain began to fall. Thunder clapped overhead and she ran for the tree line to escape the downpour that came fast and hard. But, before she could reach the safety of the trees, Emma awoke in the cage, hard rain pelting her in the darkness.

Hours had passed since she'd dozed off and, looking around the ogre camp, she saw that most had retreated into their tents for the night. Some milled about to pick through the leavings of other groups, but it was mostly quiet. None came to her, or provide her with cover, or gave her food or water and she barely had energy to ask for it anymore.

Her stomach ached and knotted fiercely as she sat

uncomfortably in the cage getting soaked. She began to cry. And as rain ran down her face, mixing with her tears, she thought of Adam and their old life that seemed so hopelessly lost.

How she longed to be with him now, lying beside him, asleep in their large hut, the sound of squabbling flappers lulling them outside, her head on his chest, his hand rested on her thigh. Had she truly lost him?

"Adam," she whispered. "I need you. Where are you?" Emma curled into a tight ball and leaned against the hard cane bars of her cage. She tried to sleep, hoping to find Adam in her dreams again, but he never appeared to her.

When Emma awoke the ogres were already on the move.

It was midday, humid and hot following the night's rain. They had ventured into the densest part of the jungle so the sun was hidden from view above the towering trees. It was a place of wild chaos where insects as large as Emma's fist hummed loudly and predatory animals waited around every corner to devour you.

Emma and Adam had found themselves in this part of the jungle on their journey to the mountain some years ago and had vowed never to return. It was here that they met their first slider and barely escaped with their lives. Thankfully it had been a yellow one, and small. If it had been red… well, she hated to ponder the outcome.

Her stomach roiling, Emma tried to get the attention of an ogre who trudged along beside her. It was a male, given the job of keeping the beast that dragged her cage moving. He looked as tired as she felt, his face twisted in an agonizing scowl as he whipped the beast whenever it slowed.

"Please..." Emma said, struggling to push the word from her lips. "I need food. Water. *Please.*"

When the ogre didn't answer, or even look at her, she sunk lower in her cage and hugged herself. She closed her eyes for a while and the sound of insects intensified. She stayed like that for a while, letting the sounds of the jungle swell around her until something more familiar made itself known to her. A chirping. Where had she heard that sound before?

Opening her eyes, she noticed something on her lap— a long slab of dried meat. She snatched it up greedily and sunk her teeth into it, tearing a large chunk away and chewing quickly. It tasted worse than it looked and was so tough it hurt her teeth as she tried to break it down and swallow.

She was almost finished when the question of where it came from finally entered her mind. Looking around wildly, she tried to figure out who had put the food in the cage for her. But the ogres continued to ignore her and gave no indication of caring enough to provide any help.

Finally she heard the sound of chirping again and knew immediately who it was. Heart racing, she peered over the side of the cage and caught sight of a dark purple tail swaying out from underneath the sled.

"KoKo," Emma whispered. "Is that you?"

KoKo's tiny upside down face peered up at her from under the sled and blinked twice quickly. Emma could tell the animal was confused and upset about her predicament.

"Koko!" she almost yelled. "Oh, Koko, I'm so

happy to see you. How did you ever find me? Can you get me out of this thing?"

KoKo cocked her head quizzically and Emma picked at the vines tying the cage together. "Can you bite through them?" she asked.

The animal pressed her head against Emma's fingers and rubbed it back and forth like she wanted Emma to scratch her behind the ears.

"No, no," Emma sighed and scratched at the vines, trying to get KoKo to look. "Can you chew the vines? Can you get me out of this cage?"

After an agonizingly long moment, KoKo climbed around the outside of the cage and sniffed at the rope vines. She pawed at them momentarily then opened her mouth and gnawed at them with her small incisors. Emma could tell it wasn't going to work. Even if KoKo could chew threw them it would take way too long. But what choice did she have but to try?

"Keep at it, KoKo," she whispered to the wide-eyed animal. "We'll figure this out together. I just hope Adam is in a better position than I am."

With her mind set toward escape once more, Emma sat back and bit off another chunk of dried ogre meat. She winced at the sour flavor but managed to swallow it. Things were looking up. With KoKo's help, she just might get out of this thing yet.

33

For his plan to work, Adam needed to waste some precious hours sneaking back to the homestead.

He'd lost his spear when he was attacked in the tunnels, so needed to rearm himself. He also needed a bellower, and some food packs.

As he moved silently back through the jungle, he hoped the ogres hadn't discovered their camp and their stores remained untouched.

Upon arrival, he stayed in the shadows of the tree line and scanned the homestead. It was still, the only sound the wailing of hungry flappers calling for their supper.

He waited for another few minutes, watching, before he crouched low and shuffled quietly up the trail and past the fence line.

As he stepped through the area, he was relieved to find everything still in its place. It was a miracle he accepted as a good omen. Now that the tribe had reemerged from their subterranean home under the mountain, he knew it was only a matter of time before they discovered it. He looked up and thanked the great gas giant above that they'd been spared that hardship for now.

Wasting no time, Adam grabbed his sturdiest long spear and strapped it across his back. He also belted a short spear and a rock stomper along his right flank. He didn't know what trouble awaited him when he caught up with the ogres who had Emma, but he wanted to be ready for anything when he did.

Now that he had everything he needed, he quickly fed the flappers and checked the camp's traps and alarms. He did this out of habit more than anything, imagining bringing Emma back and having everything exactly as she would want it to be. In truth, he was probably desperate to feel like things would be normal again.

When that was done, he took a long look at their hut. The vines covering the entryway swayed slightly back and forth in the evening breeze. Emma appeared suddenly, pushing them aside and walking out, a smile spreading across her face upon seeing him.

"Fooled you, silly," her voice said lightly. Then she laughed and vanished and Adam was along again.

He turned away and ran.

It didn't take Adam long to the track the ogres. They made no effort to hide their movements and left great roadways of trampled jungle behind them as they cut across the landscape.

Judging by their tracks and the state of the extinguished campfires that littered their way, Adam concluded he was no more than five days behind them. It was far more dangerous, but he decided to travel on the ground. If he could keep moving at a steady pace he could probably catch up with the horde in less than two full days. They would be slow in such large numbers, doubly so if they lead beasts of burden and had children with them.

He didn't know exactly how many days he'd been recovering in the mapmaker's cave, but he was suddenly struck by how closely he'd come to never waking up again. The idea made his blood run cold and he feared for Emma's safety all the more acutely.

He cursed himself for letting her out of his sight when he knew full well the dangers that lurked in the moon's shadows. She was tough, there was no question of it, but their whole lives they always worked better as a team. It was what Pin had always taught them.

How had he become so complacent over the years the ogres had vanished? If it wasn't for the nightmares that still plagued him from time to time, Adam wondered if he might have forgotten them completely.

They always come back, he thought as he picked up his pace. *Why and when was of little concern. Evil things just do, and you have to keep your guard up. I'll never make the mistake again.*

The familiar bellowing of horns woke Emma. The ogres had stopped their march to set up camp again. It was a ritual she had grown accustomed to over her days with the horde.

Once again, they broke into various groups, each with their tasks to perform. Fires were lit and tents were erected with many furrowed brows and agonizing sounds erupting from the workers.

KoKo had learned this was the best time to steal food and her wide yellow eyes appeared next to the cage right on cue, a few lengths of putrid dried meat sticking out from between her teeth. She chirped excitedly when Emma plucked them away between her fingers.

"Thanks, KoKo," Emma said weakly, tearing a mouthful off and chewing. "I honestly don't know what would have become of me without you. I think I'd have wasted away into nothing. Oh, when will this nightmare be over? It's been so long I'm almost used to the taste of this stuff by now."

Emma stuck two fingers through the bars and let KoKo nuzzle them as she tried to determine where she was and what options were available to her. There weren't many.

"You need to leave," she said soberly after some time. KoKo's ears perked up as though she understood. Emma had no doubt she did. Growing up together, KoKo had developed a surprisingly good grasp of their language and responded to most of their commands and words. "If Adam's out there somewhere you have to find him and make sure he gets here."

KoKo ran up and down the length of the cage, chirping erratically.

"I know you don't want to, but there's no other way," Emma whispered harshly. "You can't get me out on your own."

Suddenly, two male ogres—soldiers, one holding a bone club in his lower arm, the other a thick spear with a slider barb at the head—stomped towards her. She barely had time to scream before they grabbed the cage and tore it from the large cane sled.

The grey beast that was carrying it thundered a thankful groan before one of them gripped two of the cane bars and ripped them from the cage as if it were nothing at all.

Emma marvel at the ogre's strength then noticed the other one reaching in to grab her. She kicked at the ogre, but couldn't stop him from pulling her out roughly.

Fighting against his grip with all her might, Emma managed to escape and turned to run. Surprised, the ogre bellowed an anguished cry that reverberated across the camp before taking chase. Everywhere Emma looked, ogres turned to face her, but she kept moving. If she could just make it to the tree line she might be able to—

A sharp pain shot up Emma's right leg. It was cramping up from too much time in a tight space. Biting her lip, she tried to endure the pain, but her legs grew heavier with every stride she took until she felt like she was wading through thick mud. She cried out uselessly before collapsing to the jungle floor.

Strong arms grabbed her shoulders and yanked her to her feet. Two ogres held her by her feet and two grabbed her under her arms and carried her back towards the camp. As Emma screamed and struggled to pull herself away, she caught sight of something purple behind them. It was KoKo scurrying away unnoticed into the dense jungle.

Emma cried out, but onlookers turned away as the ogres continued on through the camp.

"Where are you taking me?" she screamed. "Let me go!"

Without answering, the ogres carried Emma all the way to a large tent at the front of the horde. They stopped at the entrance and put her down, making sure to hold her tightly so she couldn't run again. Her eyes darted desperately to determine what was happening, but they just seemed to be standing and waiting.

Finally, after some minutes, the tent's thick, red flaps opened and a figure came out. It was an ogre Emma had not seen before, a female, thin and quite a bit smaller than the rest. She wore an elaborate headdress made of wrapped animal hides and adorned in bones of various sizes. Her eyes were deeply bloodshot and glistened, almost as if they were weeping. The ogre pointed a long, bony finger toward Emma then beckoned her forward. The two ogres holding her let go their grip.

Emma hesitated and one of the ogres shoved her hard, sending her stumbling through the tent's entryway and into the ogre's arms.

The ogre let her go and Emma stood tall. She looked at the sickly ogre with eyes wild with terror. The ogre stared back for a long moment as though examining her before pulling her inside the tent and closing the flap behind them.

34

Inside the tent was spare. Two stone pots sat boiling next to a small, smothered fire that burned in its center. While its flames were extinguished, red cinders showed through hot, smoldering black and white ash.

The shaman ogre walked over to the fire and sprinkled something on the ashes. A spark of light erupted followed by a wave of greasy silver smoke. Amid the haze, she turned and bowed to the queen who sat oné a small throne of bones at the back of the tent, wrapped in her coverings.

"I don't understand what you want from me," Emma pleaded to the queen while the shaman's back was turned. "Please just let me go?"

Turning abruptly, the shaman grabbed her and pulled her down, pushing her face into the silver smoke. Emma choked as it engulfed her, filling her lungs.

Through coughs and sputters Emma heard the ogre muttering what sounded like strange incantations and though she fought against her grip the strange shaman was too large and strong for her to better in her exhausted state.

When she was finally released, Emma fell to the ground in a heap. Her throat burned and she spat into the dirt, trying not to vomit from the sour taste in her mouth. Rapidly, her thoughts grew fuzzy and the tent began to spin.

Emma rolled onto her back and stared up at the red, scaly ceiling. It morphed suddenly, heaving up and down as though it had come to life and was breathing. She looked around to find the tent had become like the fleshy insides of a creature. She felt like she had been swallowed.

The shaman ogre continued chanting, waving a palm frond over her. Emma felt something splatter against her face. Something wet dripped from the frond. She was sure it was blood and tried to scream, but no sound came from her mouth. She was too deep into the dark dream.

The shaman—whose face had become a contorted mess—bent closer and smeared the strange liquid across her face and around her eyes. The tent morphed again. She was back in the escape pod, but alone. She rolled on the ground clutching her stomach and groaning as her mind continued to play relentless tricks on her and the chanting grew ever louder.

Light flashed and something roared overhead. Emma looked to see a tentacle sucking at the escape pod window. She cowered and whimpered weakly, hiding her eyes from the monster.

Hands grabbed her then and she was pulled to her feet where she could finally see what was happening.

The tent flaps pulled back and there was a bright

flash as lightning arched across the sky and thunder clapped. A storm was raging. The world was chaos. Emma's eyes rolled and her mind reeled under the shaman's hallucinogenic spell.

The shaman wrapped Emma's head in vines then blew a handful of dust on her that left reflective streaks across her face that glowed in each lightning strike. Then she pulled her by the arm, leading her out into the wind and rain.

They walked between lines of small fires until they met the tribe assembled together and chanting in a single, blood curdling voice.

"Chara!" the voices of many cried at once.

"Daa!" boomed a single voice somewhere ahead in the darkness.

"Chara! Chara!" the tribe wailed as Emma passed them.

Some ogres in the crowd jumped away from her as she passed as though they were frightened to touch her. Some swiped at her with clubs and spears fits of bloodthirsty ecstasy.

Emma's eyes rolled and her mind exploded with all assortment of psychedelic images. Some were wild and colorful; others were born of true madness. It was like her subconscious was emerging like the storm itself, revealing itself in flashes of sharp lightning strikes. She faced the sky, eyes wide with madness and screamed at the red gas planet that glowed brightly overhead. Devilish faces appeared in the planet's roiling gasses and electric explosions. She coward at the sight of them, at their lust, and chaos.

All around her the chanting continued as the shaman led her through the runway of flames until, finally, they came to the end of the procession. The black probe, sitting atop the crooked wooden structure, towered over them. A raging bonfire, the largest Emma had ever seen, stood beside it, pounding her with heat.

Lightning flashed overhead and Emma fell to her knees in front of it. In her madness she felt that the sleek metal object was looking down at her, passing some kind of harsh judgement. It condemned her for believing her life was good and pure, and for trespassing upon this natural place she had no place in.

"I'm sorry!" Emma cried up at the probe, tears streaming down her face. Lightning flashed again and the shaman stood her up. As she rose, a familiar figure in bones met her eyes.

The shaman bowed and slunk away into the crowd, leaving Emma to face the ogre in bones alone in front of the tribe. She looked up at him as he called out to the assembled tribe. His eyes were bright red like the shaman's had been— like hers had now become. Looking out at the crowd of ogres she saw that all their eyes were red. She trembled at the sight and knew then that the ceremony, whatever it was, was so unnatural, so violent, it had turned them all to demons.

"Daa!" the ogre in bones boomed. His voice echoed across the high cliffs that surrounded them.

That's when Emma realized where the tribe had taken her. It was the cliffs close to where she and Adam had been raised on the beach and lagoon. Flashes of her past exploded like comets across her mind: Adam, Pin and her, all together, running across the sand, exploring the jungle, laughing at what a life they thought they might have on this tropical paradise. It was all so long ago. And just then it felt like the largest lie she'd ever been told.

Tears streamed down her face as she was overcome with fear and loss and she collapsed to her knees in front of the ogre in bones, who continued to scream at the gas planet in the stormy sky above.

He raised his arms and Emma saw he held a long silver snake that curled around his arms and melted into his skin. No. It wasn't alive. It was a long metal spike, broken off the probe and sharpened on one end.

"Daa! Tu-daa!" the ogre in bones screamed at the red planet, and Emma knew she was going to be sacrificed. For what reason, she would never know. But there was nothing she could do. She didn't run. She couldn't. Not with her mind and body so horribly infected. They'd changed her into something mad and damaged. Even if she lived, she knew she would never be the same again.

Emma *wanted* to die.

Lightning flashed again and the ogre in bones lowered his arms slowly. Then, pressing the point of the metal spike against Emma's bare chest, he called a final plea to his god above.

"Chara! Chi-Tara!" he screamed and the tribe flailed their bodies and shrieked.

Thunder cracked loudly and the ogre in bones tightened his grip around the sharp metal spike. In a moment it would pierce Emma's heart and she would be dead.

She closed her eyes and waited for the nightmare to end when a high pitched whining resounded through the air. The crowd began to quiet and Emma opened her eyes. Through tears she saw the ogre in bones looking towards the planet. Awe and ecstasy etched his face.

The high pitched whine sounded again. It echoed over the cliff face and seemed to come from every direction. The tribe looked around in confusion, grunting and calling out. Some fell to their knees and raised their arms in prayer, believing their god had spoken to them.

Still reeling, Emma let her eyes wander over the crowd. Her mind screamed out to run, but her legs wouldn't move. Then she caught sight of a familiar shape standing in the branches of a massive tree behind the ceremony. She tried to focus on it, but her mind was shutting down.

Emma heard screaming then. She turned away from the shape momentarily to see commotion in the crowd of ogres. Something was happening. She looked back at the tree and the shape was gone. Had she imagined it?

More screams erupted and the body of an ogre came hurtling through the air towards her. She held her head in her hands and screamed as it landed a foot away from her, its body broken and twisted in knots.

Emma scurried to safety under the wooden structure that held the probe and peered out at pure chaos. More ogres were thrown up into the air, tossed in every direction, some landing close by with sickening crunches.

The ogre in bones' eyes went wide when he realized what was happening. Their god hadn't spoken. Something was attacking them.

"Tu-Dita! Ru!" he yelled, leaving Emma and running towards the commotion.

At his command, a handful of larger ogres picked up spears to attack. Most tried running for cover, but quickly realized they were trapped with the cliffs at their backs. Whatever was attacking them, it was fight, or die.

As the crowd parted, lightning flashed and Emma saw something large and red tearing through the ogres. A slider—the largest one she'd ever seen—ripped bodies apart with its three tentacles, sliding over the disembodied parts to dissolve flesh and devour bones. Its body was slick with rain, making it nearly impossible to stop as it attacked quickly across the rocky ground, crazed by the feeding frenzy

Two warriors brandishing spears leaped in front of ogre in bones, screaming war cries as the slider came at them. Red blood pulsed through the monster's insides like rivers as they slashed at it with barbed spears. A high-pitched cry of anger erupted from somewhere inside the beast and it reeled up on two tentacles, towering over them.

Whipping its third tentacle towards its attackers, the slider grabbed one of the warriors by the neck and lifted him up. Once in the slider's grip there was nothing he could do but kick his legs furiously until his skull exploded with a sickening crunch.

Blood rained down on Emma and she let out a blistering scream. More cries rang out behind the warriors and she saw that a second slider—green, smaller, but no less vicious—slid along the cliff wall to attack the horde from the opposite another vantage point.

Ogres were thrown one after the other against the wooden structure protecting Emma, but it managed to hold together and keep her from being breaking apart.

She looked up to see the round probe on top of it rocking back and forth with each knock, threatening to drop to the ground. And when another body hit the tower from behind it did; rolling over the lip at the top and heaving downwards like a giant boulder.

Emma watched in horror as an ogre running for cover was caught by the probe's spikes and was impaled and pinned to the ground, left to die slowly under its weight.

Looking at it, she noticed something on the probe had changed. A hatch on the probe's side and broken open from the impact, revealing a control panel.

Rocked by an urge to run out into the open and examine the probe, Emma scanned the chaos around her. More ogres had joined the fight against the red slider, while the smaller green one was gaining ground, lumbering ever closer to her as it grappled and slid across the cliff wall. It was only a matter of time before it found her. I

If she wanted to survive this she needed to be smart and act soon. But in all the chaos, her mind still bowed to the pressure of the shaman's strange substances so couldn't decipher what action to take.

Then Emma was struck by the most horrifying thought: perhaps none of this was real at all. The sliders, the carnage— was is all in her head? Was she back in the shaman's tent, lost in the throes of a madness?

She watched as, to her right, another ogre was crushed by a tentacle and sucked into the maw of the red slider. She watched his broken body dissolved through the slider's translucent flesh as others threw flaming spears at it to scare it off with fire.

To her left, the green slider continued to grapple along the cliff face towards her. If this was all in her head, then it wouldn't matter if she moved at all. Maybe if she closed her eyes for a long time and opened them again the horror would all just vanish.

Emma shut her eyes and the sound of chaos coalesced into a shapeless blob of clattering fury. If it was real, the green slider would be upon her at any moment. But if it didn't arrive then she'd be free of the phantoms that possessed her.

She was sure it was all a trick. The thin shaman ogre just was trying to break her mind. But she wouldn't break. She would be strong. It would all be over soon. And then she would be free.

35

Something gripped Emma's shoulder and her eyes shot open.

Expecting to find herself back inside the shaman's tent, she screamed when she saw the green slider was hanging from the side of the cliff, directly above her hiding place, flailing its tentacles as though trying to grab something close by.

"Emma!" a familiar voice called and she turned just as Adam skidded under the wooden tower.

"Adam?" she asked dreamily. "Is it really you? Is this a dream?"

"A dream? Emma, have you lost your brain? This is no dream, it's a rescue! Come on!"

It was then she realized what the slider was reaching for, and why it had stayed along the canyon walls. It was chasing Adam!

"You mean you—"

"I lead the sliders here to distract the ogres! And before you say it, it's only a stupid idea if they eat us, so let's go while the ogres are fighting them off!"

Adam pulled Emma by the arm to leave but she resisted, yanking him back towards her. Their faces were close, huddled in the tight space under the wooden beams. So close now to the boy she thought she would never see again, Emma wanted to say so much to him. She thought she would never see him again and now here he was, rescuing her. But there was no time, and her head still swam with the shaman's drugs—

Emma pressed her lips to Adam's.

Electricity shot through her and goose pimples spread down the nape of her neck and along the backs of her arms despite the heat from the massive bonfire close by.

She let him go and stared into his eyes, wide and dazed like a flash of bright light had suddenly blinded him.

"What... was that?" he whispered, keeping hold of her. Now that he'd found her he never wanted to let her go again.

"I don't know," she said quickly. "But I felt like doing it."

The wooden structure shuddered and they both looked up as the top beams splintered and wood rained down. The slider was tearing apart the tower to get to them from above.

A tentacle descended down like a blood viper searching for a mud mouse in its burrow. Sharp barbs expanded along it as it grew closer to them. There was no time. They needed to run.

Giving Emma one last wide-eyed look, Adam grabbed her hand and they both scrambled out from under the wooden tower just as it collapsed, dust and dirt exploding as heavy beams crumbled into a large pile.

"There's nowhere to go!" Emma screamed as they met the chaos around them.

Adam saw she was right. Ogres fought the red slider to their right, the green slider had already changed course and was moving on them, and they were blocked by the raging bonfire.

"This way!" Adam yelled as he led them around the bonfire. "We can put the fire between us and the slider!"

Emma began to move but caught sight of the probe not far away.

"Wait!" she yelled, and, with no time to explain, dropped Adam's hand and ran out towards the large black object.

Sliding to her knees, she peered into the open hatch at the control panel inside. There were two red switches and a yellow button with letters written across it that she couldn't understand.

Catching sight of her, the slider dropped from the side of the cliff and heaved its massive body towards her. Chunks of rock exploded as it pounded its barbs into the ground, pulling itself along.

"Emma!" Adam screamed, trying to get her attention.

She looked up and saw the slider approaching. Without thinking she turned back to the probe and plunged her thumb into the yellow button. A whirring sounded deep inside the probe and she backed away just as the slider's thick tentacle descended upon her.

Rolling away just in time, it barely missed her and smashed against the probe with a sickening slap, sending it sailing through the air.

Emma didn't wait to see where the probe landed.

She was on her feet and running towards Adam in a flash.

He reached out and she grabbed his hand as she ran by. They were gone, rounding the bonfire to escape the monster hunting them.

Adam lost sight of the slider when they reached the other side of the fire. He breathed a quick sigh of relief. He knew sliders well enough to know they were easily confused. If it lost sight of them, it would likely turn its attention to the ogres and leave them to their escape. If they kept moving, they could ~~get to~~ get to the—

A tall, muscular ogre dressed all in bones stepped in front of them and Adam skidded to a halt. He found he couldn't move. For ten years he'd been haunted by the fearsome figure peering down at them with deep, bloodshot eyes and suddenly he was ten years-old again, looking pure evil dead in the face.

The ogre raised the metal spike and thundered a roaring call. "Chi-tu! CHARA!" he bellowed, about to bring the spike down in a monstrous stabbing sweep.

Something jumped from the shadows then, landing on the ogre's head and scratching wildly.

"KoKo!" Emma screamed as the ogre in bones grabbed the animal roughly and ripped her from his face. He threw the animal away and a loud yelp sounded someone unseen as KoKo hit the hard ground.

The ogre went for Adam again and Emma shot into action. Throwing herself into him, she shoved Adam out of the way and the ogre's attack missed him by mere inches.

The ogre stumbled forward and fell to one knee, grunting what sounded like a curse.

Before she could escape, the ogre reached out quickly and grabbed Emma by the neck. He lifted her into the air as he rose to full height again.

Seeing Emma in danger, Adam snapped out if his paralysis and rushed forward to try and knock the ogre off his feet. But it was no good. Using his lower arm, the ogre knocked him away with a powerful blow and Adam fell onto his back some feet away.

Fighting against his tightening grip, Emma kicked her legs and squirmed uselessly to escape. The ogre barely seemed to notice as he brought her closer to his face and roared, gnashing his rotten teeth. She saw his brow had been split open; a deep wound dripped red blood over his eyes, obscuring his vision.

She screamed as he moved her closer to the bonfire to throw her into its raging flames. Sweat dripped down her brow and hot cinders licked her bare back as he held her to the fire.

He growled once more and brought his arm back, ready to throw her.

Emma shut her eyes and readied herself for the end. At least she'd seen Adam again. Against all odds he'd come for her. Maybe this was as good an end as could be had by anyone.

She felt herself rising higher into the air and opened her eyes. They were *both* being raised and she noticed the ogre's cries had changed from anger to something closer to pain. He let her go as he struggled against his attacker.

Emma fell to the hot earth beside the fire and looked up to see the ogre in bones torn apart by two powerful tentacles. She didn't move. She could only watch and listen as he screamed in agony and his suit of bones *rattled, rattled, rattled* before breaking into a thousand pieces and raining down around her like a hailstorm.

She lay still next to the fire, doused in blood, surrounded by bones, expecting the slider to reach for her next. But for some reason it didn't see her anymore. Instead, it stuffed what remained of the ogre in bones into its maw, pulsated grotesquely for a moment, then slid away, presumably distracted by the battle raging on between the warrior ogres and the red slider.

Adam slunk in beside her and they both sat still for a long while, hand in hand and breathing deeply.

Watching the light from the fire dance off Emma's bloodstained face, Adam thought she looked very different than last he'd seen her. She was fierce and radiant like something wild had awakened within her. Why had he never seen it before? Seeing her now—*like this*—ignited a passion deep within him too and he felt, oddly, like he wanted to devour her. He wanted to bring her to him like she had done to him before. Lips to lips, body to body.

But there was no time.

"Follow me," he whispered, pulling her by the hand.

It took a moment for Emma to respond, but when she did it was with kind eyes. "I will," she whispered back, and the two of them disappeared under the fire's eerie glow.

KoKo scurried up beside them and Emma beamed. She had assumed the worst when the creature hadn't emerged from the ogre's attack. She was clearly hurt, but okay.

The three of them moved low and quick towards the hidden staircase they'd found when they were young, all those years ago.

When they reached it and Adam began to climb, Emma looked back at the carnage they were leaving behind. Piles of broken ogre bodies littered the valley, most torn to pieces. The red slider let out a deep bellow as the remaining ogres stuck it with multiple spears. She couldn't see the green slider. Perhaps it had retreated.

Emma knew that in due time the ogres would kill the red slider and all would be quiet in the valley once more. And while she would be long gone, what had happened to her there would be with her forever. And like so many things she would never understand, why any of it had happened the way it did would remain a mystery.

Anticipating the climb, KoKo jumped on Emma's shoulders and the girl turned back and towards the steep staircase. Adam was nearly halfway to the top of the cliffs now and would soon disappear over the edge. But he would wait for her there. Adam—*her* Adam—would wait for her always.

36

A sharp whistle caught Emma's ears as she reached the top of the cliff. Adam was already high in the branches of the trees, waving at her to join him.

The coolness of the stone felt sharp under her feet as she ran to the tree line and climbed the trunk quickly. Huffing deep breaths, she fought against a terrible exhaustion she'd never known before. As she climbed higher, eventually burying under the canopy of large fronds, the sounds of screams and slider bellows, and snapping spears faded into obscurity.

When she was safely hidden, KoKo jumped from Emma's shoulders and sat on a branch beside her. The way the animal looked up at her, Emma knew she was saying goodbye, but she didn't know why. Then a high-pitched chirping sang from the tree beside them and Emma turned to see a large purple animal watching them intently.

Emma tuned back to KoKo and smiled. "I think he's waiting," she said. KoKo chirped twice and Emma nuzzled her under the chin. "I'll miss you, too," she said and then KoKo bounded off and out of sight.

Emma watched after her until she joined the male and they both disappeared into the dense jungle. Then she continued climbing, meeting Adam who was watching her from higher up.

They continued onwards together, moving over tangled limbs from one tree to the next, not stopping to talk, or express the joy each felt at having found each another again. There was no time for rejoicing. Not when they each felt the cold shadow of death stalking them as they moved, invisible but ever present.

Finally, after what seemed like hours, Emma collapsed into the crook of two massive tree branches. Hugging her knees to her chest, she begged to stop. "I need to rest, Adam, I can't go on," she said in a timid whisper. "Let me sleep here. Just for a while. I'm so tired."

Indeed, they had travelled a long way, past the small waterfall with smooth black stone, but not all the way to the beach. They would have been too exposed there. Instead, they veered north into unexplored territory where the jungle was dark and wild, but there was a safety in the unbridled chaos of nature that suited them. If the ogres gave chase they would be slowed by their thick jungle, and they would be noisy.

Adam looked at Emma and knew she'd reached her limit. But there was something else, too. Her eyes seemed to stare blankly into the distance as though her mind was somewhere else entirely.

"What did they do to you?" he asked, sitting next to her and putting his arm around her shoulders to quell her shivering.

Emma looked into his eyes and found she couldn't explain. Instead, she leaned into him, resting her head on his chest. She felt his heart racing. It was comforting and exciting at the same time.

"I thought I'd lost you forever," Adam continued, burying his cheek into her hair. It smelled of smoke and fresh, night air. He was suddenly intoxicated by her. "I'll never leave you again."

Emma lifted her head and looked into his eyes. Even in the darkness they were deep blue, wide and serious. She had never seen him like this before; the cavalier boy she once knew was like a memory, replaced by someone grown up and capable.

Fronds rustled as the wind picked up. Emma shivered and pressed closer to him and he welcomed her, enjoying the sensation of their bare legs tangling up together, her arm sliding across his belly and pulling him closer.

He lowered his hand down her back lightly until it reached her hips and pulled her closer still. Then, lowering his head, he pressed his cheek to hers.

Sharp electricity pulsed through them when their faces touched, as though they had just completed a circuit long broken. They let their fingers entwine and their bodies glowed and buzzed as a strange sensation surged through them, igniting a hunger each knew they had for the other, but never knew how to express.

Emma stared into Adam's eyes, hoping he could read her thoughts, hoping he felt the same and wanted her as much as she wanted him.

He did. Anticipation took hold of him and he swallowed hard. Emma's eyes, so rich, like gemstones, seemed to invite him in and without thinking he—

A quick breath, like the flutter of a frond struck by a sudden wind storm, slipped from Emma's lips as Adam pressed his lips to hers. She folded herself around him, urgently taking him in. She grabbed the side of his head, letting her fingers burrow into his curly golden hair as they kissed fast and strong. Then, rising up, she swung her bare, right leg over his lap and sat on top of him, careful not to let their lips part for even a moment.

She felt him grow under her and became even more excited, tugging him roughly as his hands wandered down her back and settled onto her thighs. His fingers dug into her supple flesh and another surge of adrenaline shot through her and she let out a delighted squeal as they became one.

The two lovers stayed locked together for the rest of the night in the massive tree, neither wanting to separate ever again. Their hearts pounded in their chests and their skin grew hot and moist as they remained tangled throughout the night. Their animal noises were masked by the swirling sounds of fronds around them as the winds picked up, and shadows danced about like spirits as they drank each other in.

In the middle of it all, Adam looked deeply into Emma's eyes and spoke to her softly. "Do you suppose this means we're married?" he asked, his breath heavy. "I don't have anything to give you like you're suppose to, but my heart is full and this thing we're doing..." his voice trailed off then, words escaping him.

She answered with a nod and pulled him close. It was like they shared the same thought as Emma had also felt they had become joined in a way more meaningful than friend or family.

And for the first time in their lives, they let go of the confusion of being young and alone and allowed nature to lead them into a delirious ecstasy. It was a deliciousness they never imagined existed and, for this night at least, they were no longer Emma and Adam, but two creatures evolving into something new, something as old as the moon itself.

And through it all, the red planet loomed large above, roiling and raging as it watched over them. As it would continue to do until the end of time .

The next morning, hand in hand, Emma and Adam continued through the high trees northward in search of somewhere to start their life over. Neither spoke of the ogre's attempted sacrifice, the rescue by the cliffs, or the pleasures they'd shared the night before.

For four tiresome weeks they travelled together, evading sliders and all new dangers as they pushed through dense jungle towards an unknown destination.

Not once during this time did they set foot on the ground. Instead they relied on the trees to provide all they needed: protection and cover, food in the form of fruit, nuts, and eggs, and, of course, rain water to drink.

It was difficult travel for both them, but ten days in, Emma seemed to bear the brunt of their hardship. First her stomach revolted, rejecting anything she ate or drank. Her fits always started with violent convulsions, her face beading sweat as she retched. Following that, she would need to rest, sometimes even to sleep for some hours.

Adam grew worried about her as the days went on,

and watched over her in the evenings as she slept restlessly, curled against the gnarled trunks, shivering and clutching her stomach in agony.

Despite this, they carried on, often with Adam carrying Emma on his back when he could, ever loyal. And just when it seemed that the inhospitable jungle would never relent and reveal a place they could call home, they emerged from the thick jungle to find a vast expanse of grassland that undulated over low, rolling hills as far as the eye could see.

At odds with the chaos and claustrophobia of the thick jungle, the open landscape was truly a sight to behold. But this striking juxtaposition was far from the most surprising aspect.

Aligned along the edge of the grasslands, towering pillars of crystal rose some twenty stories high, some places even more. Arranged in odd, symmetrical fashion they grew from the earth like columns of bamboo and each was dotted with openings like caves.

Looking up in awe, Adam knew they could offer protection from the elements as well as from anything that wanted to eat them, but he worried about climbing up, particularly with Emma being so ill.

The crystal towers were so unlike anything else they'd seen on the moon that, if they knew to ask such things, Adam and Emma might have wondered whether they'd been set there by some intelligent life form. But nothing seemed so strange to them anymore to elicit strong reactions, and how the spires of glimmering crystal arrived to be where they stood was not as important as how they might suit their immediate needs.

Since the caves were high enough to keep a watch

out for ogres, they both decided it was worth the risk and investigate further. Exploring the spires close up, they found that one of them leaned over more than the others, offering jagged plateaus of smooth crystal they could scale up without much trouble. So after spending the better part of a day helping each other up the side, they finally found themselves standing in front a large cave that glimmered brilliantly when the sun shone against its crystal interior.

Venturing inside, Emma ran her hands along the wall. It was perfectly smooth and had a smoky opacity to it so she couldn't see the outside world through it. It was unlike anything she could have imagined and she felt immediately calm, as though something unseen inside the crystal was having an effect on her.

"Isn't it exactly like the tower in Pin's tales?" she whispered in awe, her voice echoing around them. "The magic tower the Royal Twins lived in, I mean. It's like it's come to life right here on this moon."

Adam looked confused for a moment. Then, slowly, his memory of the stories returned he said, "You're right. I haven't thought about those old stories of Pin's since I was a child."

"Something about his place..." Emma began.

"Feels like home," Adam finished.

Emma came to him then and sunk into his arms. The two of them slid to the ground and hugged each other tightly for a long time, surrounded by the warm glow of glimmering sunlight bouncing around them.

37

For a time, the two lovers lost themselves in the act of making a new home for themselves in the crystal castle.

First they brought all they needed up into the caves that dotted the natural wonder, creating living quarters for themselves in various levels of the spire. For ease, they prepared food and spent their days in the lower caves, while they slept in a cave nearer the top for safety.

The endless grasslands that spread out beyond the towers were ripe with grain, bulbous flowers that dripped sweet nectar, and thorny bushes with plump red and purple berries on them. An assortment of furry animals also called the area home, and had evolved to be small enough to hide from predators. Because of this, the only dangerous animals that visited the grasslands came from the sky above.

And indeed, all variety of flying creatures came to the fields daily to feed, swooping down to try their luck at plucking up a critter that scurried and burrowed under cover of the tall grass.

Once they realized the grassland animals were mostly foragers and grazers, Adam and Emma became comfortable hunting again. Growing far above their heads, the grass provided perfect cover, and they found they could travel undetected for long distances, hunting and trapping small game and bringing it back to their caves late in the afternoons to clean and cook.

While Adam skinned the animals they caught, Emma would arrange bundles of grass for smoking. When the grass dried, she used it to weave skirts to protect their legs and tender parts from insect bites. She also made wide brimmed shade hats to protect them from the hot daytime sun. They laughed and pointed at each other when they tried them on. Adam pretended to be the captain of a transport ship, bowing and standing at attention. They fell into each other, wheezing and sputtering with laughter. After everything they'd been through it felt good to laugh again.

Despite their good fortune, their new life was a struggle for Emma at first. Still suffering from stomach pains, she was often sick after eating.

Adam was worried at first, but after two weeks her sickness seemed to fade until she said she felt normal again, and they retuned to sharing their bodies in all manner of ways that were pure and good and, for the first time in their young lives, made them feel like natural creatures on the moon and not visitors. In these times they were as wild and free as the animals that lived, roamed, and died in the jungles and vast ocean.

Life for Adam was near perfect. Emma was back, and had brought paradise back with her. They had found a new home and a wonderful rhythm with each other. They never bickered like children anymore, and he found he was more in tune with her wants and desires than he'd ever been before.

Still, he was struck by a nagging fear. And the more he felt he had everything he wanted, the more he worried about keep it all. He knew he needed to control of their environment at all times if he wanted to keep everything as it was.

To that end, Adam kept a vigilant watch from the top-most cave of the crystal castle, which he made their lookout. Four times each day, he ventured up to scan the horizon, looking for any sign of ogres marching through the jungle behind them, or large animals that could catch them unawares in the grasslands in front. And every day his watch was met with nothing but the occasional bulbous slider hunting far in the distance, or not-bird flock breaking above the tree line to undertake their daily dance.

He didn't know why sliders and ogres never seemed to cross into the vast grasslands but, as the weeks wore on, he found he became more confident that they had found themselves someplace free of danger.

But even at his most confident, Adam couldn't shake the nagging feeling that Emma had been forever changed by the ogres at the cliffs. Oh, she had emerged radiant to him. More radiant than he could express. Every smile of hers was a paradise, and when they kissed, her eyes shined brighter than the sun in the day and the stars at night. But she had grown quieter too, and lived an internal life he couldn't understand. She worried and fussed more than he'd known her to do before, fretting about the state of their surroundings and keeping everything clean.

Stranger still, since neither had ever known shame, he didn't understand why she had started hiding her body from him.

It started when Adam had noticed her changing. He poked her and told her she was getting lumpy. Even though she looked wonderful to his eyes, she became upset, and disappeared to a different cave to spend the night alone. After that, Adam refused to comment on the changes to her body, even as they grew more apparent in the following weeks.

And the more she changed, Emma found she couldn't hunt or forage for long periods of time anymore. She became too exhausted and needed to sleep, and soon Adam was left alone each day to sweep the plains for game and supplies.

One day, when he returned home full of the thrill of a successful hunt, Adam heard sobbing from inside the cave above him. Fearing for Emma's safety, he quickened his pace as he climbed. When he reached the cave, he pulled himself up and saw Emma sitting against the back wall. She had covered herself in grass blankets and was distraught, her eyes red with tears and worry.

Adam ran to her as soon as he saw her, kneeling next to her and running his fingers through her hair to comfort her. "What's happened?" he asked. "Are you hurt?"

Emma looked at him hopelessly, her face bursting with concern. After a moment, all her silent worry exploded and she cried, "Oh, Adam! They did something horrible to me!"

Adam cradled her, letting her rest her head on his chest as she continued.

"What are you saying?" he whispered close to her ear.

"They gave me poison," she said. "That witch... She forced me to drink something and now..." Emma's voice trailed off.

"Now what?" said Adam.

Emma looked at him with red, wet eyes. Then grabbing her grass coverings, she moved them off her body slowly, revealing her stomach, round and distended. "I don't know what's happening to me. Am I dying, Adam? I don't want to die."

Overcome with emotion, Emma buried her face into Adam's chest. He held her tightly and said, "I don't know. I thought I saved you. I thought I had you back. Maybe it was too late. I don't want you to die, Emma. Please don't leave me here all alone. I don't think I could bear it."

After that they held each other closely and cried as the sun set, and the glimmering cave became dark all around them. They fell asleep that way, hopeful their dreams would take them away from their troubles for a time. Maybe even forever.

38

As weeks became months, Adam sensed that Emma's strange illness was worsening.

Though she rarely complained, she had grown pale and endured restless nights, often rising to pace the cave or venture out into the warm night to wander the grasslands. She said it calmed her mind, so Adam thought it better not to dissuade her.

Her stomach had grown somewhat larger since the day she'd shown it to him but she kept it hidden from him under grass coverings as much as she could. He could tell it bothered her but, again, chose to remain silent, not wanting to cause her further stress than she could handle.

Sometimes, while she sat stringing shards of crystals along thin vine necklaces, or mended ripped sunhats, Adam swore he saw a change in her face at times, as though something had stolen her thoughts. She would press her hand to her belly gently and breath a deep breath, almost as though she was communing with something inside of her.

Whenever he asked about it, she would only smile dismissively and go back to her task, as though nothing at all had occurred.

One morning, when the sun was hidden behind darkening clouds, Adam called for Emma to join him on a hunt. She smiled sadly and replied she would not be joining him as she usually did. She claimed she was tired and, anyhow, it looked as though it would rain again. The rainy season was upon them now and she didn't want to get wet when the weather could turn hostile at a moment's notice.

When all his protests were sufficiently rebuked, he set about packing up his things without a second thought.

Emma waved to him as he strapped his spear to his back and set his newly mended hat on top of his head. If it did rain, its wide brim would provide good cover and held his vision. She didn't get up from her spot against the wall as she waved goodbye, a thin smile crossing her face.

He waved back and said, "I'll be home before nightfall," before sliding out of sight and climbing down the crystal spire to the grasslands below.

When he reached the ground, Adam set to his usual routine. First he scanned the jungle behind them for any dangerous movement. This morning, like most others, it seemed clear. Following that, he stepped into the grass, the tall stalks enveloping him until he was completely surrounded.

As he waded further, he was surprised to discover that all new vegetation had burst and bloomed into a riot since the day before. Colorful seed pods had opened to reveal long pink tendrils that waved from their hard shells. The ground littered with thousands of them created a strange and beautiful sight to behold.

A drop of water tapped against the brim of his hat and he looked up to see rain had starting falling. He knew then the change in landscape was most likely due to the oncoming of the rainy season. Dormant life in the usually arid grasslands was awakening in anticipation of receiving new moisture needed to sustain itself for another season.

Moving on, he noticed the ground becoming soggier as it grew wet. Soon it would become difficult to walk through, so he picked up his pace. Luckily, he had committed much of the best hunting grounds to memory, so he didn't anticipate needing to be out in the rain for long.

His first spot was a large mound covered in funny holes that he and Emma had found. Upon inspection, they learned the holes were the tunnels of all the various burrowing animals, intersecting as though they'd all agreed on the location somehow. Each night he set traps around the spot and usually found them full with various animals each morning, some already dead, some struggling to life.

Following his work here, he planned to set up quietly by the large watering hole in the center of the grasslands where larger three-legged beasts often appeared to drink out of view of sliders or other dangerous blue moon predators. These were harder to kill, but with a good strike of his spear he'd been able to bring one down before. The meat had lasted them for more than a week before it spoiled. If he could get one now, it would mean he wouldn't need to leave Emma as much and avoid the rains.

Won't Emma be pleased when I come back with a tripper? he thought.

They called them trippers because of the way they always seemed to trip over their long legs when they got startled and tied to run away. They were funny creatures, too tall for their own good. He and Emma had had a good laugh one day, whispering that nature must have made them as a joke.

Thinking of Emma made Adam smile as he finished checking the traps by the large mound of earth. And even though he only found one long nosed digger with a trip vine wound tightly around its neck, he didn't let the small bounty dampen his spirits. He was cold and already starting to get hungry, but the thought of Emma back in the crystal cave waiting for him with a fire going warmed him enough to keep moving.

After tying the digger around his waist, Adam trudged onwards through the muddy ground towards the watering hole. If it wasn't for the lack of game in the traps, he may have turned back. But he had his heart set on killing a tripper and was determined to get one.

Lighting flashed overhead as he continued through the tall grass. He heard the sharp cracking of a tree trunk and knew it had been struck by electricity somewhere far away. It was something he'd seen many times in the rainy seasons— an explosion overhead as the top of a tree caught fire from a lightning strike. A moment later thunder crashed and a clouds opened up, letting loose a rainstorm that pounded the world around him.

He cursed and thought about turning back, but he was so close to the watering hole it would be a shame not to see what opportunities awaited him there.

As he approached the area, he got on his belly and slid through the mud to avoid being seen. Trippers were tall and their long necks could peer overtop of the grass and find predators. The closer to the ground you got the easier it was to sneak up on them undetected.

Parting the grass and looking through to the watering hole, he saw two trippers dipping their snouts under the surface of the water. One was larger than the other and Adam guessed it was a mother and her child. They were right in front of him and so focused on drinking that he felt confident they hadn't heard him approach. Usually very alert, their hearing was likely impaired by the heavy rainfall. Perhaps the storm was a blessing after all.

Moving his hand to the butt of his spear, Adam slowly removed it from its vine holster on his back. Then, bringing it down along his side, he clasped it tightly in the center and got ready to attack.

First he removed his hat and placing it carefully beside him. Then, moving achingly slow, he brought himself to a crouch position which would allow him to spring forward quickly.

His heart pounded in anticipation and he wiped water from his brow and eyes. He licked his lips and leaned forward onto the balls of his feet.

He was ready.

A screech from above brought everything to chaos. A large flying predator—a creature Adam had never seen before that looked more like a lizard than a bird—attacked from above, trying to snatch the smaller tripper up with its sharp claws. The tripper squealed and kicked its legs wildly as the lizard bird dug its talons into its back.

Driven by instinct, the larger tripper bounded away into the grass, leaving the smaller one to fend for itself. If Adam didn't act fast, both would be gone and he would be left empty handed.

Springing into action, he lunged from the grass and high into the air towards the watering hole. Bringing his arm back and focusing all his energy into his shoulder, he twisted and threw his spear up at the lizard bird, hoping to bring it down before it could fly away with the tripper.

The bird screeched and beat its heavy wings, angling its body to move out of the way. Water splashed off its glistening scales and its huge marbled eyeball spun widely in its socket as it twisted to avoid Adam's attack. But it was too slow. Adam's long spear pierced the leathery underside of its wing, piercing it and then plunging into the monsters' fleshy underbelly. It screeched horribly, folding its wings around its body and spiraling to the muddy ground below.

Adam pounced quickly, jumping onto the animal and ripping the spear from its body. The lizard bird flailed wildly and swung its sharp beak towards him, snapping and screeching. But Adam was faster and he struck the thing again, pounding the spear into its neck and twisting it with a deafening hunter's scream that broke through the thunderous rainstorm.

The creature's head fell to the ground and Adam watched the light of life leave its eyes before turning his attention to the tripper that was trying to hobble away through the muddy ground. It was badly injured and would soon die. Adam felt bad for it suddenly. He loved the thrill of the hunt, but hated to see an animal suffer. He had come to understand the role that death played in the cycle of life on the moon, something Pin had tried to teach him when he was young.

Striding towards it, he raised his spear to put it out of its misery. A quick death was the best he could offer the animal. And to become food was not only inevitable for any creature living on the blue moon, it was preferable to a useless death caused by starvation or accidental injury.

The tripper made a sad honking sound as its tall legs sunk deeper into the mud. Then Adam struck it through the back of the head with his spear and the chaos of the hunt was over as quickly as it had begun.

Adam heaved a deep breath then looked about. Standing between his two kills, he was faced with a dilemma. Unable to carry both back to the crystal caves, he would need to decide between taking the larger lizard bird or the smaller tripper. The smaller tripper wouldn't feed them for long, whereas the lizard thing looked to be about four times its size.

Stepping lightly over the mud so as not to get stuck, Adam picked his hat up off the ground where he'd left it before the attack. Shaking the water from it, he put it back on and weighed his options. Then he made his decision. He would drag the lizard bird back to the tower.

Bending down, Adam tore handfuls of thick grass from the roots and piled them up around him. Then, sitting down, he began the arduous task of winding them all together and tying the ends to form lengths of rope. It took a long time to make enough for his purposed, but he had time. He'd promised Emma he's be back by nightfall and it was just past midday.

It was more important to ensure he made the ropes strong enough than to rush back home. Better to come home late with dinner in hand than on time and empty handed.

When he felt he'd made his ropes long and strong enough, he bundled them up and moved back to the watering hole where his kill was waiting to be packaged. No other animals had visited the area since his attack, which was strange, but he expected eyes were watching him from the surrounding grass just waiting for him to leave.

When he reached the animal, he folded each of its long wings over its body and began to tie them down. When that was done, he grabbed the hind legs and turned the beast around so he could pull it backwards through the grass. And after tying one length of grassy rope to each of the legs, he roped another around his own waist and cinched it like a belt. He'd learned that it was easier to attach larger prey to the core of his body to drag them long distances rather than relying on the muscles in his arms.

Satisfied that he had the creature packaged in a way that would make it easy to get home, he fixed his spear to his back and took his first step toward home.

The lizard creature was heavy, but it was the mud that caused Adam the most trouble as he began the journey home. It seemed to be getting deeper by the second, and water was beginning to settle on top, trapping his feet as he trudged forward. He did his best to wade through the shallow lake that was forming, but as the rain continued to alter the environment around him, a dark realization struck him. He suddenly knew why the grasslands were so rarely visited by larger jungle predators. They had learned to avoid it because it wasn't grassland at all, but dangerous swamp—a massive bog that only spent the last days of the hot seasons as he and Emma had found it.

Adam's heart pounded in his chest as he felt his feet sinking deeper with every step. He could see the towers at the edge of the swamp in the distance now, but he was still hours away from reaching them.

Thunder crashed and he swallowed deeply. He needed to hurry but, stepping forward, he found he couldn't move anymore.

Looking back, he watched in horror as the lizard creature he was dragging behind him began to sink into the bog.

I shouldn't have stopped moving! he thought, his mind reeling.

Pulling the ropes with all his strength, Adam tried to lift the creature out of the mud and bring it forward, but it was impossible. Finally, a sharp sucking sound erupted as the creature disappeared under the surface and Adam cursed when he realized it was too late. His game was gone.

He went to untie the knot around his waist when he was forced forward suddenly and fell with a sickening *slap* onto his stomach in the mud. He lifted his head and wiped the mud from his eyes. Then his stomach lurched as he was dragged helplessly through the mud towards the stop where the bog was swallowing the creature and him down with it! He had to hurry.

Rolling onto his back Adam tried frantically to untie the knot around his waist. If he couldn't get loose soon, he would be pulled under the mud and unable to work the knot at all. But the grass had tightened in the wet and cold so his attempts were useless.

He screamed and thrashed desperately as the bog continued to pull him towards the spot where the lizard had disappeared. He grabbed onto stalks of grass as they passed by but his wet, muddy hands couldn't find a tight enough grip and he kept sliding forward.

Reaching for his spear, he managed to pull it from its sheath and drive it into the ground like a stake. Using the weight of his body, he pushed it deeper into the mud and held on for dear life. He felt the tugging of the ropes around his waist as the creature sunk deeper into the mud, but the stake held firm.

His mind raced as he tried to come up with a plan to free himself from his predicament. If he let go, he would be pulled away from the spear and sink with the creature he was tied to. If he waited too long, he had no doubt the bog would find a way to swallow him anyway. He thought about using his teeth to bite through the grass rope that connected him to the lizard, but there wasn't enough slack to raise the rope to his mouth. He was truly stuck, with little choice left but wait for the bog to take him.

Water bubbled violently all around him suddenly and he watched in astonishment as *something* seismic began to happen. He felt vibrations, small at first, but that grew to waving tremors that threw him back and forth as he struggled to keep his grip on the spear. He screamed out, then starred in astonishment as, all around him, blasts of water erupted and mud flew into the air like multiple bombs where exploding from somewhere under the surface.

What the hell was happening?

He heard the monsters before he saw them. A deep moaning sound rumbled across the entire bog before thick limbs pulled lean, muscular bodies up from the muck.

With no eyes to see and gaping mouths full of yellow teeth, the massive subterranean creatures were rising from the depths of the earth at the coming of the rainy season. These were the swampland's apex predators, emerging to eat and breed in the rainy months and retiring back underground at their end. And Adam was just unlucky enough to find himself in the middle of their awakening.

Unable to move, he shut his eyes and pressed himself to the mud in the hopes of remaining unnoticed as more of the large creatures rose around him. Blind, they mostly stayed still, waiting for the water to rise higher around them and give them cover to hunt.

A few more explosions erupted in the distance as more creatures rose and he wondered in vein what would become of him once the water rose so high he would have to let go of his spear.

Then, without warning, he was thrust violently into the air and swinging from the rope around his waist ten feet off the ground, his spear still in hand. Flailing to see what had happened, he saw that one of the bog monsters had found the lizard under the mud and pulled it free, Adam along with it.

He heard bones crunch as the bog monster took a bite and tore a leg off his game. Adam tried not to yell out, knowing the bog monster couldn't see him, but adrenaline shot through him as he panicked. Another bite and the bog monster's teeth sliced through the grass ropes Adam had tied around the lizard's legs, letting Adam fall back to the swamp, free from his bonds but still in mortal danger.

Staying low, he tried to wade away through the water, but his movements immediately caught the attention of another bog monster that barreled towards him, splashing and sniffing grotesquely through a single nostril in the center of its eyeless head.

Adam stopped moving and floated as still as he could. Hi heart pounded as the bog monster walked right over him, sniffing his body. He shut his eyes, too scared to look.

Something nudged him and he rolled onto his side. The monster was right next to him, snorting grotesquely and trying to find something that smelled like food. Maybe it was because Adam kept still, or maybe it was because he was covered in so much mud, but a moment later the bog monster stepped over him and moved away in another direction.

Adam kept dead still as more of the subterranean creatures emerged from the mud and swam around him. The water was growing ever higher and his mind raced. If he didn't get away soon he would find himself trapped in the middle of the giant swamp with no way out.

Reaching his hands deep into the water, he tried to gauge if he could still reach the muddy bottom. When he found he could, he pressed his fingers into the mud and inched himself forward, gliding smoothly and silently along the top of the rising water, careful not to drift any faster than a piece of flotsam to avoid further detection.

39

Once he was away from the watering hole and surrounded by the tall grass again, Adam found he could move through the water more quickly.

The grunts and bellows of the bog monsters soon became a distant din, but he knew if he didn't find the end of the swamplands, the entire place would be crawling with them and he would be trapped.

After a while, the water became so high that he could no longer feel the bottom and the tall grass was no more than mere inches above the waterline.

So this is why it grew so tall, he thought as he stopped to look at the horizon. *The grass needs to get above the surface of the water.*

Looking out over the top of the grass he could see the crystal towers were closer. He'd been gone so long that the sun had disappearing behind the storm clouds and it was dark. Soon it would be pitch black and he wouldn't be able to see his destination.

He wondered if Emma was beginning to worry

about him. He'd promised her he'd be back before dark and it would be much longer than that by the time he did. And, to make matters worse, he'd be returning empty handed.

In all their time spent growing up next to the ocean, Adam and Emma had become strong swimmers and, tonight especially, Adam thanked the red planet above that he was up for the task of swimming the whole way home. The muscles in his arms were beginning to cramp as he paddled through the thick swamp, but he would make it. And at least he didn't get stuck in the mud.

After about an hour of paddling, the base of the spires revealed themselves through the parting grass. He heaved a deep sigh of relief at the sight. His arms were beginning to ache and his legs had long stopped kicking.

He floating among the massive columns of towering spires until he recognized the one leaning over that he and Emma had made into the their home these past few months.

His heart was heavy as he pulled himself from the water and slid onto the first ledge of the tower. After all they'd been through, they would need to move again. Was there no part of the moon they could call home? Would they never find a place of comfort and contentment?

Something bobbing in the water caught his eye then and he stuck his hand under the surface to fish it out. When his fingers touched it, he grasped it and pulled it from the water. It was small enough to fit in his hand and seemed handmade in its unnatural rectangular shape. He wiped a layer of mud from its top, curious to examine what the strange thing was.

But when the top was finally revealed, he recognized it straight away and a sharp worry struck him. It was Emma's box, her treasure that had been with her since she was a child.

Adam opened it. It was full of water, the mechanism inside broken. Adam knew the hologram of Emma's mother would never appear again.

She would *never* have let it tumble down the tower like this unless… If something was wrong, he needed to get to her.

Adam dropped the box back into the water and let it sink below the surface. It was a sad end to something he knew Emma loved, but he couldn't worry about it now.

He started to climb up the tower, but no sooner had he taken his first step towards their cave than a familiar bellow met his ears. His heart sank at the sound.

It couldn't be!

But, sure enough, when he looked up, he saw it—a bog monster scaling the tower. He watched it disappear into one of the many crystal caves and cried out helplessly. He was too late! Emma would be caught and there was nothing he could do!

He saw another monster then, and another, and realized that the entire tower was swarming with them. *All* the towers along the edge of the grasslands were alive with the movement of those wretched beasts, burrowing into the crystal and… were they *building* more of them? Like termites building grotesque mounds, or bees constructing geometric hives, Adam realized that these monsters must have *created* the towers for some horrible use.

With no choice but to slide back down and slip

into the water, Adam did just that, and began to float away from the swamp and back towards the jungle. There was nowhere else he could think to go.

He looked up at the cave as rain poured around him, tears hiding among the drops. He prayed to the red planet that Emma had made it out alive, but, in her ill condition, how could she have made it all on her own?

Finally, after more time drifting in the water, Adam reached the edge of the swamp and pulled himself from the water. Without giving himself a moment to recover, he crawled as quickly as he could towards the tree line. He was exhausted and desperate to find somewhere to hide.

When he'd finally passed into the dense forest, he crawled underneath a thick bramble bush. He ignored the pain of the sharp thorns that scraped against his bare flesh as he pressed himself to the ground and slid underneath it. They might hurt, but the thorns would provide the safety he needed for the remainder of the rainy night.

He lay under the bush for a long while, looking out at the crystal spires in the distance. Soon they had become overwhelmed with a frenzy bog monsters.

Why does everything beautiful turn to ruin? he lamented as the rain turned from a hard downpour to a soft, continuous drizzle.

The world seemed to quiet as the rain let up and, for the first time, he could hear the jungle around him through the downpour again. But he wasn't calmed.

Faced with a renewed feeling of the larger world around him, Adam was struck by a dark feeling of loneliness. *How am I to live alone on this moon now?* he thought hopelessly. The thought angered him suddenly. *I won't do it! I'd sooner die! I'll throw myself from the cliffs and let my body dash among the rock below!*

His thoughts were disturbed by a strange sound that didn't belong among the others. It was a sound he had never heard before in all his time on the jungle moon and it caught his attention in a way that none before it had. It was a high-pitched whining that danced on the wind, echoing through the trees as it floated lightly all around him.

For some reason the sound didn't frighten him. He felt drawn to it, almost like it was a language without words that spoke directly to his heart and mind.

Despite protests from his angry muscles demanding that he stay where he was and rest, Adam was compelled to find the source of the whimpering. And so, digging himself out from under the sharp brambles, he limped deeper into the jungle, following the sound in a daze.

Perhaps my mind has cracked? he thought dreamily as he trudged on. *Perhaps I'm dead already and will walk forever and ever. Wouldn't that be funny?*

His languid, dreamy thoughts evaporated a moment later when another sound caught his ears. His heart burst to hear it, for it was a sound he'd come to recognize and love. A light humming that could bring calm to the most restless of hearts and easy the most worried mind. And only one creature was capable of making it.

Emma.

He stumbled through the jungle, frantically searching for the source of the angelic singing. He didn't care that thorns tore his flesh and thick roots tripped him up. If Emma was out there he needed to find her. He was so determined he didn't even notice that the first sound he'd heard—the mysterious whining—had stopped altogether.

He let the humming guide him.

"Emma!" he called, throwing caution to the wind as he trudged through the light drizzle. The rain had mostly abated, and the thick canopy of fronds above his head kept him relatively dry. But a light sprinkling still chilled him to the bone and he had started to shiver uncontrollably.

"Emma! Where are you?"

The humming grew louder until, rounding the trunk of a giant red gum tree, he finally saw Emma curled up against it, fronds balancing on branches above her for rain cover. She was looking down, humming softly and cradling something bundled in fronds in her lap.

She looked up when she noticed him coming closer and Adam could see her eyes were bloodshot and wild. All color was drained from her face and she looked sickly.

He was so shocked to see she'd escaped the awakening of the bog monsters that he slid in beside her without saying a word.

She kept humming and looked back down at the bundle in her lap. When Adam looked at it, he was surprised to see it move. Was it an animal? Had KoKo returned? Was she hurt?

Emma noticed him looking and removed a small fold of frond from the top of the bundle. Adam's eyes went wide with confusion. Underneath the covering was a human baby. He leaned closer. The baby was asleep and it cooed lightly and extended its fingers at the sudden feeling of the cold air on its skin.

"Where did it come from?" Adam asked, taking a closer look.

"I... I found it," Emma answered quietly.

"But... how? Was it just here?"

Emma didn't answer. Instead she covered the baby up and held it to her breast tightly. "Put your arms around us," she said to Adam, and he did.

Wrapping his arm around her shoulder, he let her and the baby snuggle against his bare chest. He began to warm up immediately and a happy glow filled his insides despite their dangerous predicament. He didn't know where they would go, or how they would survive, but the moon hadn't found a way to separate them yet. There was something good in that at least.

He looked down at Emma lying against him, the baby wrapped in her arms. "Hey, what's this?" Adam said. "There's something attached to the baby's tummy. Let me look at it—"

"Don't you dare touch it," Emma said with a start. She was suddenly fierce and protective, color rushing back into her cheeks.

Adam huffed and rested his head against the tree. He was too tired to argue. They could examine the child in the morning.

Emma fell against him again, her whole body relaxing. "You were away so long," she said dreamily as she began to drift off to sleep again.

"I'm sorry," he said. "I tried to come home sooner."

"Home..." Emma repeated.

"We can't go back." Adam's voice was shaking. "Our home is lost. I'm so sorry, Emma."

"Mmmmm... You lost your hat," she replied,

half awake, half in a dream.

He touched his head. He hadn't noticed the hat had fallen off somewhere in the swamp. "I guess I did. I'm sorry about that, too."

Emma's breathing grew heavy and regular as she finally drifted into a deep sleep, leaving Adam alone to consider the mess they were in. With no home and this new baby to care for, they would need to find somewhere to escape the rain by the next day, or he had no doubt they would all suffer grave illness.

Water pelted off the fronds above their heads as the rain picked up. Adam peered into the night to keep watch.

He wished they'd started a fire, but it was too late now, too wet. Suddenly, his eyes began to feel heavy. Despite wanting to stay awake to watch over Emma and the child, he needed sleep, and his mind would take it with or without his consent.

40

For a while, Adam lived in a dark world between dreams and reality where his mind played terrible tricks on him as he drifted in and out of consciousness.

One moment he was lying against the trunk of a red gum tree, starring into the dark jungle, and the next he was standing atop a towering crystal spire, fighting off a thousand bog monsters all at once as they swiped at him from below. When one of their claws caught hold of him, it broke his flesh and threw him from the tower.

He screamed as he fell towards the swamp below, flailing his arms helplessly. But as he grew closer to the ground, he saw a figure standing, arms held open as though waiting for catch him. It was Emma. She was looking up at him with angelic eyes and expression of pity across her face. When he fell into her, they became one and he heard her whisper something to him but couldn't make out the words.

Danger. Wake up.

Adam awoke with a start, his heart pounding. It was the middle of the night, the time when the jungle was at its darkest. He saw that Emma was awake also, but the serene expression on her face had turned to distress and her eyes burned with an intense fear. He looked around wildly but saw nothing. Then he heard a sound. It was a loud *thrashing* that reminded him of something. Something he'd heard somewhere before a long time ago.

"It's *them*," Emma said, in a screaming whisper. "The ogres have come back for me. They want the baby."

Adam couldn't argue. The *thrashing* in the dark jungle sounded just like the horde breaking through the brush. He could almost see them slicing vines and branches as they trudged forward, leaving a trail of trampled jungle in their wake.

The sound grew louder with every second that passed and he pulled Emma and the baby in closer saying, "Stay still. Keep quiet. It's so dark they'll pass us by. As long as we're silent, they'll miss us."

"They won't," said Emma. "They'll find us. They'll take our baby like they took that little one at the waterfall." Adam looked curiously ay her as she continued. "They'll rip it right from my arms and we'll never see it again."

"They won't," Adam said, trying to calm her. "They won't find us. And if they do we'll run. We'll fight if we have to."

Thrash Thrash

"It won't be enough," Emma pleaded. "Oh, Adam, don't you see? I'd sooner die than have them take me again. Promise me you'll do it, Adam! Promise you'll kill us all if they find us."

Adam looked at her in shock. "No... I couldn't," he started. "That's not how our life ends here. It can't be. What's it all been for then? What's it all been about?"

Emma's eyes were wide and hopeless and tears streamed down her face. She was overcome. "You have to. There's no other way."

Thrash Thrash

They were getting closer.

The baby woke and started to wail. Its thin cries filled the quiet night and both he and Emma became frantic. They needed to silence it, or hiding from the ogres would be impossible!

"What's wrong with it? Why is it doing that?"

"I don't know," Emma said and unfolded the frond. She pressed her hand over the child's mouth, trying to muffle its cries but the baby was stronger than she'd expected and it pulled its face out from under her palm and screamed even louder. She picked it up and held it to her chest tightly, but careful not to smoother it.

"Maybe it's hungry," Adam said and he rooted around the jungle floor hoping to find a piece of fruit or a nut that may have come from above.

Thrash Thrash

Adam pulled at his hair in frustration. That sound. It was taunting him, trying to drive him mad!

His hands touched something familiar then and he looked down to see a clump of silver-streaked rocks al around the tree. Digging his hands into the dirt, he began pulling out as many rock nuts as he could find, piling them next to the trunk.

When he was done, he had ten or twelve, not than he'd ever found in one place before. He looked at

Emma and shook his head in frustration. "This is all that's here."

"It can't eat those!" she said harshly. "They'll turn it mad. It needs something better."

She winced suddenly and her eyes went wide as though something sharp had poked her. "Ouch!" she said. "It bit me!"

"Here, let me take it from you," Adam said, reaching to grab hold of the baby.

"No, wait. It's... doing something." The baby was silent again, the only sound a quiet suckling that only they could here. "I think it's found what it likes to eat," said Emma. "Just leave it alone now."

Adam's face scrunched in confusion and concern. The baby confounded him, but he was glad it had finally quieted.

Thrash Thrash

The horde sounded like it was right on top of them. Another moment and it would emerge from the underbrush and be on them. He thought he could already see them in the shadows, his mind conjuring outlines of misshapen, bent figures with long strong limbs swaggering towards them in the darkness.

Perhaps Emma was right. Perhaps there was no point living in a world that refused to welcome them. If at every turn they were to be cast out, chased down and attacked, made to suffer for nothing other than existing, then maybe life wasn't worth living after all.

He didn't know if he did it out of a desire to protect or fulfill Emma's final request of him, but Adam reached behind his back and pulled his spear from its sheath. He set a strong grip around it and looked at Emma holding the baby to her breast.

Thrash Thrash

Slowly, Adam used the butt of his spear to pound the rock nuts, breaking them from their hard shells. When he was done, he passed five to Emma and told her to eat them.

She hesitated, but a look of understanding came to her face and she took them into her hands. Crying, she began to eat, the sweet substance underneath tasting bitter this time.

Adam finished his portion and turned back towards the jungle. The sound was louder and he could see shrubs moving.

His body came alive with the feeling of prickles all over his body as the rock nuts did their work on him. His mind began to settle and a upsetting grin came to his face.

Adam turned and pointed the sharp end of his spear towards Emma and peered back into the darkness to watch. Any moment now, the ogres would emerge in front of them. When they did he would be ready to end it all.

Hands shaking, he turned back towards Emma. She was looking down, intoxicated by the rock nuts now, humming to the baby again as it drank from her breast. She was so exhausted and focused she barely seemed to notice what was at stake. What was about to happen.

Tears came to his eyes as he watched her fuss and help the child. How could he do this? How could he harm something he loved so much.

Loved.

He moved the tip of the spear away from Emma. Watching them both, he saw past his fear to a future that was joyous and good. It was a future that was far off to be sure, but one where they were both happy.

It was a future so abstract it was like a dream. But he knew in his soul it was a future worth fighting for.

Thrash Thrash

Determination took him and he wiped his tears and set his mouth in a line. Then he steadied his shaking hands and turned his spear towards the dark jungle in front of them, towards the approaching horde.

Thrash Thrash

He balanced on the balls of his feet, ready to attack.

Thrash Thrash

If they wanted Emma and the baby they would need to deal with him first.

Thrash Thrash

Here they come!

A mass of thick brush and vines exploded as something cut through the jungle and came at them.

"Stay back, Emma!" yelled Adam as he shot to his feet.

Charging at full speed through the dark, he let a blood curdling war cry ring through the night and didn't stop until the sharp end of his spear dug into something soft and fleshy.

A shadowy figure screamed out in pain and dropped to the ground. Adam screamed, ripped his spear out of it and, jumping back, reset the point forward, ready for another attack.

He saw another large figure step forward and cried out again, ready to attack, when a blinding white light flooded the jungle. Raising his arms to protect his eyes, Adam dropped his spear and stumbled back a few steps before tripping on a gnarled root. He hit the wet jungle ground with a sickening plop, losing his balance and slipping onto his back. He groped blindly for his spear, but it was out of reach. Trying to rise to his feet, he slipped again and could do nothing but lie down, lamely trying to see what was happening.

Voices grew around him, inaudible at first, speaking all at once, until a single yell cut through the din.

"Tipton's down!" a voice called over the panic. "Let's get a med kit here!"

"Bring me a patch!" another voice answered. "I'm okay, but my suit's punctured! Damn savage tore a hole right through it!"

As Adam's eyes began to adjust, he looked around wildly, trying to see where the voices were coming from. Finally, four large figures stepped forward and bent over him. When they did, bright spotlights blinded him all over again and all he could make out were long implements in their hands that looked like spears. He covered his face in anticipation of an attack.

"Captain!" one of the figures called when they saw him. "You're not going to believe this!"

"What is it, corporal?"

A fifth figure appeared, joining the others in inspecting the thin, frightened boy at their feet covered with mud and looking up at them with wild, animal eyes.

"He's human! How do you figure it, Captain?"

The one they called Captain clicked off his lantern and bent down so Adam could finally see him clearly. His weary, bearded face peered quizzically at him from behind the smudged visor of his helmet.

"It... It can't be," he started to say before looking past Adam to Emma who was still huddled against the trunk of the gum tree, holding the feeding baby to her chest.

He clicked his lantern back on, illuminating a spotlight around her. She recoiled and turned her face away and the baby began to cry.

The captain rose slowly and stepped towards the girl slowly. "My god..." he whispered, quickening his pace. "Emma, is that really you?"

Emma looked back towards the strange newcomer who knew her name. He knelt in front of her and touched her arm lightly, unsure if he should. Unsure if the young woman in front of him was real at all.

Studying his face behind the visor for a moment she found she began to recognize it.

"Father?" she said, her voice slurring and cracked.

"Emma. My god, what's wrong with you? What's wrong with your eyes?"

"Father!" she cried, grabbing his suit and pulling at it awkwardly. "I'm sorry! I'm sorry I left you! Pin said you were dead!"

"No, Emma. Stop. It's me who should be sorry. I should have never let you out of my sight. But I've found you now." For the first time, Captain LaFarge noticed the baby in Emma's arms and called out to the others. "There's a baby here! Call Dr. Evans. Tell him we have three for the med bay. Tell him she appears to be on some kind of drug as well."

"On it, Captain," came the reply. "It looks like they're both high as the stars."

Lifting her up, Captain LaFarge moved back to where the others had already helped Adam to his feet and were inspecting him and providing some medical attention.

Then, with Emma and the baby in his arms, he

began his long walk back to the cliffs, and the valley beyond, where the probe's beacon had led them, and his team were currently setting up camp.

"I don't know how you two managed it, but you've done it, Emma. You've survived. And you've found us all a new home. This moon will save us all."

When Emma didn't answer he looked down to see his daughter—thin and wild, more animal now than girl—had passed out in his arms.

Captain LaFarge set his mouth in hard line as he forged ahead through the thick jungle. She and Adam were safe now. And there was much to be done.

A new dawn was upon them, a child had been born. The first outside of lab in more than fifty years. The revelation changed everything. What had caused it? Was it the return to a natural world? Did the moon hold medical properties yet to be discovered?

Lafarge looked up at the raging red gas giant in the sky and wondered fleetingly if all this was the doing of some ancient being. Was it meant to be? Was it the conclusion of a plan set long ago, before time itself?

Perhaps there was meaning to the chaos of life after all. Either way, he was sure that this was only the beginning of a story with no end.

Don't Miss

NEW HORIZONS

Another thrilling *StoryFix Media* adventure

In the first part of Christopher Webster's Enrollment Trilogy, a troubled teen is forced to survive off-the-grid when he is sent to a wilderness "brat camp" that is mysteriously free of adults.

> *"A new series of Young Adult stories I'm sure will prove very popular"* – Set the Tape

Available Now in Paperback and Kindle eBook

Prologue

When you're trapped in a hole in the middle of the woods you have a lot of time to think about your life and all the stupid shit you did to put yourself there.

You might think a 15-year-old boy from the suburbs wouldn't have much life to look back on but you'd be surprised how much of it floods in when you're hungry, exhausted and sitting in the dark ten feet below ground level. Fifteen years is apparently more than enough time for Old Man Karma to show up and dump a truck-load of bad memories on you so you're neck deep in regret. *That's right, just back it up, pal. You can dump 'em all right here in this hole. Don't worry about the kid down there. Nobody'll miss him.*

I keep hearing rustling above me. There are things moving through the leaves. I know it's probably just mice working overtime to keep themselves alive for another miserable day but each time I sense movement up there my heart jumps and adrenaline shoots through me like a bullet train. So, I can't sleep.

Probably for the best. They'll be back soon and I want to be ready when they arrive. Awake at least.

I've been out here long enough to know that the sounds of the forest can play tricks on a tired mind. That the smallest sound, like a seed, can sprout fear in the mind of a listener in the dark, or conjure memories best left in the past. There's a cool breeze tonight that sounds like whispers as I drift in and out of consciousness, as though the Ghost of Conversations Past has come to haunt me.

In particular, my father's words of advice seem to be playing on a loop like the greatest hits collection of some washed-up band. "It doesn't pay to be a pain in the ass, kid," was usually how he started his set list.

My father was always full of fairly useless advice. Once I called him Daisy Duke for wearing cut-off jeans and he told me, "Nobody likes a comedian." To this day, I can't decipher the meaning of that old chestnut. As far as I can tell, everyone likes a comedian. I wanted to say, "Who the hell doesn't like a comedian?" But instead I just laughed and said something typically teenaged like, "Whatever."

Well, I'm not laughing now.

For all his advice, my father couldn't keep from being a *pain in the ass* to me and my mother. He's been splitsville for over a year now and besides the occasional phone call we barely speak anymore.

I remember when the dust settled on my parents' divorce, my mother told me the judge said it would be better for me to live with her because she could provide a more "stable environment". She squeezed my hand in a weird way like she was trying to make it seem like we'd won some sort of victory together, but I knew my father didn't put up a fight. He wanted his freedom and that's what he got. Now he lives in a three-story mansion with an overly tanned 28-year-old waitress named Marlee. And me? I ended up with a stressed out mother who works sixty hours a week just to give me an allowance that barely keeps me in Playstation games, high-tops and weed. Yep, real stable.

If I'd stopped being a little prick long enough to realize life for my mother was probably much worse than it was for me I bet our relationship would have been a lot different. I certainly never thanked her for anything as far as I can remember. Not sincerely anyway. Too late now, I guess.

So anyway, my parents didn't make it. Big deal. I remember Elle told me her parents were on the rocks and thrived on therapy. She sent me a link that said fifty per cent of marriages end up in flames, so it's not like having divorced parents makes me some kind of special case.

Elle. I think of you most of all. God, I hope you're okay.
I'm drifting off again. A sound. I'm awake.

My mind is really confusing things. I can sense it shutting down. I know what Adam would say. He'd tell me to snap out of it and focus, look to my surroundings and prepare for every possible scenario. He'd say playing smart is the only way to beat the odds and avoid being another casualty of The Compound. Of course he'd be right but this time's different. It didn't take me long to assess my situation here in this 10x10 hole and realize I was in deep trouble.

The first thing I noticed when they threw me down here is that the walls are smooth, as though the hole was dug out by a machine. There are no roots to grab on to either, so there's no real way to climb out.

I carved a foothold with my fork but the dirt just crumbled apart when I stepped in it and I fell on my ass. (I've since stuck the utensil back into my underwear where I hope it continues to go unnoticed).

At least there's water seeping up from the earth beneath me; an ironic benefit to being down so deep. I dug a trough to let the liquid pool before I sip at it though. Being dehydrated isn't like in the movies. You can't just wet your lips and recover by the next scene. You have to actually fill your belly, so I've learned to be patient. Of course, you can't drink too much too quickly either or you get water-drunk and get a raging headache. Yeah, survival is that complicated.

Thankfully, I ate a squirrel yesterday so hunger's not an issue right now. We learned in school that Gandhi went more than twenty days without eating and I remember thinking that didn't sound like much time at all and probably anyone could do that if they really wanted to. Well, I didn't eat for nearly two days when I first awoke in The Compound and, let me tell you, I was so hungry I thought I might eat my own arm off. I don't remember what Gandhi was protesting about but, sitting in this hole now, it's crazy to think he had a choice in the matter; that he could have given up, just ordered Chinese food and watched TV. If I had a choice that's what I'd be doing right now. Noodles from China Magic and a Netflix binge sounds a hell of a lot better than eating worms and being lost.

But that's the big joke, isn't it? I *did* have a choice. Not one big choice but a lot of little choices that added up to me being here in a hole in the middle of nowhere with only a day (Christ, maybe less!) to live. No surprise then that my life is flashing before my

eyes.
>I'm drifting again.
>A sound.
>A boy screams in the night.

>*Pick up a copy of New Horizons today to read more!*

About Christopher Webster

Christopher Webster is a narrative game designer, novelist, and screenwriter. He lives with his wife and two children in Canada.

About StoryFix Media

StoryFix Media was founded in 2018 by four family members with a passion for storytelling across multiple genres and platforms. New and upcoming releases include the YA adventure novel *New Horizons*, its sequel *A Mark of Strength,* and the choose-your-own-adventure mobile game *The Pulse*.

Find us on Twitter *@StoryFixMedia*

The author would like to acknowledge the work of Henry De Vere Stacpoole as an inspiration for the book you are holding.

CPSIA information can be obtained
at www.ICGtesting.com
Printed in the USA
LVHW041456051119
636418LV00004B/744/P